COLD BLOOD

COLD BLOOD

D. D. BRAITHWAITE

Cold Blood by D. D. Braithwaite

Copyright © 2023 D. D. Braithwaite

All rights reserved.

ISBN: 9798870679945

ddbraithwaite@outlook.com

Cover design by DDB Designs

Firehawk logo property of D. D. Braithwaite

This is a work of fiction. Unless otherwise indicated, all the names, characters, businesses, places, events and incidents in this book are either the product of the author's imagination or used in a fictitious manner. Any resemblance to actual persons, living or dead, or actual events is purely coincidental.

First Edition

To all those who believed in me,

Thank you.

To my Eternal Beloved.

I love you.

ACKNOWLEDGMENTS

There are so many to thank for getting me to this stage over the years either directly or indirectly. Without your support, advice, friendship and everything else over the years I wouldn't have been confident enough to even do this, thank you all. Sorry if I have forgotten anyone.

FAMILY

My wife Gillian and son Corran, my niece Nicole, my father Norman, my mother Catherine, my brother Douglas, my father in law Stewart, my mother in Law Alison, my brother in law Gordon, all my aunts, uncles, cousins and second cousins who have been there for me at various times, most notably Benita, Rachel, Ifor, Wendy, Thomas Nicola and cousin in law Tracey. Also my sons Godparents to whom I consider family as well, John "He-Ro" Scott, Jay Gallacher, Jade Austin and Elizabeth Scott.

SPECIAL THANKS

Anthony Greene, Aileen Gormley, Stacey McDonald, Jason "Rifleman Harris" Salkey, Angela Thomson, Angela Hamilton, Kirstin Turner, Sharon Scally, Marco Piva, John Nelson, Kharin Klepp, Rachel Taylor, E.E. Naden, Jack Berry, Stephen Cameron, Kwaku Adjei, Suzanne Rust, Matt Weston, Phil Marriott, Gareth Holland, Debbie Craig, Kate Connell, Tracey McCulloch, Siobhan Robertson, Stuart W. Little, Iain MacIntyre, Linda McCabe, Frank McKenna, Marco Calleri, Daria Cotugno, Kimberly Benson, Richard Divers, Alix Brown, Colin Waldie, Keith Campbell, Scott Crombie, John Sneddon, John Corry, Alex Nicol, Sister Martina, Father Gerard Maguiness, Kitty Gahagan, John Bell, Mo McCourt, Rhys Kay, Luke Murray, Claire McCafferty, Bianca-Louise Little, Sinclair McCall, Brian McLaughlin, Gerry O'Donnell, Ian Gowrie, Haider Dar, Alister Speedie, Chris Cowie, Kimberley Ferguson, Amy Speirs, Gary King George Thompson Smith, Peter Dunne, Chic Anderson, Scott Walker and everyone I worked with in security and with the regular staff especially at the Esquire House Glasgow and at Tesco Extra Wishaw.

COLD BLOOD

CHAPTER 1

Netherfield House, the beautiful Georgian mansion with seventy acres of land just outside Strathaven was a welcome sight to Tegan Galloway as she stood in the driveway looking up at the place she had called home most of her life.

"Something wrong?" asked Darren, her fiance as he finished paying the taxi fare. Tegan turned to him and gave a shy half smile and sighed.

"It's nothing," she said "It's just.. you know.." she started to get flustered.

"..The first time you've been back home since everything happened?" Darren guessed and put an arm around her and gently drew her into a comforting embrace.

"Something like that." she replied softly. Darren was referring to the series of events that ultimately lead

COLD BLOOD

to them meeting up. Tegan had been abducted by local criminals working on behalf of her estranged cousin Lucy who had an old family grudge to settle. But in a bizarre twist of fate Darren had gotten caught up in everything and rescued Tegan. During the ordeal the two fell for each other and had been inseparable ever since, even moving to Dundee together to get away from the unwanted attention the ordeal had caused.

"That's not all, is it?" he said suddenly. She looked up into his blue eyes, he knew her too well.

"It's Princess, I haven't been this far apart from her before." Princess was Tegan's horse. Not just any horse, but the one Tegan had won every showjumping event she entered with and although Darren didn't fully understand the depth of the relationship between a girl and her horse he at least tried.

"I'm sure she will be fine, besides you will see her soon enough, it is only for a couple of days," he said as he stroked her long black wavy hair "Anyway, let's not keep your parents waiting.."

"Yeah," she said looking at her watch "we are a little late as it is." and with that Darren shouldered one bag and carried another, along with the backpack he already had on he looked weighed down compared to Tegan but he had insisted on carrying the majority of the luggage.

"Are you sure I can't take a bag?" she asked out of concern, she knew Darren had issues with his knees and didn't want him hurting himself.

"It's fine, honestly." he insisted as they walked the driveway.

COLD BLOOD

Tegan didn't even get a chance to ring the doorbell before Quentin, her father flung the door open and threw his arms around her in a welcoming embrace..

"You're late," he said eventually "I was so worried about you, I wish you had let me come up to Dundee to collect you."

"Dad! Please, I'm cold and tired and not in the mood for a debate," Tegan said with hints of annoyance and embarrassment "The trains weren't that bad, we just had a hard time getting a taxi from the station that's all but what do you expect? it is Christmas Eve after all." and she gave him a reassuring smile.

"I know, can't blame a man for being concerned for his favourite daughter."

"Dad," she replied as she rolled her eyes "I'm your only daughter."

"Hi Mister Galloway." said Darren as he dropped the bags on the step.

"How many times must I tell you, call me Quentin." the older man replied.

"I'm sorry, but us Douglas men were raised to respect our elders." Darren shrugged.

"Hey, less of the elder if you don't mind," Quentin said in a hurt tone but the smile let Darren know he wasn't serious. Tegan shook her head, her father was never one for formalities.

"Where's mum?" Tegan asked curiously after looking around.

"Right here," Said a voice and out stepped Olivia,

COLD BLOOD

Tegan's mother, her long greying hair in a ponytail and dressed in her casual riding attire, while both her parents had horses, her mother was the more serious rider as she competed in dressage, though not as often as she used to. The younger woman ran up and threw her arms around her mother. Quentin smiled at them and made his way upstairs to his office, he was working from home more often than not these days.

"Well, got a few things to do for work.." he started but Olivia shook her head.

"Quentin" she said "It is Christmas eve, surely work can wait.

"It is only a few last minute things to clear up, I won't be long, honestly. And anyway I have to call Bruce Ingliston about the preparations for the hunt, don't I?" he said with a shrug "He desperately wants to make this New Years hunt one of the best." Olivia nodded in agreement.

"I can see why," she added "If that law is passed in parliament.."

"Don't you mean when." Quentin countered dryly, the Protection Of Wild Mammals Act, which if passed in parliament would effectively ban foxhunting, at least in its current form in Scotland, loomed over this years preparations.

"I heard that you would still be allowed to hunt, but do things a little different." Darren offered, Quentin looked at him and sighed.

"You are right, but I know a lot of the old guard aren't keen on the restrictions, some are planning to join hunts in England..."

"...And you won't be one of then so don't get any bright ideas.." Olivia interjected with a surprisingly stern tone. Quentin put his hands up in mock surrender.

"Okay, Okay," he said good naturedly "Besides it is more the thrill of the chase for me," he then looked at his watch "Well I got things to do." and he disappeared up the stairs. Olivia looked over at Darren who was still at the open doorway.

"Darren don't just stand there freezing, come in and shut the door," she then turned to Tegan "Come on, lets get some heat into you both.

Olivia ushered Darren and Tegan into the main sitting room and they sat on the sofa.

"How have you and dad been, I'm sorry I don't call as much as I should, between Princess and coursework.." Tegan started to explain.

"...No need to explain," Olivia said as she sat on one of the fireside chairs "Your father has been out of sorts since Captain died." Captain was Quentin's horse he rode during hunts.

"He did sound really down the last time we spoke, I think it is because it all happened very suddenly," Tegan said And I think he mentioned something about the new stable girl thinking she was somehow at fault."

"Ah yes," Olivia nodded "Jill was in a right state, poor girl was only a week into the job too. I only hope this new horse lifts his mood"

"Oh that's right, he did mention Mister Ingliston had a horse he was going to sell dad and that is one reason we are going there." Tegan said after a moment of thought.

"it is," Olivia nodded "He has a thoroughbred he wants your dad to take a look at. It won't be captain though."

"I know, please tell me you didn't sent for Grayshill to deal with Captain..." Tegan started to say.

"Tegan," Olivia interrupted with a tone that she hoped sounded reassuring, Grayshill was a company that dealt with dead livestock and suchlike "We had him cremated, your dad has his ashes in his office upstairs so not need to worry." Olivia saw Tegan's shoulders sag in relief, one of the many ways Grayshill would dispose of animals was to cut the animal up as meat for pet food, something Olivia knew Tegan was not keen on. Darren however looked confused.

"But.. it's just a horse.." he started to say but Tegan turned to him and gave him a rare menacing look.

"Darren," she said in a voice that suggested she was doing her best to control her rage "We have talked about this, Captain wasn't 'just' a horse, none of them are. Horses are like family, no actually, they are family, honestly.. urgh." she screamed and got up and stormed out, grabbing a couple of their bags from the hall before going upstairs. Darren went to get up and follow but Olivia gestured for him to stay seated.

"She will be fine, just give her a moment." Olivia said soothingly. Darren just sighed and looked at her apologeticly.

"I'm sorry, I didn't mean to offend." he said sheepishly.

"I know you didn't mean anything nasty by it," Olivia reassured him "Speaking of the horses... I really should get out to the stables," she said, standing up "Let Tegan know if she wants to join me, I will be in the stables, Darren smiled and shook his head, he knew it wasn't a case of if'.. they both knew that Tegan could not resist an opportunity to be near horses, of course she would be there.

"I will." he replied and took the rest of the luggage upstairs.

He stood at the door to Tegan's old room, Gave it a quick knock then came in. Darren forgot just how big it was and it looked even bigger with the now largely bare walls. Tegan was sitting on the bed half dressed, her trainers had already been kicked halfway across the room.

"I'm sorry about earlier.." he started to explain but Tegan just looked at him and gave a slight smile

"Darren, I get it, I really do. You are still new to all.. this and I know you don't really mean anything bad but.."

"I should show more tact in the future." He guessed.

"Something like that, I take it mum is going to the stables?" her smile widened, Tegan and her mother were very much alike, Darren had decided as he saw her get changed. Tegan looked at him as she took her top off and shook her head, Yes Darren was frustrating at times but it wasn't totally his fault, he had dyslexia and dyspraxia, they also recently discovered Darren was also on the autistic spectrum so she knew he didn't mean anything malicious by the comments earlier. Tegan noticed Darren was just standing admiring her as she put her hair up in a ponytail, there had been a time that even the mere sight of Tegan undressing would have caused him to look away.

"Darren could you go and.." she started to say then shrugged "...Never mind, I will get it" And with that she got up and went to the wardrobe. Tegan selected an old pair of black jodhpurs and a pair of of her rubber riding boots she had left there for times like this. Then she went to her bag and got out the old Celtic goalkeeper top that used to belong to Darren with the name Warner and the number thirty four on the back.

"Feel better?" Darren asked as she eased the top on. He had known her long enough to know that Tegan was most comfortable in riding gear, in particular the riding boots, she almost always would wear some form of tall riding boot, even when she wasn't riding that day. Even on occasions she didn't wear them she had regular tall boots she would wear instead. It was a quirk of hers he had accepted long ago. Tegan smiled as she looked in the mirror as she adjusted the sleeves, pushing them up past her elbows.

"Much better," she replied with a smile "How do I look?"

"Beautiful as ever, I am assuming you are going to going to help your mum at the stables?" Darren said with a knowing smile, she walked forward and put her arms around him.

COLD BLOOD

"You know me too well." she said as she kissed him, he drew her in closer and guided her to the bed where they fell still in each others arms. She looked into his eyes and ran her fingers through his short brown hair.
"I love you." he said softly.
And I love you too." she replied with a shy smile. Before pulling him in for another kiss.

CHAPTER 2

Olivia was in the stables mucking out by the time Tegan got there, her mother stopped and smiled at her.

"So," Olivia said "All ready?" Tegan leaned on the wall and gave a sigh.

"For Christmas? yes I am. Darren is very easy to buy for." she then looked at her mother "For the hunt? I don't know. I'm worried about Princess, This is the first time none of us will be there to supervise her transport. What if they don't..." she started to get flustered, Olivia came over and put her am around Tegan.

"It will be fine, you gave them instructions on how you wanted her transported, they will deliver her there safe." she said soothingly "There is something else bothering you, I know you too well. It is because this is your first hunt since.. the incident, isn't it?" the last hunt Tegan took part in was the one that unfortunately ended in her abduction. Tegan gave a half hearted smile to try and reassure her mother.

"I would be lying if I said it wasn't on my mind, I still get nightmares about it," Tegan looked her her mother with a sad look in her eyes, when she and Darren escaped her captors, Tegan had been forced to stab Lucy in order to prevent her murdering Darren and in doing so killed her cousin. The courts had ruled it a justifiable homicide but due in part to some questionable reporting by the less reputable media outlets there were various other theories and versions of the events, most not kind to the couple. Tegan could feel herself starting to panic just thinking about it all. Olivia- walked over and put a comforting arm around her daughter.

"Tegan, I really wish I knew what to say, I really do." she said in a tone she hoped was reassuring "I still can not begin to fathom what it must have been like for you..."

"..You don't want to," Tegan interrupted, she could feel herself starting to panic, her mother just gripped her tighter.

"Everything will be fine," she said softly "I will ride with you and make sure you are safe. Please don't worry what people will say, anyone who knows you will know the truth." Tegan looked up and gave her mother a half smile.

"You're right," She replied "I suppose I can't hide away forever."

"Plus you will have Darren with you," Added her mother "I take it you still haven't been able to persuade him to get on a horse?"

"No, he is terrified." Tegan admitted with a chuckle "But he has been great with other things, getting my stuff all ready, he even polished my boots for the occasion."

"Really? Your father never did anything like that for me, lucky you." Olivia said with a sly smile, it was good for her to know that Darren was supportive of her daughter and her pursuits.

"Who else is going to be there anyway?" Tegan asked curiously.

"The usual suspects," Olivia said, thinking "The Campbells, come to think of it Sheena might be there too. Mrs Galbraith, The McDonalds, Beth Naden, Luke Brayson, the Molloys, you know, all the regulars plus there is apparently going to be some visitors from England and Wales too."

"It sounds like Mr Ingliston will be a kept very busy then." Tegan noted.

"That he will," Olivia agreed "I think he wants your fathers help. Oh, you might be interested to know that Tristan and Eva will be there too." Olivia added, Tristan and Eva were Bruce Ingliston's son and daughter.

"Wait," said Tegan, slightly shocked "Are you sure? Eva is going to be there? I thought she didn't talk to her dad after.. well.. you know." Olivia looked at her daughter confused for a moment then realised what she was getting at.

"Oh because of the whole hunt sab thing? No she is apparently through with that and is married now." a hunt saboteur... or sab for short... was a type of anti hunt protestor who as opposed to simply protesting hunts actually would set about disrupting them, sometimes resorting to violent acts. Eva had gotten involved with a local group of hunt sabs when she was a teenager, some people thought it was her rebelling against her parents but regardless of her reasoning it had caused a rift between Eva and the rest of her family so the news that she would be there and even taking part came as a bit of a shock.

"When did she get married?" Tegan asked curiously.

"I think it was about was about a year ago to someone called Craig Robertson, he is from Kilmarnock and a little older than her and apparently has his own company, it's something to do with computers. Your dad knows more." Olivia notice that Tegan seemed a little uneasy but was only half successful at hiding it.

"I suppose it will be good to see everyone again."Tegan shrugged.

"Oh while we are here, have you thought any more about what we discussed last time I called?" Olivia asked.

"You mean about moving back down after I graduate?" Tegan replied "Yes, Darren and I have had discussions about it."

"And?" Olivia asked with a hint of impatience "You wouldn't be living in the main house so you would have your independence. I mean the coachman's cottage is lying vacant and we would much rather have you both there than renting to some strangers or worse, just letting it sit empty."

"Darren thinks it is a great idea and I do miss

home but if I am totally honest I'm not totally sure, not yet anyway." Tegan said then offered a shy smile, Olivia smiled back.

"There's no pressure, you take your time, the offer will always be open. Tell you what," Olivia said in an effort to cheer her daughter up "Why don't we go out for a ride, you can take out Major if you like." Major was the oldest of the family horses, a large black Clydesdale with white hooves and nose, he was one of the most docile creatures Tegan had ever known. Tegan's eyes immediately lit up with excitement.

"I'd love to." she said, already heading to the tack room to get Major prepared.

Darren cautiously stepped into Quentin's office, Tegan's dad looked up from his work and waved him in.

"Come in," he said cheerfully "I managed to set things up on the computer for that game Tegan told me you play."

"Thank you," Darren said as he at in one of the chairs on the other side of the desk and stifling a yawn. "Sorry, it was just a long trip."

"I can imagine," Quentin said in a sympathetic tone. While Quentin had been cautious about the relationship between Darren and his daughter, he had not only accepted their love but also had come to view Darren almost like the son he never had.

"So Darren," he mused "New Year will be your first proper experience of a hunt, nervous?"

"I won't lie, I am a bit yeah," Darren replied "I

know I'm not actually riding but being able to help Tegan in her preparations and stuff.. I know how important this is to her." Quentin had to smile, He could see just how much his daughter meant to Darren which was going to make his next comment hurt for both of them.

"Just be aware that you will probably get some... comments from some quarters." Darren nodded silently, one of the more hurtful rumours that circulated about the couple was that Darren was in it for the money.

"Don't worry, I'm fully aware of the gossip," he said with a shrug "I'm more concerned with what people will say about Tegan."

"So am I if I am honest, although I think the topic of conversation may be Bruce's daughter Eva.." Quentin went on to explain the problematic history and the fact she used to be a hunt saboteur.

"It feels like deja vu all over again." Darren said as he looked up to the ceiling and sighed.

"What do you mean?" Quentin said, somewhat bemused.

"Is it all that common for people who are opposed to foxhunting to suddenly change their mind and take part?" Darren asked.

"What do you mean by.." Quentin started to say then remembered "Oh.. no, not really no," he recalled that on that fateful day Tegan had been kidnapped, the only reason Darren was even there at the protest was that Lucy, who was Darren's college classmate had told him she was actually protesting the hunt, partially to get out of going on a date with him and partially to preserve her reputation as something of a rebel but instead of having the intended effect of putting him off, Darren instead actually turned up in a desperate hope to impress her" Though I am curious as to why Eve has, even a little suspicious, especially after all that happened to you and Tegan."

"I assume the family has some wealth." Darren offered "She could be trying to work her way back into the family good books, maybe she had been cut off or at least was threatened that they might."

"Oh yes they are very wealthy, Bruce has many successful business ventures" Quentin nodded "And he didn't cut her off, at least not completely, he had threatened it a few times but never followed through with it no matter how bad things got, she made no attempt to hide the fact that they were related when the sabs would strike. I was there a few times myself and saw just how awkward and embarrassed he would get over it all. So who knows, maybe marriage has settled her," Then Quentin sat forward suddenly as if remembering something "Oh, I took your advice on Tegan's present, I know I wanted to get her something bigger but you convinced me and now I can understand why you said get a smaller one though I had to get Astrid's advice when it came time to get it." they heard the sound of horses outside.

"I'm guessing that is Tegan and her mother?" Darren asked, Quentin nodded and headed to the window

"I should have guessed, didn't take them long did it?" Quentin said with a smile as he looked out the window to see Tegan and Olivia head down the main path on horseback, he shook his head with a smile "I had a sneaking feeling that the two of them would go off riding."

"Yeah, me too." Darren agreed, Quentin looked down a few moments then turned to Darren

"I have to be honest with you, Christmas wasn't the same last year without Tegan."

"I can imagine," Darren nodded "But she felt it was too soon after the trial to return." Quentin agreed and went over to his computer and after a few moments stepped back.

"There you go, you have your own profile to log in to, the password is 'Tegan', I'm going to see what is on the television so have fun with your game," he headed to the door but stopped as if remembering something "Did Tegan fill you in on what we usually do Christmas Eve?"

"A little bit, she mentioned some stuff." Darren said as he went over and sat at the computer.

"Well, the agenda for tonight is once they get back from riding we will phone for a takeaway then watch Muppet Christmas Carol..." It was Tegan's favourite Christmas movie so no surprises there Quentin went on listing the nights activities " ...Then later on we go to midnight mass." Darren nodded in understanding. Midnight mass.. or church service.. was a special Christmas service many churches had, Darren and the Galloways were all devout Roman Catholics.

"Sounds good to me," Darren said as he logged into the computer. "My family have different traditions, Evening mass on Christmas Eve, come home via the chip shop and we would open our gifts after we had our food."

"Wait, you'd open your gifts at Christmas Eve?" Quentin asked puzzled.

"Well yes but we didn't always do that, only once my brother and I were grown up but if I'm honest I prefer waiting until Christmas Day, especially with Tegan, her enthusiasm is infectious."

"That it is," Quentin nodded "One last question before I go, what time did Tegan get up to open Christmas day last year?" he asked.

"She was out of bed and opening presents by half past six, despite promising to wait for seven o'clock." Darren replied with a smirk.

"Ah, same old Tegan," Quentin smiled as he left "enjoy your game, What is it anyway?"

"Tribes Two," said Darren, "Its an online sci-fi first person shooter, most of my online mates play it."

"I see," Quentin replied "Okay, well have fun." and with that he left Darren to his gaming.

COLD BLOOD

CHAPTER 3

It was a beautiful starry night and the first thing Tegan done when they returned from midnight mass was to stand outside at the hedge that lined the driveway and looked up at the stars. She felt more at peace with herself than she had in a long time. It was when, everyone was watching TV earlier and then at mass during Father Devine's sermon, she looked over and saw her parents and Darren, the three most important people in her life, and they were all together,she started to smile to herself. As she looked back at Darren, who was getting out of the Range Rover, Tegan also noted that ever since they became a couple, the anxiety attacks she had been prone to having were happening less often and weren't as bad as they used to be. She waved him over and smiled.

"There it is," said Darren as he put an arm around her "Orions Belt." she turned and kissed him, the first night they met, when he helped her escape he told her that he always looks for Orions Belt in the stars, something she had found herself doing lately too. They stood looking up for a few minutes until Quentin called them in.

"Come on, you will catch a death of cold out there." he said.

"Coming!" Tegan shouted back and took Darren's hand as they headed indoors.

After some hot chocolate it was time for bed, Tegan got changed for bed, she wore an old pair of Celtic away shorts from the nineteen ninety six to ninety seven season and an old black tshirt with the Lanarkshire Pony Club logo on the front. Darren just wore a pair of grey pyjama bottoms and a white tshirt. Usually they would wear less but they were staying with Tegan's parents so a bit of modesty was called for. Tegan cuddled into Darren, her head on his chest, listening to his heartbeat.

"Excited for tomorrow?" Darren asked.

"Oh yes." Tegan said smiling widely, Darren thought about Christmas last year, even though she was twenty one, Tegan still treated Christmas Day with a wide eyed wonder. And even though they had elected to stay in Dundee and had a low key Christmas Day that year Tegan was still up early opening presents.

"How early are you getting up this year?" he asked dryly, Tegan looked up.

"Seven o'clock at the latest." her smile widened and she kissed his cheek. "It's okay, you can go back to bed after the presents are opened, my parents won't mind."

"Thank you, have I ever told you how amazing and beautiful you are?" he said and kissed her forehead.

"A few times but once more won't hurt." and she kissed him full on in the mouth and pulled him in closer...

It was quarter past six in the morning and Tegan sat crosslegged on the floor of the sitting room next to the tree as she opened her presents. The first few presents she opened were the usual array of toiletries and gift sets from relatives until she got to a couple of large rectangular boxes, the first one had a tag saying it was from her mother.

"I wonder what this could be." she half stated, half asked as she looked up at her mother, who was sitting on the sofa with a cup of coffee in hand smiling back.

Only way to find out is to open it." she said with a smile. Tegan ripped open the wrapping paper and opened the box, it was a pair of riding boots, very expensive ones by the quality of the leather, they had a small metal 'P' on the top , the outer leg being taller than the inner (A feature known as a Spanish cut). Tegan ran her hand up and down the leather and held one up.

"Oh my.." Tegan said as she looked at it in awe "Petrie Windsors," she looked up at her mum with a huge smile Petrie Windsors were the riding boot of choice for many dressage riders and while Tegan was more of a showjumper she still liked that style "Thank you mum, I always wanted a pair." and she got up and hugged her mum

"Hopefully that will mean you won't be begging to borrow my pair any more." Olivia said dryly as she smiled back at her daughter who resumed her present opening.

"From Darren, I wonder what this could be," she said to herself and she tore off the wrapping and it was another box, inside were another pair of riding boots, but these were different as Tegan took one out and examined it and noticed straight away these this pair had a zip fastening up the back, Tegan smiled and shook her head. She had said to Darren more than once how hard it was to take off her traditional pull on riding boots. Darren must have assumed she was hinting.

"Are they okay?" he asked as he sat on the floor close by, she leaned over put an arm around him and kissed his cheek.

They are perfect," while they probably didn't cost as much as the ones her mother bought her, it was the thought that counted "Where's my gift to you?" she asked looking a the small pile of gifts Darren was opening. He reached over and grabbed a bulky parcel and tore it open. Inside was a black Celtic goalkeeper shirt with green trim and the name Douglas and the number twenty on the back, he eagerly put it on before leaning close and kissing her cheek.

"You know me all too well." he said smiling widely, also in the parcel was a signed photo of the Celtic goalkeeper Robert 'Rab' Douglas (no relation to

COLD BLOOD

Darren).

"I couldn't resist after that day at Wetherspoons." Tegan replied. Quentin, who had just came through to the sitting room from the kitchen with a tray of the Galloway family traditional Christmas Day breakfast of sausage and bacon rolls. Looked at Tegan curiously.

"Oh, what happened like?" he asked, picking up his mug of coffee.

"Well, you know how Rab Douglas used to play for Dundee?" Tegan started.

"Yeah.." Quentin said, kind of guessing where it the conversation was going.

"Well," Tegan continued "We had just been to /Tannadice park to see Celtic play Dundee United and we went for dinner at Wetherspoons, anyway, Darren goes to pay and drops his card and someone, a Celtic fan apparently, picked it up. When he saw Darren's surname, he thought he was related to Rab and offered to buy him a drink despite Darren repeatedly telling him he wasn't." Tegan shook her head as she laughed.

"The guy wouldn't take no for an answer." Darren shrugged

"Could be worse," Quentin said "You wouldn't believe the amount of times people think I own Galloway Cheese." Darren and Tegan locked eyes and burst into fits of laughter. Quentin looked at them slightly puzzled not realising that when they first met that was exactly what Darren did think. Quentin just shook his head and picked p a roll.

As the present opening continued, Tegan got a Celtic home shirt with the name Larsson and the number seven on the back from her father, a Celtic golf style pullover jacket, some new jodhpurs in various colours, a crucifix necklace and various horse riding accessories. Darren got a collection of Star Wars novels, some DVD's and assorted clothes. There was one last gift on the floor, a small box addressed to Tegan, she picked it up and shook it gently, something moved inside.

"I wonder what it is." she said curiously.

"Only one way to find out." Quentin said exchanging a wink with Darren, it was the gift they had spoken about earlier. Tegan ripped the wrapping off and opened up the small box, inside were a set of carkeys attached to a keyring that was the Volkswagen logo. Tegan turned to her dad.

"You didn't.. did you?" she asked, her face one of surprise.

"Take a look out the front door and find out." And with that, Tegan headed to the front door, stopping to slip on the rubber riding boots she had left at the door. Outside was a small car, a black Volkswagen Lupo to be exact.

"It's yours," Quentin said with a smile, Tegan "I thought to myself, now that you passed your test you should have something to get you out and about. I was going to get you a Land rover but Darren convinced me to get something smaller." Tegan turned to her dad and hugged him tight.

"Thank you dad, it is perfect," she then turned and hugged Darren "thank you," she said and kissed him on

COLD BLOOD

the cheek before running up to her new car and getti8ng in the drivers seat. Tegan just sat in awe and ran her hand over the steering wheel. The dashboard was compact and there was a CD player and Tegan had noted that someone had already put some of her favourite CD's in the open glove compartment, Darren joined her in the passenger seat "Was this what you and dad were talking about on the phone a while back?"

"Yeah, he wanted to do something for you passing your test, so going to take her for a spin" Darren asked, smiling.

"But I'm in my nightwear and so are you." Tegan protested, though her eyes told him she really wanted to.

"It's Christmas Day, the roads will be empty and nobody will see us." Darren reasoned, Tegan thought for a moment, put the key in the ignition and started the engine.

"Okay, you convinced me." she smiled widely and kissed him before driving off down the driveway.

After a short drive they returned to the sound of Christmas songs coming from the sitting room CD player. They went up to Tegan's room and Darren went back up to bed as Tegan dressed in the nearest Jodhpurs that came to hand, slipped her boots back on and she put on her new Celtic top.

"I'll come back up and wake you in a few hours, okay?" Tegan said and gave Darren a kiss "Oh and remember, phone your mum..

"Yeah, thanks. Love you." Darren replied.

"Love you too." Tegan said and headed down the sitting room, where her parents were sitting, relaxing before a start was made on dinner.

"Where's dad?" Tegan asked.

" So," Quentin asked "Like the car?"

"I love it," Tegan replied as she took her gifts and put them in a neat pile, she looked at the riding boots boxes longingly..

"Oh go on, try them on, you know you want to." Olivia said knowingly, Tegan grinned and first tried on the Petries.

"Oh these feel amazing," Tegan said as she walked across the sitting room to get a feel for them "will need to break them in first before I do any serious riding in them, thanks again mum." and after she got them off she tried the pair Darren bought her. As she pulled up the zip at the back she looked at her mum with a bemused look on her face.

"What is it?" Olivia asked.

"Nothing, just feels strange zipping up riding boots that is all," Tegan replied "She then walked up and down in them "They are actually very comfortable." she sounded pleasantly surprised.

"It seems like Darren has good taste and knows what you like." Olivia said with a smile, Tegan sat and unzipped them, making sure to carefully put them back in the box

"Well at least he knew to get me dress boots, you know I don't like the ankle laces on field boots." Tegan said as she put her old rubber ones back on, the difference between dress and field boots were that field boots had a lace detail at the ankle which was usually favoured by showjumpers as it allows greater flexibility of the rider's ankle, however Tegan wasn't a fan of the style and preferred dress boots. As Tegan looked through her presents again she came across a keyring Darren had bought her, it was something he picked up at a marketplace in Dundee. It looked like a little grey winged human with pink hair, it was apparently sold as a pixie charm. Tegan thought it was cute and fished her carkeys from her pocket, looping the pixie keyring onto it.

"Well I better get dinner started." Olivia said as she got up.

"Need a hand?" both Quentin and Tegan asked at almost the same time.

"Not yet, will give a shout later if I need it." she replied. Olivia had every detail of dinner planned to the point you could almost set your watch by her so there was no real need for help, but they always offered none the less.

After Tegan had woke him up, Darren was on the phone to his mother as she grilled him on what he had gotten for Christmas. Darren's mum was spending the day at his brother Charlie's house, when he came off the phone Tegan looked over at him.

"How is your mum?" she asked.

"She is fine," he sighed "But sounds like she is driving my brother up the wall," Darren turned to explain to Quentin "It's Christmas dinner, my mum knows exactly what she wants and how she wants it and it's not always the way my brother likes it either so you can imagine how that is going."

"Sounds like fun." Quentin commented dryly, from the interactions he had with Kate, Darren's mother, Quentin had come to the opinion that while she came across as an unassuming woman, she was quite formidable when the notion took her.

"She wanted to know if you liked her gift," Darren said to Tegan "What did she get you anyway?" Tegan look a moment to think.

"Oh, it was that towel bathrobe with my name on it." she said "And chocolates too." she added. Olivia came into the sitting room, taking off her food stained apron and with a smile proclaimed.

"Dinner is ready."

In the middle of the dinner table were several serving dishes. Darren could see there was a selection of meats in turkey, gammon and lamb. As for vegetables there was potatoes, peas, carrot, brussels sprouts, corn and onions with not one but two gravy boats, everyone took their place at the table and said grace as was the family tradition on Christmas day.

"We don't do it all the time, only on Christmas day." Tegan had explained.

If there is one day you should take a moment before eating and be thankful for what you have it is today." Quentin had added. As they ate Tegan looked up at her dad.

"Dad, why are we going as early to the Inglistons?" she asked "I know mum said Mister Ingliston may need help and of course there is the new horse but why so early?" Quentin finished off his mouthful of turkey then replied.

"Tegan, you have to keep in mind this may be a bigger hunt than usual and he could do with all the help he needs." he answered "I think having us up early and allowing us to make use of his facilities and the hospitality is his way of thanks."

"Does Tristan still live with them?" Tegan asked.

"He does yes, well when he is at home anyway." Olivia replied.

"What does Tristan do?" Darren asked curiously, so far he had heard a lot more about Eva.

"He is in the navy, a sub-lieutenant onboard one of the frigates, H.M.S. Sutherland I think." Quentin said

"It's good they gave him some leave to come." Tegan nodded.

"He had saved it up, there was no way he was missing this hunt." Quentin informed her as he helped himself to some Turkey.

"So what are you two going to do while we are there? You will have a few days to do pretty much anything." Olivia asked Tegan.

"Apart from the obvious, some things are not to be discussed at the dinner table." Quentin added.

Well, there is one thing we had in mind," Darren said after looking over at Tegan with a smile "We were going to bring a tent and go find a secluded spot and if it is a clear night we will look up at the stars." Quentin looked relieved, Tegan had noticed his worried expression when Darren started telling them.

"Don't worry dad," she said with a smile "We have been wanting to do this sort of thing for ages." her smile widened.

"Okay," Quentin said with a sigh, not sounding fully convinced "Just be careful."

"Lighten up Quentin," Olivia said, winking at Tegan "We were young once too, remember that time we ended up sleeping in the stables because your parents were out and you forgot your key."

"We didn't get much sleep if I remember right." he replied with a grin., Tegan rolled her eyes.

"Not this story again, please." she pleaded. Her parents just laughed. Tegan then turned to Darren "I have heard this story way.. way too many times to count.."

"Now now, Darren hasn't heard it before," said Quentin as he turned to Darren "We had not long been engaged and we had been out..."

After dinner was finished and they had gathered around the TV to watch a movie it was decided that it would be a good idea to get an early night as it had been a long day and they had a long journey the next day. Darren and Tegan took their gifts up to the bedroom to pack them away for the morning. Darren held up a portable DVD player.

"Who got us this?" he asked as he opened it, it was noted it had an adapter to be used in a car as well as a regular plug.

"I think that was your mum." Tegan said, trying to remember "want to watch something on it in bed?" she said with a smile.

"Yeah," he replied and looked at the new DVD's he got "What do you want to watch?" he handed over his new DVD's to Tegan who had a look through them."Battlefield Earth? Who got you that?"

"My brother Charlie, he told me it's so bad it's good." Darren replied with an amused look on his face as Tegan handed over the DVD.

"Okay lets watch that." she said as she stretched. Once they were changed and in bed, Tegan cuddled into Darren, her head on his chest as she looked over at the screen, she didn't see much of the movie as she fell asleep soon after he started the DVD.

CHAPTER 4

The sky was still dark when Tegan woke up, she was just pulling her rubber boots on when Darren stirred and woke up.
"Where you going?" he said half asleep.
"I'm going to see if mum needs help at the stables," she said "You don't need to get up."
"I know better than to get between ladies and their horses." he smiled at her and put his head back on the pillow. Darren could clearly see that Tegan was in her element. Back up in Dundee, Tegan did try and spend as much time at the stables as she could but he knew it wasn't ideal for her due to the stables being a bus journey away from their flat. Tegan was a very hands on horse owner and wasn't keen on trusting others with Princess's welfare, she needed to be close to stables.
"What time are we leaving anyway?" asked

Darren.

"One o'clock I think," Tegan answered "Well that's what mum said anyway. I take it we are all ready and packed?"

"More of less," Darren said as he sat up on the bed "It is just really the Christmas presents and a few small things. When I get up I'll take the luggage downstairs."

"Thank you." she replied as she left the room, closing the door behind her, Darren slid back down and pulled the duvet back over himself.

It took them a while to get the trailer ready to transport Lolita.

"It's too early to load her in just yet. Olivia said as walked down the ramp "But we should make a start on things." Tegan then decided to start packing the car up for the journey ahead. She soon came to the conclusion that the Lupo was a lovely car, Tegan thought but the car boot was laughably small, in fact it literally only had enough space for a pair of boots.

"How am I going to fit all our stuff?" she sighed and opened the passenger side door and took a look at the back area, her thinking was drastic but necessary in her mind, take out the back seats. After retrieving a toolkit from the stables, Tegan set about examining the rear seats and saw the bolts at the bottom holding the seats to the car. As she tried to find the correct spanner size to take them off, Tegan felt someone tap her boot, she looked up to see Darren leaning on the open door and was looking down at her with a perplexed look on his face.

"What are you doing?" he asked, clearly amused.

"Isn't it obvious?" Tegan said, looking at Darren in confusion "I love this car, I really do but have you seen the car boot? It is tiny, how am I going to transport feed? Or a saddle? or.. anything really?"

"I know, but.." Darren started to say.

"Don't just stand there, give me a hand," Tegan said in frustration.

"You really don't want to use the back seats do you/" Darren asked.

"I would have thought that was obvious Darren, come on, I can't be expected to do all this by myself can I?" Tegan was getting angrier

"Well you could.." he started to say but was cut off by Tegan's continued ranting

"I mean I know it is just the two of us so we don't really need the back seats and we would get a lot more storage..." She trailed off as she saw Darren trying in vain to suppress a laugh.

"Tegan, did you read the manual? the back seats fold down flat." he said once he composed himself.

"What?" she said as she got out the car and stood facing Darren.

"The seats can.." he started to say but got in the car and reached over to the back of the rear seats, after removing the headrests and dumping them in the backseat footwells, Darren then pushed a couple of small levers the seats folded down flat "...See?" Tegan looked in and then looked back at Darren in disbelief.

"That is all you needed to do?" Tegan sounded shocked.

"Pretty much and there is no need to actually take the seats out," Darren said trying not to sound like he was gloating and was only partially successful "Would you like me to load up the car?"

"Yeah, could you? I think mum will need help with loading Lolita into the trailer, she has never liked going into them."

As he was finishing the loading of the car, Darren saw Quentin come out with some luggage.

"Need a hand?" he asked, Quentin nodded.

"Yes, thank you." was the reply and Darren took one of the heavier cases.

"So, is anyone looking after the place while you are gone?" Darren asked as they loaded the Range Rover.

"Oh, we asked Astrid if she could look after it, could you do me a favour?" Quentin asked.

"Sure," Darren said "Anything."

"Can you tell that idiotic boyfriend of hers to behave himself." Quentin said then after a moment continued with a sigh "I'm sorry, I know he is your friend but..."

"... He can be frustrating, trust me I understand, I will have a word with him, don't worry about that." Darren reassured him as best he could. Jason Gallagher was one of Darren's best friends from college and he met Astrid, the Galloway's stablehand, during the abduction crisis and had been together ever since despite Jason's reputation as a bit of a playboy. Quentin sighed and took a deep breath.

"Well, I don't know about you but I'm going to grab a cup of coffee, want one?" Quentin asked.

"Sure." said Darren and they headed inside.

Later on a silver Volkswagen Polo pulled up outside Netherfield house and out of the car stepped Astrid, already dressed to work in the stables with her boots, Jodhpurs and a quilted jacket, made her way inside.

"Hello Astrid," Olivia said with a smile "how are you? Have a good Christmas?"

"I did yes.." she started.

Is Jason there?" Darren interrupted as he came down the stairs. Astrid stopped and looked around.

"Oh, he must be getting his things out the car." Astrid replied before continuing her conversation with Olivia. Jason was just coming in the door as he saw Darren, he had a holdall in one hand and a case of beer under the other.

"Hey mate," he said with a wide smile, Jason was his typical scruffy self, his messy ginger hair in a ponytail and beard he looked older than his twenty one years, he was sporting baggy jeans and the new Rangers home shirt worn under green parka jacket. Darren beaconed him over "How's things?"

"Things are alright." Darren replied then looked at Jason knowingly "Jason please promise me you won't do anything stupid."

"Don't worry.." Jason started to say.

"..And no sexual olympics either," Darren added, sexual olympics referred to Jason's stories of having sex in every room of a girlfriends house, Netherfield would be quite a challenge for Jason, one he would gladly accept. Jason rolled his eyes.

"Darren, come on, look at the place, its bloody huge, besides who is to know?" Jason replied.

"I'll know," Darren said "I know you too well."

"I can't promise anything," Jason said with a smirk "besides Linda will be calling in during the week anyway. When are you lot back?"

"The third I think." Darren said after a moments thought then looked at Jason suspiciously "Why, not planning a wild party or something?" Jason looked over at Astrid.

"Wild yes," he said to Darren with a smile "Party, no." Darren just shook his head.

"Look, just please don't do anything in Tegan's bedroom, it is the one on the top floor." Darren pleaded.

"Okay, okay, I promise." Jason said with a smile.

"Liebchen!" Astrid called out "Can I get a hand in here?"

"Coming my little Bremen beauty." Jason called back and hurried in. Darren just shook his head. He didn't want to know what Jason had planned for when they were gone.

Everyone was standing outside the front door with Olivia giving Astrid some final instructions while

Quentin talked to Tegan..

"Now Tegan, you do know where you are going?" Quentin said cautiously.

"Yes, dad, we have a map too and I will be following you anyway." she said rolling her eyes, this was about the fourth time he had asked her.

"I'm just checking." he said holding his hands up.

Quentin!" Olivia said in a half stern tone "Tegan knows what she is doing." and guided Quentin to the Range Rover. As Darren and Tegan headed to the Lupo, Darren thought for a moment.

"Tegan, do you have your phone? Last I saw it you had it on charge in the bedroom." he asked. These days Tegan carried a mobile phone around with her for emergencies, Tegan patted her pockets and pulled out a Samsung A300 flip phone.

"Got it." she said with a smile before getting in the car. Astrid and Jason waved them off at the door, Jason oblivious to the stern look Quentin was giving him as they drove past.

"So where exactly is this place anyway." Darren said as he looked at the map.

"Glen Tachur, it is near Barrhill." Tegan said, keeping her eyes on the road and careful to keep her parents in sight, the Range Rover was towing the horse box with Lolita so hopefully they wouldn't lose sight of it.

"I take it you have been there before." Tegan nodded.

"A few times when I was younger,, it was alright, Eva and I would be at the stables..." Tegan said.

"Of course." Darren muttered knowingly. Tegan ignored it and continued.

"..Tristan would hang out with us sometimes, At least that was when he wasn't out with friends. More often than not they visited us

"Fair enough, how'd the family make their money anyway?" Darren asked curiously.

"Mister Ingliston owns BICon," Tegan said, BICon was one of the biggest construction companies in Scotland "And Missus Ingliston owns a chain of jewellery stores."

"So both are quite well off then." Darren shrugged.

"Pretty much," Tegan replied

"How long will it take us to get there?" Darren asked. Tegan thought for a moment then replied.

"About an hour and a half I think." she said as she reached down to the CD player and inserted her Runrig The Big Wheel CD and pressed play, it was a good thing her and Darren shared the same musical tastes.

"Good choice." Darren nodded.

"Thank you." Tegan replied and smiled, this was going to be a good trip.

It was a rather uneventful drive, just a long one but they eventually arrived at Glen Tachur. It was a a large white walled country mansion that was initially built in the mid nineteenth century but unsurprisingly considering Bruce Ingliston's line of work, there looked that were had been a lot of work done to it over the past few years. Bruce and Hannah were waiting outside, Bruce was a tall stocky man with balding brown curls and Hannah was a slim woman with her long blonde hair in a severe ponytail. They were all miles and waving.

"Hey Quentin how have been keeping?" Bruce shouted as Quentin got out the Range Rover, the two men walked towards each other grinning from each to ear and shook hands then Bruce pulled Quentin in for a back slapping hug.

"I'm doing alright." Quentin replied as they turned to the others who were joining them.

"Olivia, always a pleasure" Bruce said with a formal nod then looked over at Tegan " Oh Tegan how you have grown, I'm glad you could join us... and this must be Darren." he then stretched his hand out to Darren who shook it cautiously "I'm Bruce Ingliston and I have heard a lot about you." he said with a smile and a wink.

"Pleased to meet you Mister Ingliston." Darren replied, looking unsure about what to say.

"Well let us get in out of the cold, shall we?" Bruce said after a moment and walked toward the front door, gesturing everyone to follow.

The interior of the house had tartan carpet and wood panelled walls.

"Oh my.. I've died and gone to a shortbread tin." said Darren as he looked around, Tegan slapped his arm.

"Darren!" she said, trying to sound angry but holding in a laugh, as they entered the sitting room, they were greeted by a young man in his mid twenties, he was a little taller than Darren with short dark brown hair and was wearing smart jeans and grey sweater over a blue shirt.

"You remember my son Tristan don't you?" Bruce said as the younger man shook Quentin's hand

"Ah yes, good to see you again Tristan." Quentin said with a smile then looked around.

"Eva is running a little late," Bruce said, anticipating Quentin's question "She should be here soon."

"Did Princess arrive? Where is she?" Tegan asked, Bruce smiled.

"Don't worry, she is here," he said "and settling into our stables."

"Come on," Hannah said as she headed to the doorway "I was going over to check on the horses myself anyway." and with the Tegan eagerly left the room after handing the carkeys to Darren, Tegan was followed out the door by Olivia.

"Better get Lolita settled too." she said before disappearing.

"So," Quentin started "What is this horse you were wanting me to have a look at?"

"Ulysses?" Bruce replied "Oh I think you will like him Quentin, a good all rounder. I'll take you to see him in a while." Bruce kept looking out the window and was looking a little worried.

"Dad," Tristan said knowingly "I'll let you know when Eva arrives."

"No, I want to be here for her arrival," he turned

to Quentin "Despite all that we have been through, she is still my little girl."

"I understand." nodded Quentin. There was silence that was broken by the sound of a vehicle coming up the driveway.

"That'll be her." Bruce commented with a smile "Tristan, go get the door will you?"

"This should be interesting." murmured Quentin to Darren as Tristan went to open the door, a few minutes later in walked Eva, was a sight to behold, she was short and slim, her waist length hair was in red dreadlocks, she wore a green quilted jacket with a black polo shirt under it, maroon coloured jodhpurs and a pair of brown knee high riding boots.

"Eva, so good to see you," Bruce said as he walked towards his daughter "I was worried something had happened.

"Sorry, we had.." she started to say when a voice behind her said.

"Sorry we are late," a short man with close cut balding hair and designer stubble appeared beside Eva wearing a polo shirt and jeans "but her horse was being difficult..."

"Marco was not being.." Eva tried to interrupt, anger clear in her voice but he continued.

"Then the drive here was a nightmare, but we are here now."

"I should go get Marco settled." Eva said almost in a whisper.

"Yes you do that." Craig said with surprisingly nasty tone. He then turned to the others with a wide smile.

"Craig," Bruce started "You already know Quentin, don't you?"

"Of course, it was a pleasure to do business with you." Craig said and he shook Quentin's hand., Bruce then gestured to Darren.

"And this is Darren, Quentin's future son in law, and I believe he works as a librarian in Dundee, Darren this is Craig Robertson, my daughters husband and owner of Thistle Computing." Craig held out his hand and Darren took it.

"I know who you are," Craig said with a morbid curiosity "You were very brave, not all who interfere in the business of the Donnelly gang live to tell the tale."

"Any decent person would have done the same in my position" Darren said with no hint of pride. Craig smirked and shook his head.

"Maybe," Craig said then gave an oddly cold smile "I should go see how Eva is getting on." and he left without awaiting a reply.

"I suppose we better get the luggage out the cars" sighed Quentin "And then, if its okay, I wish to see this horse you have been telling me about."

"Of course, just let me know when you are ready and I'll take you to see him." Bruce smiled.

CHAPTER 5

As Darren and Quentin were unloading the luggage from the cars Quentin turned to the younger man.

"So, what do you make of them?" he asked referring the the Inglistons.

"They seem nice enough," Darren replied "though I admit it looks like despite everything, Eva seems to have done well for herself." Darren noted "Married to a guy who seems like a successful businessman with his own.. what?" He noticed Quentin shake his head.

"Depends on how you measure success." the older man said as he pulled a large case from the Range Rover.

"What do you mean?" Darren asked curiously.

"Bruce asked me about a year ago as a favour to give Craig's company the job of upgrading the company computer systems, let us just say I was not impressed."

"Oh.." Darren looked a little surprised.

"Yeah, had to get another company in to redo half the work." Quentin continued.

"Oh that doesn't sound good." Darren said shaking his head.

"No it wasn't, cost me a fortune." Quentin told him "It was a nightmare."

"Oh well, I suppose we better get these cases inside." Darren said, Quentin nodded in agreement.

"I suppose, then I should talk to Bruce, see if this horse is everything he says it is." Quentin said as he checked one of the bags and shook his head.

"What is it?" Darren asked curiously.

"I packed some extra riding gear and it seemed Tegan's mother has..oh wait, typical Olivia, she has repacked the bag and put it right at the bottom. Typical." Quentin sighed with relief and with that they headed inside with the luggage.

The guest room they were assigned was next to the one Tegan's parents were using and was one of the smaller rooms, though it did have a shower room attached. Darren sat the bags down and was careful with the ones containing Tegan's riding attire, he glanced over at his fiancee who had just came in the door as he was already unpacking and hanging up her blazer, smoothing it over.

"They seem a nice enough family," Darren remarked "Though your dad was right, that Eva seemed a little.. different."

"That is an understatement," Tegan replied as she sat on the bed "It wasn't always the case though."

"What happened?" Darren asked as he laid out her riding boots, she had chosen to wear her Cavallo brand ones that she had started to wear during competitions as they had been sufficiently broken in.

"Hard to tell exactly, I had known her for a while and she used to compete in showjumping when we were younger. I remember the last time I saw her, It was one time her parents came over to visit and she was there, I had not long turned seventeen and she was dressed a bit.. grungy to say the least and she tried to tell me how foxhunting was wrong.. amongst other things." she looked over at Darren and shrugged.

"I can imagine that went down like a lead balloon." he stated, Tegan nodded.

"Soon after that I heard she had moved out and then I remember dad coming back from a hunt and telling me he saw Eva amongst the hunt sabs." Darren shook his head.

"I have to ask, how long has she had that.. hair?" Darren asked.

"Don't know, I was surprised to see her when she turned up at the stables earlier looking like that." Tegan said with a sigh "There was something else that bothered me though."

"Like what?" Darren asked.

"The Eva I knew was always cheerful, chatty and outgoing, it looked like all the joy had been drained out of her, she barely spoke at all and it was worse when her husband showed up, he came in, introduced himself and said to her it was time to get back to the house and unpack and she just meekly left with him."

"What do you think of him?" Darren asked curiously.

"If I am honest, there is something about him I don't like, I'm not sure exactly what though." Tegan answered as she sat on the bed "You know I really should go for a shower, but it has been a long day already." she flopped sideways onto the bed, her head perfectly landing on the pillow and she swung her legs up onto the bed, thankfully she cleaned her boots before she came in the house. Tegan fell asleep almost immediately, Darren looked at his watch, they had a few hours until dinner so he just reached into one of the bags, got out one of his Star Wars books and sat on the bed, he would wake Tegan up later.

Dinner that night was a somewhat formal occasion and as such everyone dressed up a little. Darren wore a plain black tshirt with his best jeans, Tegan decided to wear a dark green turtleneck sweater, black skirt and a pair of plain leather knee high boots with a slight heel. Quentin wore one of his business suits and Olivia wore a long dark blue dress with matching shoes. As they came into the dining room Darren saw that Bruce, Hannah and Tristan were already there and suitably attired for the evening, Hannah had an apron over her dress as she was just bringing the food out.

"Perfect timing," Hannah said with a smile "Dinner is ready." just then Eva and Craig walked in, Craig was wearing a shirt and dress trousers while Eva was still wearing her riding gear from before, just changed into a black long sleeve top

"Something smells good." Craig said as he walked over at Hannah took her hand and kissed it, taking her by surprise, Hannah blushed at the flattery as he went to sit down.

"So," Bruce started "What do you think of Ulysses?" Quentin looked over at his friend and smiled.

"A fine horse and a confident jumper, can't wait to take him out on a hunt." he replied "Though I seriously doubt any horse could ever match Tegan's Princess for jumping."

"Ah yes," Bruce said with a smile "She is a fine creature. Irish sports horse am I right?"

"She is Mister Ingliston," Tegan answered, a little bit of pride creeping into her voice then turned to Eva "Correct me if I'm wrong but is yours a..."

"Oh it's some Welsh horse." Craig interrupted before Eva had a chance to answer.

"It's a Welsh Section D." Eva said softly but Craig turned to her, looking visibly annoyed.

"Yes, yes, that is more or less what I said, stop being pedantic," he turned to Darren "What are these horsey types like?" Darren didn't look too pleased to be included in this conversation.

"I don;'t know, I've always been supportive of Tegan's riding activities." he said pointedly, Craig looked Darren over a few moments then shrugged and returned to his dinner. As everyone ate the conversation flowed. Quentin and Bruce discussed their respective businesses highs and lows, Hannah was talking to Olivia about a new line of jewellery coming to her stores while Tristan announced that he was receiving a promotion to Lieutenant, something that filled Bruce with pride but Darren noted how quiet Eva was, which was strange considering that it had apparently been a long time since she had spoke to anyone else in the family. As everyone finished their meal the conversation moved on to the upcoming hunt.

"This New Years hunt will be the end of an era, that reminds me, Eva," Bruce said "You aren't really serious about wearing those brown riding boots to the hunt are you?" Eva nodded and went to speak when Craig cut in.

"I have been trying to talk her out of it but you know how headstrong she is," he said rolling his eyes. Eva looked at Craig annoyed but he seemed to ignore her gaze "I told you, I even offered to get you some nice new black ones, so you would look smart for once but no, you insist on wearing those old brown ones like some tramp or something." Craig said to Eva, Bruce shook his head in dismay.

"Bruce, I think you can allow this break in dress code," Quentin suggested suddenly "Just this once, for your daughter. I know I won't mind"

"I suppose," Bruce smiled weakly "I just want this last big New Years hunt to go without any issues I guess., I can only hope the hunt sabs don't stir too much trouble." Bruce then side glanced Eva who looked shocked.

"Dad!.." she started to say.

"Oh she doesn't talk to that crowd any more," Interrupted Craig, then turned to her in an almost aggressive tone said "Do you?" Eva looked like she was going to say something but instead just shook her head and fell silent.

"But Surely Bruce your hunt will continue under the new regulations." Quentin asked curiously as he looked over at Craig and Eva then exchanged a glance with Darren, both noting how Craig repeatedly kept answering for her.

"Of course it will, but you know what some people are like, I've heard a few people have already talked of quitting and others are talking of going to England to take part in hunts down there." Bruce sighed as he stabbed at his food with his fork, silence fell on the table. Craig looked over at Tegan, his eyes lingering on her a few moments before he spoke

"So.. " Started Craig "Tegan, I was told you are training to be a nurse?"

"That is correct yes," Tegan said as she laid down her fork, there was something about Craig's gaze that made her feel uncomfortable but she looked over to Eva and smiled "I hear your artwork is doing well," she said to Eva "you were always quite the artist from what I remember."

"What kind of art do you do?" Darran added curiously/

"Well.. " Eva started but Craig cut in.

"It's apparently the sort of artwork gets paid thousands of pounds for, isn't that right my dear?" his voice had an almost mocking tone to it.

"It's.." she started to reply.

"Not bad for a little hobby." Craig continued

smugly and put his arm around her shoulders, Darren noted the grip her had on her seemed a little too tight. Eva shrugged the arm off.

"Craig.. stop it, I can't take it any more, not here, not now. I have had enough of this you never let me talk. I can speak for myself, you know how Important my art is to me! you know how important this week is for all of us! Why are you are always doing this to me. You uncaring.... seggfej." Craig's features hardened briefly but then he smiled at her.

"Oh just lighten up Eva." Craig said and he playfully slapped her on the arm but Eva's response surprised everyone, she stood up suddenly and shouted at him.

"Stop it!." She stared at him angrily for a few moments as if she was going to say something else but eventually just murmured "just stop." and stormed off, tears forming in her eyes. Everyone just looked at each other stunned, unsure of how to react, just then Tegan stood up.

"I'll go see if she is okay." and went after Eva, Craig went to follow but Darren motioned for him to sit back down.

"Let Tegan handle it," he said as Craig's eyes darted from Darren to the door the girls had left through as if silently debating if he should follow them or not. "Trust me, let her handle it." Darren repeated in a more insistent tone.

"Yes, let Tegan talk to her, might be what Eva needs." Bruce agreed.

"Yes, let her cool off a little." Quentin added.

"It has been a long day for everyone." Olivia noted.

"She will cool off eventually." Tristan said knowingly.

"I'm sure she will be fine Craig." Hannah said with a soft smile. After a few tense moments Craig sighed and sat back down dejectedly and and looked to the other diners.

"Sorry I don't know what has gotten into her lately." he offered with a shrug though Quentin and Darren exchanged looks. Darren could tell that Quentin was not impressed by Craig's antics.

"Well Quentin," Bruce said after an awkward silence "I have a new bottle of scotch in the study, care to join me?"

"What kind?" Quentin asked

"Glenfiddich of course." Bruce answered with a smile.

"Of course," Quentin echoed "lead on."

CHAPTER 6

Tegan caught up with Eva just as the latter got to her room.

"Eva, what's wrong?" Tegan asked as she closed the door behind them.

"It's nothing, honestly." Eva said unconvincingly, her eyes welling up with tears "I should really get back.." she made to leave the room again but Tegan stood in her way.

"No, there is something wrong. Look, anything you tell me will stay between us, I promise." Tegan said "I know something is wrong, I heard you swear in Hungarian, you only would do that if really mad or upset."

"I don't want to talk about it," Eva said in a desperate tone then her shoulders seemed to sag as she sat on the bed and she looked down a the floor in silence.

Tegan sat next to her and put a comforting arm around her.

Can I ask you something Tegan, if it is okay?" Eva said suddenly, the dreadlocked girl's eyes red from crying.

"Of course." Tegan said and walked over to sit on the bed next to Eva.

"Look, I will understand if you don't answer but what was it like.. the.. you know?" Eva stammered, Tegan sighed and looked down at the floor, she knew what Eva was asking about and while she didn't really want to talk about it, even after all this time, she thought it might help Eva open up.

"It was like a nightmare I couldn't wake up from, I still remember the look of hate on Lucy's face." Tegan said softly

"I can't even begin to imagine how you must have felt. I remember you two were really close back in the day, in fat most people thought you were sisters instead of cousins." Eva interjected. Tegan looked at her sadly and sighed.

"That is what made it all the worse," Tegan looked at Eva then suddenly smiled "Thought I will admit, the strange thing is, if it hadn't happened I'd have never met Darren."

"He does seem like a really nice guy. " Eva said with a weak smile as she tried to dry her eyes with her hands.

"Yeah, I probably wouldn't be alive today if it wasn't for him." Tegan said softly.

"So, if it is okay to ask, how did you two..?" Eva

started.

"Fall in love?" Tegan said, anticipating Eva's next question "Well..."

Darren sat in the sitting room, the peace and quiet was welcoming, suddenly bottle of beer was sat down on the coffee table in front of him.

"I want to apologise for earlier," said Craig, who took the seat across from Darren in the sitting room "Eva can get a little.. passionate and stubborn at times. I shouldn't have said what I did though."

"No you shouldn't have," Darren replied with an edge to his voice but in a more softer tone continued "How long have you two been arguing?"

"In all honesty, too long," Craig said as he pulled out a mobile phone from his pocket and looked like he was texting someone on it, it was one of those Nokia phones Darren had seen advertised that had interchangeable cases. This particular one was purple "Sorry, business stuff" he shrugged apologeticly "I assume you have been told all about her past? Being a hunt saboteur, her criminal record.. all that." Darren nodded slowly.

"Some of it but surely you knew about all this when you married her." He said as he picked up the beer bottle and took a drink Craig looked down at his feet and gave a dramatic sigh.

"I did, but I thought she would settle down a little. She had given up the whole hunt saboteur stuff when we met but it is like there is this urge not to conform to..

anything really," he then thumped the arm of the chair with his fist "Sorry, but here is only so much a man can take."

"Easy there, it can't be that bad surely." Darren said as he started to make calming motions with his hands.

"Sorry," Craig said as he ran his hand over his close cropped hair "You don't know Eva like I do, it is not just that she would help sabotage hunts, it is the fact she used to sabotage hunts her dad took part in and made it obvious the hunters knew who her father was. You should have heard the way she would speak about it all." Craig explained.

"So, why did she stop doing the hunt sab stuff?" Darren asked.

"Her story is the local group she was part of started taking things too far, finding out where hunt attendees lived, threatening them, that sort of thing, she said it was getting out of hand," But Craig gave Darren a look that suggested he didn't believe her "But as you saw earlier I'm not sure her father is fully convinced that is true."

"Oh, well I can understand that why she left them but why was she invited if there was still bad blood between them?" Darren looked at Craig confused. Craig leaned forward and sighed.

"When we first met, she was this relentlessly positive vibrant young lady but as I got to know her..." Craig stopped as if unsure if he should confide in Darren "but she is unhappy, she is sinking deep into depression and I didn't know what to do. I got her a horse as she said she was always at her happiest when riding, that helped but she hadn't spoke to her family for years and I could tell it was eating away at her inside so I suggested she contact them, one thing lead to another and here we are but you saw for yourself, mark my words it won't end well." Craig remarked.

"Surely It won't get that bad." Darren tried to reassure Craig as Tristan walked in and sat on the sofa. Craig stood up and stretched.

"We will see I guess," he said dryly then looked at his watch "Anyway, it is getting late and should see if Eva is okay." as Craig walked away Darren shook his head, there definitely was something about Craig he wasn't sure of.

"Something on your mind?" Tristan asked Darren, Darren looked at the fireplace then at Tristan.

"It's probably nothing." Darren said with a weak smile as he picked up his beer bottle, regarded it a moment and took a drink.

"...So yeah, he was selfless, caring and you know what? I wouldn't be alive today if it hadn't been for Darren. I love him with all my heart." Tegan looked down a moment then looked back at Eva "Anyway, what have you been up to? Last time we spoke must have been..what?"

"Ninety seven I think," Eva said after some thought." Well, let's see, where to begin..."Eva was starting to open up, she talked about joining the hunt sabs and leaving home. She even rolled up her sleeves and showed Tegan her tattoos that she designed herself, some very beautiful and intricate, they reminded Tegan of Indian mehndi designs. Tegan however did also notice bruising on both arms but elected not to say anything but in general she found Eva was talking more freely, that is until Craig knocked on the door.

"Eva, Is it okay to come on?" he asked, Tegan looked over and saw Eva suddenly become nervous and tense.

"Yes.. of course." she said shakily, he walked in and looked at Tegan surprised.

"Oh, I didn't realise you were still here." he looked as if he was barely hiding his frustration, he then turned to Eva "I thought you would be in bed by now." Tegan looked at Eva confused.

"I usually go for a ride first think in the morning before breakfast..."

"Yeah and probably wake me up at seven in the morning every time with her alarm." Craig interrupted dryly.

"It is okay," Tegan said as she stood "I was just going anyway, talk to you tomorrow." and she looked at Eva with a sad smile, Tegan was sure Eva was going to tell her something before Craig came in. As Tegan walked down the hall she could hear raised voices from the room she had just left, She just hoped Eva would be okay.

Later when he walked into their room, Darren saw Tegan was already there and was laying on the bed still fully dressed.

"So... what happened?" he asked and sat on the edge of the bed. Tegan sat up and looked at Darren sadly.

"I'm worried about her Darren, I really am," she started "It took her a while to do so but she really started to open up a bit, I started to see glimpses of the old Eva again.."

"Then Craig showed up?" Darren guessed and raised an eyebrow.

"Something like that, yeah." she replied with a sigh.

"While you two were talking, Craig struck up a conversation with me." Darren said as he took his trainers off.

"Oh, how did that go?" Tegan asked with a curious tone to her voice.

"It was odd," Darren replied with a shake of his head "The stuff he was saying, his general demeanour, how long have they been married?"

"Let's see, about a year I think." Tegan replied after thinking about it.

"Well, it sounds like the magic has already gone out of the relationship..." He went on to tell Tegan what Craig had said to him earlier "... I know everyone has arguments at some point but this felt different somehow. Ever notice how Craig never really gives Eva a chance to speak?" Tegan sat up and nodded.

"I had noticed, kinda hard not to, I did kind of notice something else too but didn't want to say and I'm not sure it is what I think it might be." she said cautiously.

"Oh? what was that?" Darren asked, sounding quite intrigued.

"Well," Tegan started with a hint on uncertainty "I thought it was a trick of the light at first when I saw her in the stables but then at the dinner table and after I noticed the area around her left eye seemed somewhat discoloured."

"Discoloured? How so?" Darren looked a little confused.

"It was like she has used some foundation or concealer but hasn't quite matched the makeup with her skin tone, y'know?" Tegan said, doing her best to describe it.

"Are you saying what I think you are saying" Darren said slowly "That he is hitting her and she is hiding the bruising?"

"It is possible, I did see other bruises too but I dunno," Tegan sounded unsure, as if suddenly doubting herself "But as you know bumps, bruises and scrapes are part and parcel of equestrian life." Tegan was second guessing herself and Darren knew it, if he was honest it wouldn't surprise him if Craig was abusive in that way to Eva.

"What can we do though?" Darren said eventually "It's not like we can ask her with him always hanging around," he looked over at Tegan who looked deep in thought "Tegan.. Tegan.. you okay?"

"Oh? Yeah just thinking," Tegan said as she snapped out of her thoughts "Eva goes out for an early morning ride about seven o'clock. I could always join her..."

"Ah very clever and hopefully she might talk some more if she is away from him? Certainly worth a try," Darren said as he stifled a yawn "Well, it's getting late.."

"I know and I have to get up early to catch Eva." Tegan agreed as she slowly started to get changed for bed.

The alarm went off at seven o'clock and Tegan sleepily got up with a yawn, pulling on the first pair of Jodhpurs that came to hand which happened to be her black pair and Tegan then put on her Warner thirty four Celtic goalkeeper shirt on. She struggled to get her first rubber riding boot on, managing in her fifth attempt. She then went looking for the other boot, which she found under the bed. Tegan then pulled it on first time, stood and tied her hair up in a ponytail. As she opened the door, Darren stirred and woke up, looking at her with heavy eyelids and smiled.

"Morning." he said sleepily.

"Morning," she replied and smiled back "Just going to try and meet Eva, will let you know how I get on when I get back."

"Okay." he replied and settled back to sleep as Tegan made her way to the staircase, Glen Tachur was eerily quiet first thing in the morning Tegan found as she headed down the stairs as quietly as she could as not to wake anyone. It was still dark as she stepped outside but Tegan noted that the Ford Mondeo she had seen parked next to her Lupo earlier wasn't there any more as she made her way to the stables. It was oddly quiet as she stepped inside. Tegan walked up to Princess and stroked her muzzle.

"How are you girl," Tegan said as she looked around Princess stood out amongst the other horse with her dapple grey colouring "Up for a ride?" she noticed Marco, Eva's Welsh Section D stallion, with it's dark brown, almost black and white colouring was still there so maybe Tegan had arrived early. Something out of the corner of Tegan's eye caught her attention. It looked like somebody's foot sticking out of one of the unoccupied stables, she looked around cautiously and walked forward slowly.

"Hello?" she said shakily, her anxiety was rising "Who is there?" As Tegan got closer she could make out in the dim light. It looked like someone was laying face down in the stable in fact it looked like Bruce Ingliston " Mister Ingliston, are you okay..." she was about to say when she saw the blood...

CHAPTER 7

By the time Detective Sergeant McManus arrived on the scene forensics were already on the scene. Detective Inspector Duff, a young woman with short brown hair came up to McManus with some urgency.

"So," McManus said "What are we dealing with here?" Duff flicked through her notes.

"Mister Bruce Ingliston, found dead at quarter past seven this morning. Looks like he was bludgeoned to death with a spade that was found next to him at the crime scene."

"Okay," McManus said thoughtfully "Who found the body?"

"A Miss Tegan Galloway, she was staying at the house as a guest of the deceased." Duff answered sharply.

"Galloway? Why does that name ring a bell?"

McManus looked at Duff curiously.

"Remember that kidnapping that happened February last year?" Duff replied.

"Oh, I see" McManus said as he remembered "I remember it now, the Donnellys are still trying to recover from that incident from what I hear, was a strange affair by all accounts, did she see anyone else at he scene?"

"No and we have discounted her as a suspect due to she wouldn't have had the time to do it, plus I cant see any motive." Duff shrugged.

"I take you took initial statements from everyone in the house." McManus stated.

"We did and they are waiting inside for you, well all but one," Duff said as she once again consulted her notes "Bruce Ingliston's daughter Eva...."

"Wait, Eva Ingliston?.." McManus interrupted.

"...Robertson she is married now." Duff quietly corrected him.

".. Yeah whatever. You see, Bruce was heavily involved in the local foxhunting scene, his daughter however was a bit of a rebel it seemed and became a hunt saboteur." McManus explained.

"She wasn't, was she?" Duff looked genuinely shocked.

"She was," McManus said with a knowing glance "Multiple arrests, most for disrupting hunts her father was part of. Of course he would refuse to press charges. Oh yes our Eva was quite the firebrand at one point."

"you don't think she had anything to do with this?" Duff said with a sense of disbelief in her voice.

"Let's see, her father, an important figure in foxhunting is found murdered days before one of the biggest days on the hunt calender. His daughter, a known hunt saboteur and a violent one if her past is anything to go by, was staying in the house at the time and is now nowhere to be seen, "McManus explained in a gruff manner, Duff was still relatively new to this and had a habit of trying to see the best in people "I'd say it at least makes her our prime suspect, don't you? Who else is here?"

"Well, there is Hannah Ingliston, the deceased's wife. His son Tristan Ingliston, an officer in the navy here on leave. The son in law Craig Robertson who is the owner of Thistle Computing. Miss Galloway's parents and a Mister Darren Douglas..." Duff read from her notes.

"… Douglas? Why does that name ring a bell?" McManus asked and Duff quickly checked her notes again

"He was the guy caught up in the kidnapping of Miss Galloway and..." she started.

"Oh yeah, aren't they engaged or something?" McManus remembered. "I suppose we better go see what the others have to say." he said as he started to head towards the the house.

"Sir," shouted a young redheaded officer "We found something." and held up a clear evidence bag with a purple Nokia phone in it...

McManus sighed as he looked at everyone assembled in

the sitting room, being called out to a murder was not how he imagined starting his day. Duff stood next to him ready to take notes.

"I can't believe this is happening." Hannah said through her tears, Olivia was comforting her with Tristan also nearby. Quentin and Craig were on the large sofa and Darren and Tegan were standing, Darren holding her protectively. McManus noted Craig would occasionally glance at Hannah, though she didn't really seem to notice.

"Missus Ingliston, I regret to say that after analysing the crime scene and taking all the evidence available to us it would seem that the number one suspect in your husband's death is your.."

"Eva? No, she couldn't, she wouldn't." interrupted Tristan, anticipating what McManus was going to say next.

"Unfortunately it does look like she is our number one suspect. Her criminal record doesn't help matters, she has been charged with violent acts in the past and take it from me it would take someone a lot of hate and resentment to the victim t attack him in such a manner. Your husband was facing his killer when it happened."

"Yes, he was struck on the left side of his face it seems." Duff added as she consulted her notes

"Of course this was found near the body." McManus said as he took the evidence bag with the purple Nokia phone out of his pocket, Craig looked up at the phone with a shocked expression.

"That's Eva's phone." he said eventually.

"Where is your wife now?" McManus looked at

Craig intently.

"I don't know, all I know is my carkeys weren't were I left them and my car is gone."

"Ah yes," McManus casually flicked through his notes "A dark green Ford Mondeo, This does not look good Mister Robertson, your wife is nowhere to be found, her phone found at the crime scene," McManus started to pace "Can anyone think of a specific reason why Missus Robertson would attack her father?" he asked and to his surprise, Craig spoke up.

"Well," he started slowly "I know they didn't see eye to eye for a long time. As I'm sure you know she used to be a hunt saboteur you see and had interfered in some of the local hunts in the past."

"So why was she invited then.. if they had such bad blood?" McManus asked with interest.

"It was shortly after we got married, they started talking again and everything seemed fine, she told him she had cut ties with her hunt saboteur friends and apparently they wanted to make a fresh start." he looked like he didn't believe that was true.

"You had your doubts?" the Detective Sergeant asked.

"I don't like to speak ill of my wife but it wouldn't surprise me if she was still in contact with them," Craig shook his head in disbelief "But it was also the little things they were arguing over, they even argued because she was insisting on wearing her old brown riding boots." McManus looked confused. Quentin offered an explanation.

"It is tradition to wear black boots when hunting,

some may wear ones with a brown top but all brown? It is not the done thing usually."

"Yes," Craig said nodding "She also seemed as if something was on her mind and became confrontational at the dinner table," Tegan exchanged glances with Darren, the reason she seemed that way was because Craig wasn't letting her speak for herself but he continued "Then after it we did have a bit of an argument."

"What about?" Asked McManus, looking more alert than before.

"This and that and everything in between," Craig shrugged "I don't think she was all that happy being here." McManus shook his head and held up the purple mobile phone.

"There was a text sent from this phone to her father last night asking to meet her in the stables in the morning."Anyone know anything about this" he looked at everyone in the room in turn.

"No," answered Tegan shakily as she cuddled into Darren, who in turn did his best to keep her calm. Tegan was nervous about talking to police ever since her own experiences with them after the kidnapping.

"Ah yes, Miss Galloway, you are the one who found the body did you not? In the stables?" McManus asked as he checked his notes. she nodded

"Why were you there? If you don't mind me asking?" he asked.

"I was checking to see if princess.. my horse.. had settled into the stables," she then looked around as if wondering if to continue "And to talk to Eva, she likes to ride before breakfast"

"I see, did you want to talk about anything in particular?"

"We had spoke last night and it looked like she was wanting to tell me something but couldn't." She answered, Darren noticed Craig look over at her with interest.

"Any ideas what that could have been?" asked Duff, looking up from her notes.

"Not really, can't say for certain, only something was upsetting her greatly." Tegan side cuddled into Darren and he put his arm around her protectively. McManus sighed.

"Okay," he turned to Craig "Do you know who a J. Quinn is?" said "There does seem to be a few messages from this person on you wife's phone."

"I have no idea, one of her saboteur buddies maybe?" Craig replied then suddenly put his head in his hands "I just wish I knew where she was, I'm worried about her, about what she might do."

"I see," said McManus as he rubbed his temples "Well, if she returns or tried to get in contact with any of you let me know immediately, in the meantime we will do everything we can to solve this case," H handed out cards with a direct number to him and before leave McManus turned to Hannah "We will do everything we can to catch your husbands killer, I promise you that."

After the officers left, Quentin turned to Hannah.

"If you need help with anything, funeral

arrangements, whatever, I'm here for you" he said, his voice full of concern.

"Thank you, I think I will need all the help I can get." Hannah said as she dried her eyes "I know one other thing you can do, if you are up to it of course, Bruce would want to hunt to go on without him, you know this." she said as she dried her tears.

"I know.." Quentin started.

"Really? You are still going through with the hunt? But.." Darren started to interrupt.

"Yes," Hannah said, looking over at Darren sadly "Bruce would have wanted to to continue, and he would want you to lead it Quentin."

"Me?" Quentin said, surprised "Surely there is someone already part of the Ayrshire Hunt who could take over?"

"I have no doubt there would be, but Bruce would want you." Hannah said almost pleading.

"Okay, okay, I will do it," Quentin said with a sigh "who do I contact to discuss it with?"

"Alexander McVitie and don't worry I will tell him, I have to.. break the news..." Hannah said as she started to cry fresh tears.

As they headed to the car, McManus turned to Duff and sighed loudly.

"So? What do you think?" McManus asked.

"All evidence points to the daughter, it's really hard to see past her at this point," Duff shrugged "Nobody else has any real motive."

COLD BLOOD

"I know, neither the Galloways or the Douglas boy have any real reason to kill him, his wife by all accounts was a loving partner and owns her own business, I can't see it being the son, what about the son in law?" McManus mused.

"He did seem very critical of her actions to say the least." Duff admitted. McManus shook his head and looked back at Glen Tachur house.

"You know, I grew up in Maryhill, family didn't have much but you know what? We were bloody happy," He said almost absently "look around you, it feels like a different world doesn't it? They would have you believe it is a better life but you know what? It doesn't make them any happier."

"What do you mean?" Duff asked, slightly bemused.

"They still have the same arguments and issues as the rest of us," McManus said and shrugged "We better get a list of all associates of Eva Robertson and while you are at it, circulate images of her to the stations in the area and the ferry ports."

"You really think she would..." Duff started to say but was interrupted by McManus.

"I'm not taking any chances, let's get back to the station." he said as he climbed into the car.

CHAPTER 8

As everyone dispersed from the sitting room. Tegan made her way up to her room with a sense of urgency with Darren following, as he walked into the room, Darren saw her curled up on the bed softly humming Loch Lomond to herself.

"Tegan, what's wrong? It must be bad as you are humming Loch Lomond." he said as he sat on the edge of the bed.

"I keep seeing his body.. lying there.." she stammered as tears rolled down her face. Darren lay on the bed behind her and put a comforting arm around Tegan.

"Tegan, it's okay. I'm here for you." he said as she turned around and cuddled into him.

"I thought I was over all this, the panic attacks, the humming..I've not done that since.. you know.."

Tegan stammered as she pressed her ear against his chest, listening to Darren's heartbeat always settled her.

"Look," Darren said as softly as he could "You just saw a dead body, a reaction like this is fully understandable. I'd actually be more worried if it didn't bother you." Tegan looked up at him teary eyed and gave a weak smile.

"You always know just what to say." She said.

"I try my best, you know what?" Darren said after a few moments thought "Let's grab the tent and get away for a night or two, just the two of us like we planned. It is going to be busy around here with the police coming and going." Tegan nodded.

"I'd like that." she said in barely a whisper.

"That's settled, I'll go let your parents know." Darren said as he got up.

"Where will we go?" Asked Tegan as she propped herself up on one elbow.

"Don't know," Darren shrugged "But we will find out when we get there."

Hannah was looking out the window of the sitting room, alone in her thoughts when Craig came in.

"Sorry, I didn't see you there.." and he turned as if to leave.

"What's wrong?" she asked as she faced him.

"I'm wondering if it would be for the best if I left, considering everything that has went on.."he started but Hannah walked forward and took his hand in her hands.

"Craig," she smiled sadly "You are still family, at

least stay until the funeral, please. Bruce would have wanted it, he was so pleased to hear Eva had married and settled down with a man like yourself."

"Thank you, her father was lucky to have such a beautiful and kind wife. Okay, I'll stay." he relented with a smile "Excuse me, I just need to make a few calls." he said as she turned back to the window, not noticing how he looked her up and down, his smile broadening as he left the room.

While they were concerned and worried about Tegan, her parents understood why Darren thought getting away from everything would be a good idea. As he was walking back to tell Tegan they were okay with it, Darren bumped into Tristan.

"Hi, is Tegan okay?" Tristan asked.

"Yeah," replied Darren "I think the shock of it all, plus dealing with the police again has overwhelmed her a bit. I'm going to take her out camping. Hopefully it will help her relax a bit." Tristan nodded and looked in thought.

"Does she still like to stargaze?" he asked "I remember back in the day hearing her mention doing it a few times." Darren nodded.

"Yeah she does, why?" he asked curiously.

"Well there is a place Eva and I used to go when we were younger on camping trips, its not too far from here, only about forty five minutes in a car. Galloway Forrest Park." Tristan answered.

"How fitting." Darren said, raising an eyebrow,

Tristan just looked at him.

"What do you mean?" Tristan said looking slightly confused then smiled "Oh.. I see, never thought of that. Give me a few moments, I'll drop by your room with one of my old maps pointing out the spot we always went to, It is perfect, unspoiled view of the star as night, Tegan will love it."

"Thanks." Darren said with a smile, he hadn't been too sure about Tristan at first but he seemed like a decent guy.

Darren came back into the room to see Tegan back the rucksack they had brought with them with various supplies.

"I see you've been busy, I wasn't gone that long was I?" He said noting all the tinned food and bottles on the bed.

"I thought it would take my mind off things." she replied. The tent was stored in the rucksack along with a blanket, food and other equipment, two sleeping bags were attached to it on the outside with straps. They decided to take another bag, Darren's backpack and have a change of clothes and toiletries just in case they needed them. Darren changed into comfortable, mainly old clothes with the exception of his Douglas Twenty goalkeeper top. He had some old Reebok trainers, black Umbro tracksuit trousers and opted for his faithful black bomber jacket. Tristan dropped by with the map and soon they were ready to go.

"So, are we ready? Have we got everything?"

Darren asked as he looked around the room to see if anything had been missed. Tegan nodded and held up her carkeys.

"I'm Ready." she said with a smile.

It didn't take long to pack the Lupo with the camping equipment, as he shut the car boot door Darren looked over at Tegan, she had on her rubber knee high riding boots, black jodhpurs, the Warner thirty four Celtic goalkeeper shirt on under a green and black Umbro branded jacket that went nearly to her knees and had a drawstring waist. She noted he was looking at her boots and sighed

"Darren I know what you are thinking but these are really comfortable to wear, trust me." she said, anticipating his question, they both remembered the last time they were out in the countryside, which of course was when they were fleeing Tegan's kidnappers, she had on a pair of her more expensive leather riding boots, which was an issue as while they were excellent for riding, the stiff leather and thin soles made walking long distance very difficult. Darren considered it for a moment then shrugged.

"Only if you are sure," he said eventually "we got everything?" he asked.

"Should have," she replied "I mean we are only going to be out for a night or two at most anyway." she shrugged.

"And you know were we are going?" he continued to ask.

"The directions Tristan gave me were pretty easy to follow," she fished into her jacket pocket and produced the map Tristan gave them map and a piece of notepaper "I should be able to find it based on these directions." she said with a smile as she opened the car door. Soon they were back on the road and heading to Galloway Forest Park. Ten minutes into the journey Tegan suddenly cursed under her breath and shook her head.

"Oh no," she said "I forgot my phone, I left it on the bed."

"Tegan it's okay, I'm sure we will be fine," Darren reassured her "It is not like we are going to run into trouble... damn!" he suddenly said louder than he intended.

"What is it?" Tegan asked.

"That is what was bothering me earlier, it was the colour of Craig's phone, of course." Darren said after some thought.

"What about it?." she said, not sure where he was going with this,

"Tegan, he was using a grey phone this morning." he explained.

"And?" Tegan asked shaking her head.

"He had a purple one last night.. like the one they said was Eva's." he said earnestly but Tegan rolled her eyes.

"Maybe she left it at the table when she stormed off during dinner," she offered "Darren, can we just put all this to the back of our minds just for one night? Please." Darren shrugged but she could see he wasn't fully satisfied but managed a smile.

"Yeah, you're right," he said and started to study at the map "Let's just enjoy ourselves."

They were close to the park when the car started to slow.

"What's wrong?" Darren said, looking a little bit confused.

I don't know," Tegan said, then looked at the dashboard "Oh, erm.. I forgot to get petrol." she pulled to the side of the road and looked at Darren apologeticly, Darren just smiled back.

"Well," he said looking at the map "If we are where I think we are, we can easily walk there." but Tegan just looked at him confused.

"So what do we do about the car?" she asked nervously.

"It should be safe here for the night and we can go to a petrol station and get one of those little plastic bottles with the funnel for petrol and fill it up and come back" Darren shrugged "Would give us enough to drive and get it filled up properly."

"I'm not sure about leaving it overnight, what if someone comes, breaks in and drives off with it?" Tegan said with worry in her voice.

"Tegan, think on it," Darren said with a raised eyebrow "How are they going to drive off, the car has no petrol."

"Oh, sorry," Tegan said with a weak smile "I wasn't thinking straight."

"It's okay," Darren said as he got out the car "We

probably better get to the camp before it gets dark." They got the bags out of the car, Darren took the larger rucksack and Tegan took the backpack. Before they left, Tegan quickly written a note and put it on the dashboard for people to see stating it is out of petrol and they will be back soon.

"Don't want people thinking it is abandoned." she shrugged.

"If I'm reading the map right," Darren said as he studied the map carefully "we head this way." and he pointed deep into the trees.

"Okay, let's go then." Tegan said with a slight smile, Darren's map reading, even without the use of a compass was surprisingly good despite the fact when they met he wasn't really the outdoors type. she linked arms with him as they walked. It was quiet and peaceful, just the sounds of their own footsteps breaking the silence, yes this is definitely what she needed, Tegan thought away from everyone and everything, only her and Darren.

Back at Glen Tachur, Craig was in the sitting area staring at his phone, alone in his thoughts when Tristan walked in.

"Hey, you okay?" Tristan asked as he went to the window to look outside.

"I've tried calling home and everywhere I know Eva will go," Craig said with a deep sigh "I'm still waiting to hear back from some of the people but so far she is nowhere to be found. I guess I'm just trying to make sense of it all, to be honest I'm surprised you still want me around."

"Craig, you are still family," Tristan assured him with a smile "regardless of what happens you are always welcome here."

"That's what Hannah said too. Thank you, it really does mean a lot," Craig said and put his head in his hands with a groan "I Just don't understand why would she do this? I know Eva didn't get on well with her father but this?" Tristan walked over and sat in one of the vacant chairs.

"You are asking the wrong person." he said "The Eva I knew growing up was a fun loving cheerful person, a little too free spirited at times for the rest of us but that was just her way." Tristan looked over at Craig sadly.

"I just wish she would come back," Craig sighed "At least let us know why she did it." he then stood and paced around and rubbing his temples.

"Yeah, I just don't get it,"Agreed Tristan "I have heard them have worse arguments over the years." Craig slumped back on one of the chairs then looked around with a slightly confused look.

"Hey," he said eventually "Where is... erm... what's her face..?"

"Tegan?" Tristan asked

"Yeah, her and that man of hers too. I haven't seen either of them since before lunch." Craig said with an nod.

"They have went away to camp overnight, Tegan is a bit of a stargazer and Galloway National Park is perfect for it." Tristan explained.

"Oh," Craig shrugged "Have you ever been there yourself?" Tristan sat back and gazed up at the ceiling thoughtfully.

"Oh yes, Eva and I used to go there all the time when we were younger. Dad used to take us at first but eventually when we were older, we would go ourselves." he leaned forward "She liked going there to get away from it all, especially after..." Suddenly Craig's phone started to ring.

"Sorry," Craig said as he went to answer. Tristan sat patiently as Craig had a short conversation "That was jut the owner of the local stables, Eva hasn't been round there either."

"Hopefully she will turn up somewhere," Tristan sighed as he stood up, I'm just going to check up on things, will you be okay?" Craig looked up and smiled weakly.

"I'll manage." he replied, when Tristan left Craig frantically texted a message a number on his phone as quickly as he could, his hands shaking.

It had been quite a trek but they eventually got there in the end.

"How's your feet?" Darren asked.

"They are fine honestly." Tegan said "I told you my rubber boots are way more comfortable than the leather ones, there is a reason I wear these as often as I do." and she gave him a look that suggested he should have known really this by now, she then looked around, it was a small clearing with a fallen tree. Tristan had suggested setting up the tent near the tree to act as a wind breaker of sorts, suddenly something had caught Tegan's eye.

"Tegan, what is it?" Darren asked as he noticed her tense up..

"Look." she pointed to the edge of the clearing, someone had draped a large tartan blanket over the roots of one of the fallen trees and the corners held in place with stones "Someone else is here." Suddenly the sound of a twig snapping made them both turn to the direction of the noise and into the clearing walked a figure, short and slim, long red dreadlocked hair, a tight black turtle neck sweater with a green padded gilet,a small beige canvas backpack with brown leather straps, trim and fasteners. She was also wearing maroon and black jodhpurs and brown leather knee high riding boots, it was Eva Robertson...

COLD BLOOD

CHAPTER 9

Tegan couldn't believe her eyes.

"Eva! What are you doing here?" she said in shock and slowly backing away cautiously, her eyes darting around. Darren placing himself protectively between the Tegan and Eva.

"I had to get away from everything for a bit, get away from him, I was going to go back tonight.. I just needed space.. I'm actually glad to see you as the car is.. wait, why are you acting so weird? What is going on?" she asked as she noticed them both staring at her in shock

"Eva, Your father is dead." Darren said with little to no tact "and as much as I hate to say it but all signs point to you as the main suspect." Eva looked confused, then shocked, she staggered back and put her hand on the fallen tree trunk to stabilise herself.

"What?" she said in a whisper then in a louder tone continued "How?"

"You tell us." Tegan said in a cold tone, her arms crossed.

"Tegan!" Eva shouted as tears welled up in her eyes "Come on, you know I didn't do it," she said repeatedly her expression a mix of sadness, fear and panic "You have to believe me. Please."

"Calm down," Darren said as he held his hands up "Eva, Your father was found dead in the stables and your phone was found next to the body."

"My phone?" she replied looking confused.

"Yeah, the purple Nokia." Darren remarked, Tegan looked on, her expression was one of cautious curiosity.

"I thought I lost that a few days ago." Eva said after some thought "Wait... You said it was found in the stables?

"Apparently." Tegan added, her expression getting more curious as if she was trying to figure out Darren's thought process.

"And you definitely lost it, you didn't have it at all yesterday? Right?" Darren asked, his mind racing.

"I'm positive, why are you asking." Eva was starting to look confused.

"I'm now certain that Craig had your phone last night," Darren said "He texted someone on it.

"You didn't tell me he was actually using it." Tegan said with a frown.

"I didn't see why it was... oh," Darren replied "There was a text to.."

"Wait, hold on, what are you trying to say?" Eva interrupted "Just tell me."

"Well," Tegan said as she stepped forward slowly "Your dad apparently received a text from your phone last night but from what Darren has said.."

"Craig texted him with my phone? why?" Eva interrupted then fell fell silent and started to cry. Darren looked over at Tegan and shrugged, she gave an equally confused look then Darren remembered what Quentin said about Craig's business.

"Eva, I know this might sound inappropriate with your dad dead, what happens to the family wealth?" Eva looked back through bloodshot eyes from crying and sniffed pitifully.

"The money from his estate would be shared equally between myself and Tristan." she said after a moment.

"What about your mum.." he started but Tegan shook her head.

"Darren, there is something you should know, Hannah Ingliston is not Eva's mother." she said, Darren looked confused.

"Hannah and my father have only been married five years, my mother's name was Katalin, she was a Hungarian gypsy immigrant. She died when I was nine." Eva told him.

"That word you called Craig at the dinner table before you walked off, was that..." he started to say.

"Hungarian? yes, Tristan and I can both speak it, mother thought it was important we learn the language." Eva explained.

"Darren, what are you getting at?" Tegan asked as she looked at Darren then Eva in confusion.

"Tegan, it's okay, all will become apparent soon enough. Eva, one more question, if you don't mind." Darren said with a look that suggested he knew what he was talking about."Would I be right in saying you have a joint bank account with your husband?" Eva nodded, Tegan looked at Darren in shock, realising what he was getting at, by her expression Eva was coming to the same conclusion.

"You don't think.." she started, Darren nodded with a sad smile.

"That Craig might have done this? Yes, yes I do," Darren said with confidence "Think on it, business not going well, for all we know he owes people money. Craig then realises his wife is in line for a large sum from an inheritance..."

"Are you sure?" Eva asked, trying to make sense of it all "About the business I mean. According to him, business was going well, he mentioned a new investor." Darren shook his head.

"No, if what I have heard is anything to go by, business is not going well at all."

"Even then, why would he do this? Why would he blame me? he wouldn't be capable.." Eva started but Darren shook his head.

"Eva, Tell me if I'm wrong here," said, looking at Eva intently "But has Craig has been beating you? Or worse?".

"What do you mean?" Eva looked at both Tegan and Darren in surprise.

"Eva, it's the little things, the concealer round the eye, the long sleeve tops to cover the bruising on the arms, the way you reacted to his punch to the arm at the dinner table..." Tegan started to say and would have continued but suddenly Eva just burst into tears, Tegan went over and comforted her, there was no need for her to answer "How long as this been going on." Tegan said after a while. Eva looked down and then, in soft voice spoke.

"A long time," she started to cry fresh tears "A week before the wedding we had an argument, he lashed out but said he didn't mean it that the stress of his business and the wedding just got to him and he vowed not to do it again."

"But it did, didn't it?" Tegan said softly. Eva nodded again.

"On our wedding night, I was too tired but he wouldn't take no, once he had.. punished me as he put it.. he...he.." she struggled to say the rest her shoulders sagged and she whispered "If I do anything he doesn't like or approve of..." Tegan had heard enough held her close, letting Eva cry on her shoulder.

Craig nearly leapt right out of his seat when his phone suddenly rang.

"Hello there Craig I got your text, I assume you have some good news for me, namely that you have the money you owe me." said a voice with a heavy Glasgow accent.

"I do, or at least I will have soon, let us just say I

am about to come into some family wealth..." Craig started to say.

"Oh?" the person on the other end sounded impressed "So you dealt with the old man then? I didn't think you had it in you to do it, I must admit I'm glad I was wrong." the other person interrupted "Do they suspect you?"

"No, I managed to convince everyone it was that stupid bitch of a wife of mine..."

"Clever, is she in custody?" the other person asked.

"Well, actually that is why I needed to talk to you. No, she ran off..." Craig then explained exactly what happened "… So, that's what happened, we had a row and she ran off."

"Idiot, what if someone saw her drive off or has some other proof that she wasn't there?" the other person sounded angry.

"I figured she would come back after an hour or two once she cooled off but for whatever reason she hasn't and nobody we know has seen her. What do you suggest I do?" Craig asked "Do I wait until she returns and .."

"No,It is too risky. listen I can make this problem go away but it will cost you." the other person interrupted.

"I can afford it.. well I will be able to.". Craig said with a smirk.

"Good, all we need to do is make it look like an accident and ensure the body is found after the will has been settled but that should be no problem." the person said "Do you know where she is?"

"Well, Not for definite but let's be honest, she stands out a mile with that hair so she will be easy to spot. However if you are looking for a good place to start I'd recommend Galloway National Park. I have it on good authority she used to go there when troubled in the past, it's close by and as I say I've tried everywhere else. Just look for my Ford Mondeo, she managed to take that. I mean there are a few people she would have contacted if she had her phone but she doesn't."

"Oh yeah?" said the voice dubiously "I'll send my brother Raymond over there to check it out and don't worry about this Quinn character, as you say she's pretty bloody distinctive, we will find her."

"Oh yeah? What about that incident.." Craig started to say.

"Shut it! You are getting brave for someone who has unpaid debts with us" said the voice sternly "And besides, Andy was a stupid, horny fool who really should have known better. Anyway if he had just come to us at the start things would have turned out completely different."

"I'm sorry Michael, Speaking of that actually, If she is there you may need to... dispose of some others too" Craig said carefully.

"keep this up and you won't have much of an inheritance left." Michael chuckled humourlessly "Who else are we to dispose of?

"Well," Craig said slowly "Look out for a Volkswagen Lupo in that area, let's just say it belongs to a Miss Tegan Galloway."

"You have to be kidding me? Right? Why is she there? I assume he is too." Michael said in a tone of disbelief.

"Michael. I'm tell you the truth," Craig said in a tone he hoped was reassuring "Would I lie about something like this? Her family are.. or were.. guests of my now late father in law."

"Well you are right, if they have met up with her, we can't have witnesses." Michael said thoughtfully then his tone changed to a more threatening one "You better not mess us around and you better pay up or you will find out first hand what happens when you double cross a Donnelly." and he hung up on Craig. He flopped on the bed, looking at the ceiling. He knew getting involved with a crime family like the Donnellys was dangerous but if it saves his business, in Craig's head it was worth the risk.

It took a while but Eva was finally able to compose herself enough to think straight.

"I feel so confused," she said as she sat and took off her backpack "I can't believe it, yet I can. It all makes sense, he was really keen on me getting back in contact with my dad, he was determined I go and take part in the hunt. He planned all of this didn't he?" Darren nodded.

"The fact he used your phone to frame you too suggested it was definitely planned in advance." he admitted

"If that's the case what do we do now?" Tegan asked, Darren looked up at the darkening sky.

"Well, as we have no mobile phone and the car is out of petrol, I'd say it is best we wait until the morning before we do anything," Darren replied "Plus we don't really know too much, only that Eva here didn't do it." Tegan had to admit that Darren did make a persuasive argument, she had been sceptical about Eva not knowing about what happened to her father she trusted Darren's judgement on this.

"We should probably get the tent set up then," Tegan shrugged as she looked over again at Eva's makeshift effort with the blanket "You are welcome to join us, better than that thing if the weather turns bad." Eva looked back at her effort too and sighed.

"It was all I had in the car that I could use, I don't want to cause you any more trouble than I probably already have." Eva said with a nervous smile.

"Don't be silly," Tegan said in a tone she hoped was reassuring "I mean it is supposed to just hold two but it should be fine." she then helped Darren unpack the tent.

Soon the camp was set up, it would be a tight fit in the tent with the three of them and there were only two sleeping bags but Darren suggested unzipping one fully and he and Tegan use it as a sort of duvet and giving Eva the other one. Darren had also gathered enough wood to build a small fire.

"So, earlier you mentioned something about your car, where is it?" Darren asked Eva as he at next to Tegan.

"Oh, you see there is a narrow dirt road that leads near to this spot, unfortunately due to the rain last night and the fact the car isn't a four wheel drive..."

"It's stuck?" Tegan said.

"Not sure but we can look at it in the morning I suppose. Actually, why are you two out here anyway?" Eva asked as she huddled near the fire with the tartan blanket she was initially going to us like a tent draped over her shoulders.

"After finding your father and the police being round," Tegan started "I needed to get away for a night or two and we were planning to do something like this anyway..."

"No," Eva interrupted "Why are you here in this spot specificly?"

"Tristan told us about this place, said you two would come here when you were younger." Eva looked downcast at the mention of her brother.

"What must he think of me right now, what must everyone think?" they believe I did it, don't they?"

"Tristan seemed in denial about it, they all are, they don't want to believe it but Craig seems to be doing a good job of painting you as the prime suspect." Darren said with a sigh.

"What has he been saying?" Eva asked. As she flicked some mud off her boot.

"A lot of little things, suggesting you are still in contact with hunt sabs, that you and your dad argued over things the night before." Tegan answered.

"Yeah, he even told them about you insisting on wearing brown boots, what is the deal with that anyway?" Darren asked curiously.

"Darren, just take a Look at me, I'm not a typical rider am I, dreadlocks... tattoos..." she pulled up her sleeves to show Darren her tattoos "Besides, wear brown boots mainly because I remember when my mother would ride, she wore brown boots." she went quiet.

"So, what actually happened this morning, if you didn't go to the stables." Tegan asked.

"I was planning to go there but as I was getting ready Craig just started to have a go at me, First he was annoyed my alarm woke him up then he continued by saying I ruined dinner last night, saying I embarrassed him," Eva's voice started to tremble "He started to hit me and knocked me to the floor, I spotted the carkeys next to his shoes, grabbed them and ran out the door, got in the car and just drove off. I just knew I needed to get away from him, from everything. I didn't know where else to go..."

"So you came here to think about what to do next?" Darren asked, Eva nodded.

"Something like that." she replied "I needed to be alone with my thoughts".

"I don't get it, there is nothing I have seen that suggests he is in any way a likeable person. Eva why did you even marry him in the first place?" Darren looked at her in surprise.

"He wasn't always like that," Eva said with a sigh "Or at he very least he didn't act like that, not at first. As I told Tegan, we met as he came into the store in Kilmarnock I sold my paintings at, we did talk a few times, then one day... he asked me out, I said yes and.."

she stopped and looked up at the sky "You have to understand that I was at rock bottom, mentally I mean, when we started talking properly. At first he was charming, wining, dining. Romantic trips away, shopping sprees. Craig made me feel special, he made me feel wanted. I found myself smiling a lot, I felt happy but then he slowly changed."

"It's not just beatings is it Eva? There's more to this isn't there?" Tegan asked. all concern.

"No, I don't have many friends and the ones I do have I am barely allowed to see. When he has his guests round, well you see what he done last night, its the same thing. My house.. I can't even call it a home now.. has become a prison, even Jazz has told me for ages to leave..."

"Wait, hold on," Darren said suddenly "Who is Jazz?"

"Sorry," Eva said as she shook her head "Jim Quinn, but he prefers to be called by his nickname Jazz." Darren and Tegan looked at each other, so that was who J. Quinn was.

"Is he one of your old sab friends?" Tegan asked cautiously.

"Jazz? No," Eva looked surprised at the very suggestion "However it is complicated. You see I met Jazz online before Craig and I started dating, became good friends and we get on really well but Craig hates him."

"Why?" asked Darren, looking intrigued.

"I suppose I should tell you the whole story," Eva said as she held her head in her hands. "Just after I was married I noticed Jazz wasn't talking to me as much, in fact he stopped completely when I asked him what was wrong, he confessed he developed feelings for me. The truth was I did have feelings for him too, in fact if anything if I thought Jazz thought the same way I would never have went out with Craig, don't get me wrong I believe he does love me in his own way and I guess I love, no, loved him but with Jazz, it's different, I could talk to him for hours about anything and everything, he cares deeply for me, makes me smile."

"Does Craig know any of this?" Tegan asked.

"He... sort of knows Jazz and I are friends," Eva shrugged "But he thinks Jazz is just some guy from the stables and nothing more. I hide how often Jazz and I are in touch, we phone each other most days. It is innocent, friendly chat but even then it would be enough to make Craig angry and jealous..."

"Does Jazz know Craig hurts you?" Darren asked. Eva nodded sadly.

"He does, he even said I should leave Craig and come live with him but.. I don't know.." she trailed off and sat in silence.

"We should try and get something to eat then settle for the night, it looks like it might rain, or worse." Darren noted as he looked up to the sky.

CHAPTER 10

Darren cooked some beans with mini sausages on the gas burner and handed out some bread to Tegan and Eva. As there was three of them and they only had two of each of the eating utensils and utilities Darren volunteered to eat straight from the tin with the serving spoon and let Eva use his bowl and fork. Eva ate it ravenously as it was the first thing she had to eat all day.

"I really needed that," she said as she sat the empty bowl down. "It's bringing back memories of when Tristan and I would come up here, you know there was one time dad decided for a change to coo using the fire..." she trailed off into silence.

"Are you okay?" Tegan asked.

"I'll be fine," Eva sniffed as a tear rolled down her cheek "I.. I will never be able to tell him just how much times like that meant to me, how a lot of my happiest moments involved him.." I'll be fine." she repeated and stood up wiping the tears away and let out an involuntary shiver "I suppose we should get inside the tent, it's getting cold." Darren and Tegan nodded in agreement.

The tent was a tight squeeze, Eva eventually got into her sleeping bag then Darren set up things for him and Tegan, A blanket below them and the unzipped sleeping bag on top.

I'll just do a quick check," Darren said as he grabbed a torch from the rucksack "Just make sure everything is okay." and he stepped out the tent. Eva propped herself up on one shoulder.

"I see what you meant last night." she said admiringly.

"What do you mean?" Tegan looked at Eva slightly confused then remembered "Ah, yeah when Darren gets going..."

"Tegan, can I ask you something?" Eva asked as she nervously played with one of her dreadlocks.

"Sure, of course." Tegan said.

"Did you think I had done it?" Eva just came out and asked.

"I'm going to be honest, I wasn't sure," Tegan said thoughtfully "On one hand there was a lot of evidence, the phone, the way you are your dad argued. However after our talk last night.. let us just say it gave me just enough doubt that you would have done such a thing. Can I ask you a question?"

"Sure." Eva replied wondering what Tegan could possibly ask that has her so nervous.

"And please be honest," Tegan said, her voice slightly trembling "You were genuine about patching things up with your father, taking part in the hunt.. all of it, right?"

"Tegan," Eva said sitting up as best she could, the sleeping bag unzipped halfway "Yes I was, why would you ask..." Then she remembered what happened with Lucy, how she took part in the hunt just to get a chance to kidnap Tegan "...I see, Tegan trust me there is no ulterior motive." Tegan looked intently at Eva a moment then shook her head.

"Sorry, if I'm honest it was the hunt sab stuff that was making me suspicious." Tegan admitted.

"I can understand that but..." Eva started but Tegan held out a hand to stop her.

"No, you don't understand, what I didn't tell you was, believe it or not, you know how I told you Darren was only there because he was at the protest?"

"Yeah.." Eva replied and gave Tegan a curious look.

"He was only there because he and Lucy were college classmates and Lucy had told him she would be there… to protest the hunt."

"Oh," Eva said as she realised "Were Darren and her..?" Eva stopped when she saw Tegan's shocked look.

"No, nothing like that." Tegan said and hurried to explain "Yes he did have a crush on her but... look the thing was she told him, and others apparently she was protesting, then I find out that you.. an ex hunt sabis joining the hunt.."

"..Oh I get it now, trust me, please I wouldn't do that sort of thing. If anything I wasn't sure I wanted to go. I had thought of going to see dad at another time, a less stressful time, maybe just him and I but Craig was insistent I came for the hunt and he was determined to come too and that surprised me." Eva said rubbing her temples.

"Why? Because he isn't into horses? Darren isn't but he always comes with me for stuff like competitions, not that I compete as much these days." Tegan guessed.

"No, it's not just that," Eva explained "He doesn't show an interest in anything I do as it is but, despite buying Marco for me, Craig just refuses to help or understand at all... Hey, is Darren okay out there?"

"Oh, he will be back, he is just probably double checking the surrounding area, I'm used to it. When we go out anywhere he checks the door is locked about five or six times before." Tegan shrugged. As she adjusted the sleeves of her goalkeeper shirt.

"Tegan?" Eva said curiously "what is the deal with that football shirt?"

"This?" Tegan asked looking down at it "I have always wore Celtic stuff, you know that."

"Yeah but most of it fitted a lot better from what I remember." Eva countered noting it did look a little too baggy, even if Tegan did like her clothes loose fitting.

"Okay, It used to belong to Darren, it was his lucky shirt and it is the first thing he ever gave me..." and proceeded to tell Eva the story about how he initially gave her the shirt to make her look less conspicuous to their pursuers "...and he then said later on that I could keep it meeting me was the luckiest thing to ever happen to him so it has already brought him all the luck it ever could."

"That is actually quite sweet." Eva said smiling.

"Yes it is, isn't it." Tegan agreed with a smile of her own.

Darren came back in, torch in hand.

"Everything is okay, there's nothing moving out there, not even a fox?" Darren said as he sat and zipped the tent opening shut and carefully put a padlock on the zips."

"No Reynard? Aww." Tegan pouted in a dramatic fashion.

"I'm sorry, who?" Eva said with an eyebrow raised "Who is Reynard?" Tegan and Darren looked at each other as if silently deciding who would tell the story.

"A few times when we were being pursued, a fox would appear.." Darren started.

"And it was the same fox each time.." Tegan said pointedly.

"We can't be certain of that.." Darren interjected.

"Anyway I ended up calling him Reynard." Tegan said as she elbowed Darren playfully in the stomach. Eva laughed and shook her head.

Dinner at Glen Tachur was a sombre affair with many

empty seats.

"I was on the phone to the police, they should be able to release Bruce's body to the undertaker soon, so that's something." Quentin said to break the silence.

"Thank you again," Hannah said, she was doing her best to stay strong but the slight tremor in her voice betrayed her emotional state "I had a quick word with Alexander and he said he can make sure everyone turns up but is happy for you to take the lead on the hunt itself . He suggested that everyone wear black armbands for it." Quentin nodded.

"Seems only fair," Quentin said then looked over to Craig "So, how are you bearing up?" Craig looked up from his barely touched food.

"Sorry, was in a world of my own. I guess its not every day you find out your wife is a killer." he said/

"We don't know for absolute certain." Olivia said knowingly "not everything turns out as it seems." when Tegan had been kidnapped there was no initial reason to believe Lucy had any involvement, it was only later they discovered just how involved in it she had been.

"No offence," Craig said dryly "But it seems all the evidence says otherwise."

"Craig, it really does sound like you have all but given up all notion of her innocence." Tristan said cautiously

"Just being realistic I guess." Craig muttered then in a louder tone "I don't know how everyone can be so calm about all this." Hannah looked over and shook her head.

"Craig, I lost my husband today," she started

slowly "And yes it does look like Eva may have been responsible but until we hear her side..."

"...Her side?" Craig sighed and stood up "Excuse me, I seem to have lost my appetite." As he walked out, Craig's yes lingered on Hannah but the others were too stunned to notice.

"Unfortunately I think he might be right," Tristan said "I want to believe she is innocent, I really do but it doesn't look good." Quentin took a mouthful of pork before replying.

"I know but until Eva comes back or the police find her we won't know for sure, it is best to focus on the things we have control over, like the funeral and the hunt." he said wisely.

"When do you think the funeral will be?" Tristan asked.

"Not sure, will know more when the body is released but it won't be until after the hunt I don't think."

"In a way it would be a perfect send off." Hannah said, smiling sadly.

"Yes, yes it will." Quentin agreed.

"Well that was awkward," Quentin said as Olivia was getting ready for bed "There is something about Craig that is starting to really bother me." Olivia slipped on her night dress and turned around.

"Quentin, his wife may have killed his father in law and he is dining with her family, of course he is going to seem a little tense." Olivia said with a sigh as if willing her husband to show some compassion for the younger man but Quentin instead paced around the bedroom deep in thought.

"No, still something not right." He said as he sad on the bed and pinched the bridge of his nose "Look at Tristan, I feel sorry for the boy, on one hand he has lost his father, on the other he is hoping his sister hasn't done what he thinks she has done. Its tearing him apart, you can see how he looks and carried himself but Craig? It is like he is outright refusing to believe she may be in any way innocent."

"Do you really think that?" Olivia turned to him and asked curiously.

"Okay, Imagine if I was accused of killing my father. How would you react? And be honest." Quentin asked.

"Your father? Honestly I'd be helping you hide the body." Olivia said in a droll tone. Olivia was a nurse from a humble background when she met Quentin. Most of his family, including his father, did not approve of her and made it very clear on a regular basis. So there was no love lost there.

"Okay okay, bad example," Quentin admitted "But you get what I mean, at least you would give me some benefit of the doubt until it has been proven one way or another."

"Probably," Olivia said "Sounds like you are doubting she did it."

"To be honest I really don't know what to think," Quentin replied "But I do remember when Bruce received that text, we were in his study and he was telling me how that despite his misgivings that he was happy that Eva had come and was hoping to spend time with her."

"She did seem more upset at Craig than anybody else I will give you that," Olivia said thoughtfully "but if not her who else has any motive? Look none of us are thinking straight right now, maybe this is not the best time to speculate anything. It has been a long day, you should get some sleep" Olivia said in a soft but firm tone then climbed into bed.

"I suppose," Quentin said as he climbed into bed, switching off the bedside light as he did.

In his room, Craig lay on top of his bed staring at the ceiling. Entering into what Michael Donnelly referred to as a business agreement was something he needed to do to save his company, it wasn't his fault things weren't that good this year but he had some, nice contracts coming up. Craig needed time the Donnellys weren't going to give, he had thought about Eva's life insurance but he would be the number once suspect if anything happened to her, however she had told him about the inheritance she stood to gain if something happened to her father before they married, he never thought much about it at the time but now it could be just what he needed and much more besides and she made no secret that there was bad blood between her and her father. Killing him was the hardest part. The older man was quite surprised to see Craig and not Eva at the stables, the first blow was the most difficult one to do but it knocked Bruce down, after that the rest was easy. The strange thing Craig found was that he felt no remorse for what he did to Bruce or for what may happen to Eva, he did have however have a little bit of regret for what may happen to Tegan and Darren, after all it wasn't personal but if they had indeed come across Eva, well some things can't be helped. Craig looked over and saw a small well used notepad on the bedside table on Eva's side of the bed, out of curiosity he picked it up.

"what's this?" he said to himself. It was a list of phone numbers, Eva must have forgotten to pick it up. Craig smirked, if she didn't have this notebook and her mobile phone taken by the police as evidence, she had no way at all to contact any of her friends. He tossed it back on the bedside table and smiled then decided to get changed for bed. It was hard work pretending to be the wronged husband and grieving son in law.

Eva lay in the sleeping bag looking up at the dark interior of the tent, Darren was on the far side of the tent asleep on his side and Tegan was cuddled into him, her head pressed against his chest. Eva was still trying to process everything, her dad.. Craig... all of it, it was all so overwhelming. Eva felt fresh tears build up in her eyes as she cried herself to sleep.

CHAPTER 11

It was cold and the sky was still quite dark when Darren exited the tent. He didn't get much sleep, a combination of the hard ground and the recent events rolling around in his head kept him up. He heard movement in the tent and as he turned around Eva came out rather clumsily. And stretched her arms.

"Morning," Darren said "How did you sleep?"

"I struggled at first," Eva admitted But once I settled I was fine, It has been a while since I had done anything like this."

"Fair enough, is Tegan awake yet?" Darren asked.

"Tegan's still asleep, should I wake her? She asked.

"No, oddly this is the first time in a while she has had a good long rest." Darren smiled a little as he tried to tidy up the campsite as best he could.

"I didn't know you were friends with Lucy." Eva suddenly said as she sat on the fallen tree trunk, Darren looked up a little surprised then shook his head.

"Friends... is a very interesting way of wording it." Darren said as he sat next to her.

"What do you mean?" Eva asked as she looked at Darren curiously.

"Well, the thing was I thought Blondie.."

"Blondie?" Eva interrupted.

"Sorry, Blondie was Lucy's nickname at college.. anyway, I thought we were friends and had wanted to asked her out for over a year and when I did she said no, because.." Darren continued.

"She was going to protest a foxhunt?" Eva made a guess "Tegan had told me that part."

"Well she was known for her activism at college so it wasn't so hard to believe, I thought she might be impressed, you see, while I saw her as a friend, I was just useful to her, I could do the parts of Blondie's coursework she couldn't or didn't want to do, that was all she saw me as. I guess I wanted her to see me in a new light, didn't happen that way, don't regret going though."

"Let me guess, because of Tegan?" Eva asked as she tried to tame her dreadlocks into a ponytail..

"Basically, you know the strangest thing?" Darren said as he smiled "In those days Tegan and I spent together trying to get away from her kidnappers I learned more about her as a person than I ever knew about blondie in a ear and a half of knowing her. Tegan is kind, beautiful, we share so many interests and she just... gets me as a person and I love her with all my heart." Eva couldn't help but smile, Darren truly loved Tegan, that much was clear to her.

"She is lucky to have someone like you." Eva said sadly "I honestly thought Craig would be good for me, I really did."

"I assume you will be leaving him." Darren said after a pause.

"You think?" Eva raised an eyebrow "I put up with it all, the abuse, hoping maybe eventually it will stop, maybe he will see sense, realise just what he was doing to me and stop.. I dunno. Yet the more compliant I got, the worse he was. My only worry is where to go? Back home to Glen Tachur?"

"What about Jazz?" Darren asked "He offered you a place to stay."

"I don't know, the truth is we only have physically met the once," Eva said nervously "But the truth is I would speak to him nearly every day on the phone for over an hour at a time. When we did meet it felt wonderful, natural and the truth was he made me feel more cared for and wanted than Craig ever did." Eva's eyes stared off into the distance as if fondly remembering a memory.

"You really love him, don't you?" Darren asked. Eva looked at him initially shocked b then slowly nodded.

"I have feelings for him but.." she said looking confused then she suddenly looked at Darren intently "Yes, I love him, the more I think on it... I do, but he knew I was suffering yet didn't..."she trailed off when Darren shook his head.

"Eva, don't mistake his lack of action for lack of caring. If what you say is right and he does love you then I say go for it and follow your heart," Darren said as he looked around "look at it this way, Craig as beaten and abused you and much more for a long time. Has Jazz done anything remotely as bad as that?"

"I would get beatings if I was caught on the phone to him and Craig went crazy when he found out I actually had went to meet Jazz..." She tried to explain "If I hadn't.. then..."

"You can't blame Jazz for that." Darren said with a stern tone that even surprised him "You want my advice?"

"Please." Eva said.

"The first chance you can talk to Jazz, even if it's just a phone call, work something out. You only get one shot at life, the question 'What if' is the most soul destroying question you can ever ask yourself. If you let Jazz go you will be asking that question for the rest of your life, trust me." Darren said with surprising conviction. Eva looked down in silence, as if she was contemplating everything Darren had told her. Eva then looked up at Darren.

"You sound like someone who is speaking from experience." She said eventually.

"You could say that, it is the main reason I went to Netherfield House that day," Darren explained "In my head if I didn't go I would spend the rest of my days asking what if I had went and I had too many moments like that in my past."

"Yeah but you didn't go there for Tegan." Eva

commented but Darren just smiled.

"True but did you expect to fall for Jazz?" he asked, Eva shook her head.

"No," she answered truthfully "He contacted me after seeing some of my artwork online and, we got talking.. and... well.. the more we spoke the more we realised we shared so many mutual interests but because he never seemed to want to take things further I guess I was too scared to destroy what seemed like an amazing friendship by making the first move..." she trailed off and gave Darren a weak smile

"Well there you go then, sometimes it is just fate." Darren said as Eva nodded silently.

"Thank you." she said in almost a whisper.

"Hey," came a voice, they both turned to see Tegan get out the tent with a yawn "how long have you two been awake?"

"Not that long," Darren replied as he walked up and gave Tegan a hug "You were too comfortable and I didn't want to wake you.

"Aww," She said then turned to Eva "Usually it's me who is up first and I end up waking him," Tegan explained "So, what do we do first?" Tegan asked as she released her hair from her ponytail.

"I'd say we get something to eat then work out a plan of action." Darren replied and kissed Tegan in the forehead.

The phone had been busy all morning with people calling to offer Hannah their condolences. Quentin went to the kitchen to make himself a fresh cup of coffee and to make Hannah some tea when Craig came into the room.

"Hi," said Quentin politely "Need anything? Tea? Coffee?" Craig shook his head.

"Oh hello, No, I'm okay thanks." He looked a little distracted.

"How is business these days?" Quentin thought he may as well indulge in small talk while the kettle boiled.

"We did ave a bit of a slump earlier in the year but it is now doing well, had some new investors and I have some big contracts coming up so here's hoping." Craig said in a way that did not convince Quentin but he smiled at the younger man anyway.

"It's good to see things finally take shape, I remember how hard it was for me starting up, mind you I did have my brother with me, well, at first anyway bur he wanted out after a while" Quentin started "The point is you will get there, if you persevere," he could tell Craig was only half listening as the younger man stood gazing out the window "Something on your mind?" as if snapping out of a dream, Craig suddenly looked at Quentin, regarding the older man almost like he was seeing him for the first time.

"Sorry, just got a lot on my mind," Craig shrugged weakly "But yeah, it has been hard financially but it is amazing how things turn out I guess, if you'll excuse me..." And with that Craig walked out the kitchen. There definitely was something a bit off with the way Craig was acting and now that he thought about it, the way Bruce talked about Craig's business woes that time he convinced Quentin to give his company the job of upgrading the Galloway Haulage computer systems it sounded like the company wasn't doing well, yet suddenly out of nowhere that all changes. Quentin shook his head, he had been in business himself long enough to know that something wasn't right. he went up the stairs to retrieve his mobile phone just as the kettle finished boiling.

As they packed up the tent Eva looked over at Darren.
"So, what do we do now?" she asked hopefully.
"Well," Darren said "It is risky but I really think going back to Glen Tachur is your best option at this time"
"But won't she be arrested?" Tegan asked "Someone is bound to phone the police."
"Yeah," Agreed Eva "I really can't see anyone rolling out the welcome mat if I showed up, especially Craig..." she continued, but Darren was already thinking ahead.
"Let me finish," Obviously we would have to get you back without Craig knowing," Darren said with a deep sigh "Plus it is actually the last place anyone would look. I'm sure there is some corner of the place we could smuggle you into until we are ready." Eva looked at Darren as if he was mad.
"I'm not sure about this." Eva said doubtfully, her hands shaking.
"Where are you going with this?" Tegan asked, more for Eva's sake than her own, she had a half idea

where Darren was going with this but was seeing Eva start to panic

"I am, look I have been thinking of this, Craig was counting on Eva being arrested before anyone told her anything about the murder..." Darren tried to explain.

"..Yes but then she would be able to tell them.." Tegan tried to interrupt but Darren shook his head.

"You remember what it was like for us, the questions, the atmosphere and even with a lawyer there it is quite a daunting experience." Darren continued, Eva nodded.

"You are so right," she said knowingly "And I have to be honest, without you I wouldn't have figured out as much as I have. I doubt I could have convinced the police of my innocence, Especially if they take my previous arrests into consideration."

"I know, Even with what we know it still might be hard to convince them but that is why we have to get back to Glen Tachur without Craig seeing you. Then we can phone the police with our suspicions, maybe try and find some evidence that will hopefully increase your chances of being found innocent, we have to at leat try," Darren sighed and looked at Eva intently "Eva, I just have a horrible feeling that the minute Craig sees you he will .. I dunno..he could prepare an alibi or something before anyone has a chance to call the police... threaten you into silence.. or worse."

"What do you mean?" Tegan asked.

"Yeah," Eva said as she rubbed her temples trying to make sense of it all "What are you trying to say, just tell me, please.

"Well he has killed once..."Darren started, he didn't need to finish. Both Eva and Tegan looked at Darren in shock. Eva started to cry, Tegan went over to sit beside Eva and comforted her.

"It's going to be okay," Tegan said softly "If anyone can get you out of this situation it's Darren, I'd trust him with my life and already have in the past."

"How did my life get like this?" Eva said tearfully

"Eva," Said Darren as he crutched in front of her "I really don't know what to say, only that Tegan and I are here for you."

"Yeah," agreed Tegan "We will help you through all this." Eva just buried her head in Tegan's shoulder.

"Thank you." sh e muttered softly.

The three of them made their way to Eva's car as soon as they were finished.

"It doesn't look too bad." Tegan said as they walked up, she then looked at the slippery dirt road "You did well getting this far all things considered."

"Thank you," Eva replied "Would you believe me if I said I don't have a drivers license?"

"Really?" Tegan asked, surprised.

"Well I took a few lessons, well actually a few friends showed me a couple of years ago," Eva smiled weakly "I know, it was a silly risk, but I just saw those carkeys and saw.. a way out, I just had enough I guess." she sighed and looked down.

"You did the right thing," said Darren who was just ahead of them and was walking around the car

"There is no sign of any..hold on." He said suddenly and squatted down next to the front. Eva and Tegan jogged closer.

"What is it?" Tegan asked as she saw Darren give the wheel a slight push,it moved freely.

"Looks like you have broken the axle or something," he said shaking his head "This car isn't going anywhere soon, how did you manage that?"

"I think I mist have hit something," Eva said looking back and noticed a tree stump "Oh, must have hit that somehow."

"You are lucky that is all that happened." Darren said getting up stiffly.

"How are your knees?" Tegan asked, Darren had a condition called Chondromalleca Patelle, basically the back of his kneecaps were like sandpaper. The pain and stiffness could get unbearable but Darren rarely complained, even barely took the painkillers he was given to help with the pain/

"I'm fine, for now anyway." he said, trying to reassure Tegan, he knew she worried about him.

What do we do now?" Eva asked.

"Well," Darren said thinking "Could always go back to the Lupo, dump our stuff and walk to the nearest petrol station like we were originally going to do."

""What about me? Eva said, slightly concerned "I'm hardly inconspicuous am I?" Darrcn thought for a minute.

"You won't like it, but you could always hide n the back of the car while we are away with a blanket over you? I's not like anyone is going to stop and look too closely." he said eventually.

"It's not ideal but I'll give it a go." Eva shrugged "Wait, the Lupo is your car?"

"Yes, why?" Tegan asked.

Well, no offence but I thought it belonged to one of the stablehands when I saw it parked up near the house at first, I don't know why but I thought you would have driven something bigger," Eva explained carefully "The storage space is.."

"I know, trust me I know," Tegan agreed "We had to put the back seats down fully but I like it. I don't like I could cope with something bigger, not yet anyway."

"Well," Darren said as he rubbed his knee "We should probably get a move on, It is going to be some walk to the petrol station."

"Darren if your knees are playing up.." Tegan started to say.

"No, I'm not letting you go alone." Darren said with a defiant tone as he made his way back through the trees. Eva looked at Tegan curiously.

"Does he know where he is going? He has read a map of the area hasn't he?" she asked.

"Oddly enough he does and yes he has," Tegan shrugged "He has an instinct for this sort of thing, come on, sooner we get to the car the better."

COLD BLOOD

CHAPTER 12

As they neared Tegan's car Darren heard noises and immediately ran to the cover of a bush, gesturing for the others to follow.

"What is it?" Eva asked in voice Darren thought was a little too loud, he put his finger over his lips to signal both of them to be quiet as he peered through the bush. There was a black car, he couldn't make out the model and three men, the ones who came in the car Darren assumed were looking around the Lupo. One turned round and looked like he was scanning the area with his eyes for something or someone. Darren looked intently at the man as he looked familiar.

"Come on, back to the camp." Darren said as softly as he could and made his way back the way he came but had stooped to a crouch.

"Darren.." Tegan started to say but he turned

around and said in a harsh whisper.

"Just trust me we need to go.. please." and with that Tegan and Eva followed Darren, keeping low until they were out of sight of the roadside.

Raymond sighed as he walked around the Lupo.

"Well, that confirms it." came a voice behind him, it was Luke Sanders, the big Englishman nodded to the car as Peter Reynolds, one of Raymond's oldest friends looked at the note that was left.

"It certainly does, and they must be close." Peter said.

"Just proves the Galloway girl is here," Raymond shouted back as he brushed his dark hair back with his fingers

"Yeah I suppose and we still need still to find … who is it again?"" Luke said with a sigh, looking a little bit disappointed.

"Eva Robertson, apparently we will be able to spot her easy." Raymond replied

"Oh yeah," Luke said remembering "She is the one with the long dreadlocks in that picture Michael showed us."

"Yeah, her," Raymond said "We still need to find her car. If she isn't here we leave them alone, Michael's orders."

"Why?" Luke asked "Thanks to them Andy is in jail."

"Andy was a fool, he did the whole thing without telling us, plus revenge for revenge's sake isn't really our style."

"Yeah, unless it's against the Lyles or.." Peter started.

"Okay, seeking revenge on a rival is one thing, but Michael believed there was nothing to be gained.. and I agree, however if they have gotten caught up in all this.." Raymond said with a grin.

"...Ah," Luke nodded "I understand now."

"Yeah, anyway I think we should start by checking out that dirt track just up the road that looks recently used. Good a place as any." Raymond suggested as they walked back to his car. The Vauxhall Vectra may not be the most glamorous car in the world but Raymond preferred function over style plus Vauxhalls were good enough for his parents so they were good enough for him. Raymond sighed as he opened the car door.

"What is it?" Peter asked.

"I won't lie," Raymond said as he got in the drivers seat "A very real part of me kind of hopes this Eva isn't here."

"Oh?" Luke sounded confused as he smoothed his goatee with his hand "Why is that?"

"I have no desire to go roaming about the woods chasing some woman. All because her husband has promised to pay Michael more than he owes us to kill her off." Raymond shook his head and started the ignition.

"I don't know," Luke said as he stared out the windscreen "Didn't Michael want her death to look like an accident? It would be a lot easier to make it look like a bad fall or something out here, why is Michael entertaining this guy anyway?"

"It's typical Michael, he is going to do this for the guy and instead of asking for more money he will demand to be made his business partner" Raymond explained.

"What sort of company is it anyway?" Luke asked curiously.

"Something to do with computers," Raymond said after a moments thought "I can see what Michael is thinking, the more legit businesses we have an interest in, well the more we have to fund our .. other activities, if you get my meaning."

"Fair play," Peter said thoughtfully "It's a smart move too, it seems everything is done on computers these days."

"Exactly, Michael knows what he is doing," Raymond agreed as he put the car in first gear "Let's see what is up this dirt road anyway."

"Darren, what is going on, please tell me." Tegan said as they neared the clearing they had used to camp the night before.

"One of the men we saw at the Lupo, is one of the Donnellys." he blurted out.

"Really? Are you sure?" Tegan asked, Darren nodded.

"I seen his photo in the papers during the trial, the question is what is a Donnelly doing out here now?" then he turned to Eva.

"Eva, you said Craig had a new investor, did he

mention a name?" Darren asked carefully.

"Yes, once," Eva said as she tried to remember "Michael, that's who it was, I only heard his first name, why?" Darren shook his head.

"Michael Donnelly," Darren said slowly "I remember his name from the paper and news reports, He's the leader of the Donnelly gang."

"Oh no.." Tegan said and instinctively went over and cuddled into Darren, he could feel her shake.

"What's wrong.." Eva was about to say then remembered something Tegan had told her.

"Andy's big brother? Was that him we saw just there?" Eva asked.

"Yes it is Andy's older brother but the one we saw was another Donnelly brother, cant remember what his name was." Darren explained.

"What do we do now?" Tegan said shakily.

"I have an idea but you wont like it, either of you..."

As he kicked the broken wheel on the Mondeo, Raymond let out a groan. Luke pointed at the footprints Darren Tegan and Eva had left in the mud earlier.

"They must have been here recently too." Luke Noted

"Damn I was hoping not to find this." Raymond said despairingly.

"Why not?" asked Peter "We have as good as found her."

"Yeah but she is very likely with the other two if

what I was told was correct and that is not good news, trust me." Raymond said as he stared up at the sky."I remember the first time I visited Andy in prison and he told me that when the two of them escaped from the house they had them holed up in, instead of heading to Strathaven which is where the girl was from, instead the guy took her to Bigger instead."

"I remember reading some of that in the papers, they were in the middle of the lead hills and didn't the guy choose Bigger because it was closer or something like that?" Luke said, remembering.

"Yeah," nodded Raymond "it was barely closer but it was also in the other direction, meaning any attempts to head them off failed miserably."

"So what now?" Luke said as he drummed his fingers on the roof of the Vectra.

"I'll contact Michael but I think the best thing we can do is work out where they made camp then work out the most direct way to get to that big house, Glen Tachur or whatever it is, That is were they came from, Luke, you and I will take that route and either get there before or catch up to them." Raymond said with a sigh "Peter, I'm trusting you with the Vectra, go as close to Glen Tachur as you can without being seen and set up camp overnight, if we don;t get them you will, you know what to do, don't you?" Raymond asked, Peter nodded "II wondered why Michael suggested I pack one." Raymond concluded.

How come he gets a tent?" Luke said as Raymond opened the car boot and started to change his shoes to a more practical pair before pulling out a large backpack and crammed two sleeping bags and a few small tins then slipped the now bulging backpack on.

"You always like to be prepared don't you?." Luke commented dryly.

"After years of working with Michael you learn to prepare for any eventuality," Raymond said then tossed Peter his phone "Peter when you get into position, let Michael know the plan. Come on Luke, let's find their campsite then we take it from there." Raymond leaned into the car and pulled a map out of the glovebox before the two of them headed off.

Tegan shook her head frantically.

"No," she said "there has to be another way." but Darren was adamant.

"Tegan, remember the trial, when we found out that Andy was acting on his own when he abducted you, that the others weren't involved?" he reminded her, she nodded.

"Yeah." she said softly

"Well I'm willing to bet that this time the full Donnelly crime family and their resources will be dedicated to finding her." And Darren pointed to Eva. Tegan paced around while Eva, who was sitting on the fallen tree trunk stood and walked towards them.

"You two have done more than enough," she said in a resigned tone, "I'll just go and give myself up..." she started.

"No," Darren insisted "They will no doubt kill you..."

"Okay, we will go to the police.." Eva tried to reason.

"No, not until we get the evidence you need," Darren said in a frustrated tone "You need to trust me." Eva looked at Tegan, who in return shrugged with a nervous smile.

"Eva," Tegan said "trust him, please."

"Okay, what is our first move. If we move now we still have a good head start, that is if they plan to follow us." Eva asked.

"You won't like it." Darren replied

"Why?" Eva asked.

"Honestly? It is because I don't like it either..." Darren started.

A while later Raymond and Luke turned up at the camp.

"They were here, look," Luke said, pointing to the flattened ground where tent had been and the remains of the fire "I'd say they only left recently too."

"Okay," Raymond said and took out his map, laying it out on the tree trunk and pointed to where they were "So, we are here and they are probably heading here," he pointed to Glen Tachur on the map "So.. they are probably going the most direct route." he then took out a pen and marked out the best route to take on the map.

"We should get a move on if we hope to catch up to them," Luke said "Do you think Peter has it in him to get the job done if we don't get to them first?"

"yes he has and he knows the deal," Raymond

said as he picked up the map "Make it look like an accident."

"Might be a bit harder with three of them." Luke noted.

"Okay, murder suicide then," Raymond shrugged "They find her, she kills them to stop them talking, realises the true extent of what she has done and takes her own life.. must I think of everything?"

"In that case we better start moving," Luke said "we don't know just how much of a head start they have."

Once he was sure they were gone, Darren emerged from his hiding place in the bushes near the clearing helping Tegan up who gripped him tight as she stood.

"Please can we not do that again," she said as Eva made her way out of the bushes too holding the tartan blanket they had covered themselves with as extra camouflage.

"It was a risk we had to take, now as it stands they are in front of us and we now now they are taking the more direct route so we know how to avoid them."

"I suppose, but what if they had seen us." Tegan said as she but her head on his chest.

"It was either that or constantly be looking over our shoulders, where is Eva?" he said and they turned to see her on her knees crying.

"they really did come there to kill me, didn't they?" she said as Tegan walked over and squatted down to put her arm around Eva.

"Eva, we won't let that happen," Darren said "I can not let that happen."

"But why, you don't know me.." Eva started to say.

"You are a friend and that is good enough for me." Darren said as he too squatted down and smiled.

"Really?" Eva said in surprise.

"Of course you are," Tegan said with a smile "We never really fell out, I mean we stopped talking once you joined the sabs obviously." Eva pulled Tegan in for a hug.

"Thank you, for what it's worth I'm really sorry I tried to fill your head with all that hunt sab propaganda crap back then."

"It's okay, we were both young and.." Tegan started to say.

"..Foolish, I know." Eva finished for her and looked over at Darren who had pulled out his map and was holding his house keys. Eva wondered why until she noticed one of his keyrings was a compass.

"Okay, I say we head north west until we need to make camp then we head to Glen Tachur which would roughly be south west of where ever we eventually make camp."

"Can't we go get petrol for the Lupo now?" Eva asked but Darren shook his head.

"Too risky, who knows what the police or the Donnellys have told people." he said, Tegan noted Eva's confused look so decided to explain.

"When Darren and I escaped our captors we went straight to a local farm, but it turned out the couple who lived there had been told by them I was a potential Olympic rider they were detoxing me of drugs that Darren was apparently supplying.. something like that.. and if the couple saw us to contact them right away." Tegan said.

"And the couple believed it?" Eva said shaking her head.

"well, in all fairness I was in the papers a few times back then with the reporters claiming I stood a chance." Tegan shrugged.

"Oh yeah I remember seeing some of those articles." Eva said after some thought. Darren dragged the rucksack out of its hiding place in the bushes and put it on.

"Come on, we have a fair distance to cover so the sooner we start..." he said before helping both Tegan and Eva up to their feet.

"Is he always like this?" Eva asked curiously.

"Yes," said Tegan with a slight smile "Yes he is"

CHAPTER 13

The offices of the main Galloway Haulage depot just outside Bellshill were quiet as Linda McKay made her way to her office. She was the dispatch manager and was in to catch up on paper work. She was also one of Darren's old college friends along with Jason and she got offered a job with Quentin after seeing her determination and loyalty in trying to find out what happened to Darren during the whole abduction incident, even turning up at Netherfield House in order to find out any information on Darren's whereabouts. Linda quickly won Quentin over with her hard work and soon gained promotion into management. As she sat at her desk the phone started to ring.

"Hello, Galloway Haulage, Linda McKay speaking." she said as she answered the phone.

"Linda, it's Quentin, how are you?" said the voice

on the other end.

"Things are well, just in today catching up on paperwork." she replied as she looked at the pictures on her desk, one was of her and her partner Ellen on holiday and the other of her Jason and Darren, even though she was older than the other two, she was in her thirties, the bond between the three was very strong.

"Ah, I hope it is not taking you away from anything important." Quentin said.

"Oh no, Ellen is visiting her sister Andrea for a couple of nights, I just dropped her off at the train station and I didn't want to be rattling around the house on my own, she will be back for new years though, weather permitting. How are things with you, you are at that big hunt in Ayrshire aren't you?"

"I am and that is what I want to talk about." Quentin replied "Have you read the papers yet or seen the news last night?"

"We were out last night so not seen the news and I have a paper, hold on," and she pulled out a Daily Record newspaper from her bag and saw the headline and started to quickly look at the article in growing horror "Oh, don't tell me that's..."

"Yes, the same Bruce Ingliston who invited us to stay with him and his family," Quentin confirmed "I'm helping out with the funeral arrangements and with helping to organise the hunt."

"Ah," Linda said "So, how are Darren and Tegan handling it all?" While Darren was her friend from college, Linda had quickly accepted Tegan into her friendship circle and had almost became like a big sister to her.

"Darren is okay, Tegan was the one that found the body." Quentin said with a sigh.

"Poor girl, I hope she is okay." Linda asked, all concerned.

"She should be, Darren has taken her out camping for a night or two to calm her down a bit."

"He mentioned something like that, I said he was made for camping in the middle of winter but if that's what floats their boat who am I to argue. Anyway, is there anything I can do?" she asked.

"Well there is," Quentin said "Do you remember the owner of Thistle Computers? Craig Robertson was his name."

"Don't remind me," Linda groaned "What about him?"

"Well that's Bruce's son in law, married to Eva.." he started to say.

"..Wait, so his wife has just killed her father?" she said as she looked at the article again.

"Apparently so but there is something bothering me, well a few things." Quentin admitted

"Like what? " Linda asked, she could hear on the other side movement and doors being closed.

"Sorry, wanted to make sure nobody could overhear," Quentin started "Before it all, he was essentially showing controlling behaviour over Eva, not giving her a chance to talk, being overbearing, you know the sort of thing. After it happened and she emerged as the main suspect, he has repeatedly done everything to to convince everyone that she must have done it."

"That does sound odd." Linda had to admit.

"Don't get me wrong, she does have motive.. long story, but there is something about his attitude."

"I know, I'm surprised he still has a business if I'm honest." Linda said.

"He days he has new investors or something along those lines but something doesn't add up." Quentin said in a low voice.

"What like? It's doubtful that he would be desperate enough to.. say.. murder his father in law for a shot at the inheritance money or something like that. I mean he is a prick but he's not..hello?" Linda stopped as Quentin had suddenly went silent.

"The inheritance, of course," he replied suddenly "Linda you may be on to something, can you try and find any and all information you can on Thistle Computing, especially anything financial."

"Sure," Linda said, excitement creeping into her voice "Anything else?"

"Yes, do me a favour please" Quentin said with a sigh "Check in on Netherfield House, Astrid is looking after the place but nobody is answering my calls."

"Sure, don't you trust her?" Linda asked "She might just be busy in the stables.

"I do trust her, but she has him staying over too." Quentin replied.

"Ah,"Linda said knowingly "Jason is a worry to us all unfortunately." She could understand Quentin"s concerns, Jason, before he met Astrid at least, was a bit of a playboy known for his many female conquests despite his protests that he wasn't as bad as people made him out to be. Quentin's main issue, apart from a bad first impression when Jason did a poor job of describing Darren's reasons for being near Netherfield House that day, was an incident where Quentin came back early from a ride to find Jason and Astrid in the stables in a.. compromising situation. Linda believed there was more to the story and didn't understand why Quentin was as upset. Astrid was close to her employers and apparently Quentin promised her family back in Germany he would look after her but it did seem excessive.

"That is one way to describe him, I better go but thank you and I should be back at the office next week." Quentin said.

"Okay, If I find anything out about that Craig Robertson I will let you know and I will drop by the house." she said as Quentin hung up. First thing Linda did was to go online and start searching the internet for any information on Thistle Computing.

Quentin had just finished the call just as Olivia walked in on him.

"Going out riding with Hannah, she could do with a break." she said as she started to get changed. Olivia pulled out a large bag from the bottom of the bed which contained her riding boots, three pairs in total. Her rubber ones and two pairs of leather Petrie brand ones the same as the pair she bought Tegan for Christmas. Now as far as knee high leather riding boots went Petrie was the only brand Olivia wore. She had brought a relatively new pair she wore when competing plus she was planning to wear for the hunt and an older pair just in case she needed them. Quentin shook his head, like mother like daughter.

"Yeah, she could do with a break," Quentin said "She okay about going into the stables with all that has happened?" Olivia finished putting on her black and grey jodhpurs and sat down.

"I said I'd bring Dandelion out to her," Olivia replied, Dandelion was Hannah's personal horse "Just so she doesn't need to actually go inside in case it upsets her." Olivia retrieved her bootpulls from the bag and selected older pair of Petrie boots and started putting them on.

"It will do her good to get out in the fresh air too." Quentin noted.

"Who were you on the phone to anyway?" Olivia asked curiously.

"Just Linda at the office." Quentin said with a shrugged.

"How is she?" Olivia asked as she put on her black quilted gilet and tied her hair up in a ponytail.

"She is doing well," Quentin said "She is going to check up on the house later."

"You really do not trust Jason do you?" Olivia said as she shook her head "'he is Darren's friend and like it or not Astrid is fond of him." she then scooped up her helmet and crop.

"Quentin, the house will be fine, Astrid will be fine." she said as she left.

"I wish I could believe that." Quentin said dryly.

As Hannah was heading out she bumped into Craig.

"Oh, sorry," she said, all flustered "How are you feeling today?" Craig looked at her and gave a sad smile.

"I'm still trying to work that one out," he said with a theatrical sigh "I take to you have heard nothing yet from the police too?"

"No, I haven't." Hannah said sadly. Craig put a hand on her shoulder in a way he hoped would come across as comforting.

"I'm sure the police will catch her soon," he said but Hannah just shook her head.

"Craig, a very real part of me can't bring myself to blame her for this. There has to be a reason." she said sadly.

""I dunno," he smiled weakly "If it was me, I wouldn't be as forgiving. Listen, I am here for you if you ever need to talk" he then walked to the sitting room.

"You aren't that much forgiving as it is." Hannah said softly to herself once he was out of earshot.

"Are you ready?" said Olivia as she came down the stairs and saw Hannah stare into space.

"Oh." Hannah said, sounding a little startled "Sorry, was in a world of my own there for a moment."

"It's okay, come on, it has been a while since I went for a ride out this way." Olivia said with a smile she hoped was reassuring.

As they walked to the stables Hannah turned to Olivia.

"Before you came down,"She started "I had a run

in with Craig." she said nervously.

"Oh, what did he say?" Olivia asked.

"It wasn't what he said, its how he acted," she said as if uncertain as to what she was trying to say "I don't know, he has his own issues right now I suppose."

"Everyone is trying to cope as best they can I guess," Olivia said as she adjusted the straps on her helmet "I wish I knew what advice to give you, I really do but we are always here for you, okay? I wouldn't worry too much about Craig if I were you." Hannah smiled back at Olivia and started to walk towards the stables.

"Thank you," she said "You and Quentin have been such a great help already." Olivia stopped a moment as if unsure of something but shook her head and followed Hannah up to the stables

CHAPTER 14

They had been walking for a couple of hours when suddenly Darren stopped and rubbed his knees.

"What's wrong? Your knees?" Tegan asked, Darren nodded.

"Yeah," he said grimacing "And I forgot my painkillers, I didn't expect to be trekking about."

"Right, we need to take a rest," Tegan said, a slight tone of authority in her voice "Okay?"

"Okay... Okay." he said eventually. And they looked for a good spot to rest up.

"What was that all about?" Eva whispered to Tegan who explained the full extent of Darren's knee problems and also how hard he pushed himself when he was getting Tegan to safety.

"...It's just, when he gets like this he doesn't think about his own well being."

"Oh?" Eva said "why not stop over there? I looks okay" she pointed to a slight slope next to a tree where the roots had been partially exposed.

"Yeah," Tegan agreed and said to Darren who reluctantly agreed. As they all sat on the slope, Tegan looked curiously down at Eva's right hand

"Hey that is a really nice ring," Tegan said as she pointed to Eva's hand "where did you get that?" Eva looked at Tegan surprised then after a few moments pause held up her hand then smiled.

"This?" she gestured to a ring on her finger that was a silver fox head with red stones set in the eyes "Jazz got me that when we met, he called it a vixen ring."

"It is lovely," Tegan noted admiringly "Did he ever tell you why he gave you it?" Tegan could see Eva blush and hide her face behind a dreadlock curtain of hair.

"He told me I was his little vixen and that it was something to remind me that someone out there loves me for who I am." she admitted.

"I'm surprised you even went back to Craig if being with Jazz was as good as it was." Darren said as he stretched out a leg, the knee joint cracked a little as he did.

"I did think about it," said Eva, her tone sad "But.. I dunno.. I don't know if it was fear or what..." she then fell silent, Tegan put a comforting arm around Eva and drew her in close..

"It's okay." Tegan said softly.

"No, it's not. I let my own fears enslave me," Eva

said, she sounded on the verge of tears "Craig tells me I should be thankful I have him in my life, that he has my best interests at heart."

"Eva, he doesn't, you must know that, don't you?" Darren said. Eva looked up dried her eyes with her sleeve and gave a weak smile.

"I do now.. can we talk about something else, please?" she said, trying her best to sound somewhat happy. Despite the tears then looked down at her feet with a pained look "Damn my feet really hurt." she rubbed her foot though the leather of her boot.

"Could be worse, I had to walk about the hills in my regents for nearly a week." Tegan said.

"Was that when you were.. y'know?" Eva asked, Tegan nodded.

"I feel your pain," Eva said eventually, full hunt or competition riding attire, especially the boots aren't really idea for trekking across the countryside on foot "I love wearing these but I do have other ones for just every day wear."

"I'm the same, love my leather ones but these for every day." said Tegan as she stretched out her boot encased leg.

"You always seemed to wear a pair every time I saw you, even if you weren't riding," Eva smiled at Tegan "Nice to see some things haven't changed, I won't lie, missed our visits, you were one of the few real friends I had." Eva looked at the ground as Tegan put an arm around her.

"I'm still your friend." she said as Eva looked up at her and sighed.

"That means a lot, it really does." Eva replied. Darren had been silent, as if thinking something over in his head, then suddenly picked up a stone and tossed it over to Eva.

"Eva! Catch!" he shouted, Eva stretched out her left hand and caught it instinctively "Ah, thought so." he said simple, Eva just looked bewildered at Darren then at Tegan and back to Darren.

"What was that about?" she asked.

"Sorry I was just checking." Darren replied "You are left handed."

"Yes, you could have asked though." Eva said in a bewildered tone.

"True but this way I know for certain." he said in a cryptic tone, "Is Craig left handed? I didn't really notice earlier" Darren asked.

"No, he is right handed, why? Darren just tell me what is on your mind, please." Eva said as she shook her head.

"Darren just tell me." she said almost pleadingly. He sighed and looked over at her.

"Eva, the police said your dad was hit on the left side of his face," He said, then continued when he noted both Eva and Tegan looked bewildered "They also said he was facing his attacker, if you had attacked him, chances are he would have been struck on his right side, but he wasn't." Eva turned to Tegan and gave her a puzzled look.

"Darren has a habit of noticing details other people miss, " Tegan said with a shrug "I've gotten used to it, comes in handy."

"I bet it does," Eva said looking over at Darren, she couldn't help but admire the guy after all he didn't know her, yet he was doing everything he could to stop her going to prison for a crime everyone else thinks she committed. Eva could see why Tegan fell for him "I'm actually quite jealous of you."

"Why?" Tegan said looking bemused.

"You have a guy who loves you and will do anything for you, has literally saved your life and I ended up with an abusive narcissist who only thinks of himself." Eva said as she stood up and stretched her legs and looked up at the heavy clouds "I suppose we should get going." Darren stood up too, a little stiffly for Tegan's liking and helped her up, it was obvious His knees were still sore.

"This way?" Eva asked as she headed off in the direction they had been walking, Darren looked at the map, looked at his compass keyring for a few moments and nodded.

"Yeah," he said "We should try and make up as much ground as possible before night fall".

The Vectra moved slowly up an access path near Glen Tachur and came to a stop under one of the larger trees. Peter got out and once he was satisfied he couldn't be seen from any of the buildings on the estate proceeded to set up the tent. As he put it up, he thought about what to do when he does see them, if it is all three it will be difficult but not impossible. Peter had a few tricks up his sleeve, he knew if he managed to get hold of one, threatening the others into compliance will be easy. Once he was finished pitching the tent he reached into the car and pulled out the sleeping back, his backpack and a long but narrow bag, in the backpack was Peter's tools of the trade. In the backpack was various blades but it was the narrow bag that was the most interesting and probably the reason Peter was chosen to lay in wait. In the bag was Peter's trusty hunting rifle, if all else fails he would be able to shoot them before they got too far away. Peter had been hunting with his father and grandfather since he was eight and was a crack shot. In recent years he would go off on hunting trips with Luke old Malcolm Devlin, that was until Malcolm was jailed for his part in the Galloway girl kidnapping. Peter did think of arguing that his hunting expertise would be better used tracking them but Luke had experience too and he suspected Raymond needed his shooting skill here instead in case the others were not able to catch their prey.

"Well Peter," he said to himself "Better make yourself comfortable." and he sat just inside the tent and pulled out a book from in his backpack, it was Firefox by Craig Thomas and he started to read, taking advantage of the peace and quiet.

Craig looked at his phone, no texts or missed calls from Michael. That could be a good thing or a bad thing, either way Craig was not going to tempt fate by calling him. As he looked out the window Craig saw Olivia and Hannah returning from the stables in a good mood.

COLD BLOOD

There was something about Hannah, from the moment he first saw her something in him just... he couldn't fully explain it, all he knew was he desired her. Yes she was older than him but she was still something of a beauty. He watched as she stamped her foot to knock the worst of the mud off her riding boot. Unlike Eva, her stepmother had class, Hannah didn't go out in some old scuffed and worn brown boots and mismatching attire. No, Hannah was wearing Black leather ones that were polished to a sheen, navy and black two tone jodhpurs and a navy quilted jacket. As she teased her hair out of the ponytail and let her blonde hair cascade over her shoulders he smiled. Why couldn't he have met a woman like her? Beautiful, successful in business, charming to talk to. He knew there was an age gap between her and Bruce, with Bruce being older by about fifteen years or so. Maybe, if he played things right, after giving her a suitable period of time to mourn her loss of course, who knows where things might lead. A cruel smile formed as Craig thought about Hannah and the things he would like to do, he was a man who was used to getting his own way and this was going to be no different even if he had to play the long game. He took another look at his phone, still nothing. If he was honest Craig hated all this waiting around but not much he could do about it. He sighed and went to sit on the bed and think of his next move.

"Thank you for suggesting that we go for a ride," Hannah said "I think I needed that."

"The fresh air does wonders, doesn't it?" Olivia said as she removed her helmet and smiled "Sometimes I fond when it all gets a little too much for me nothing beats going out for a ride on Lolita helps me relax and focus."

"It is a pity Tegan couldn't join us," Hannah said as they walked back to the house "I wish she didn't feel the need leave like she did."

"Unfortunately she has been through a lot these past few years and I think the combination of finding Bruce and the police presence unsettled her." Olivia explained, truth be told even before the abduction attempt and the media circus that followed, Tegan was a quiet person who preferred her own company always had been despite Olivia and Quentin's many efforts to get her to mix with others, competitions, pony club, university, none of it really worked. Apart from her cousin Lucy and children of family friends like Eva, Tegan didn't socialise much and on the rare occasions she did were usually unsuccessful for one reason or another.

"It is good she managed to find someone like Darren," Hannah said nodding "It is obvious he cares deeply for her. I remember when I first started dating Bruce, Tristan was okay with it from day one and I thought Eva was too until I found out she was saying rude things to me in Hungarian. But she did warm to me eventually but it was admittedly quite tough going for a while."

"Eva took her mother's death hard if I remember" Olivia said as she opened the door for Hannah "You have to remember she was only nine years old at the time and was very close to her mum, I think she would have reacted that way to anyone." Hannah stepped inside followed by Olivia.

"I know that and I did my best not to take any of it personally, though there were times I did wonder if it was worth the effort but I'm glad I stuck it out. I wouldn't swap those years with Bruce for anything." Hannah went and sat in the sitting room, not bothering to change, Olivia followed suit.

"Anyone want a cup of tea?" said a voice from the doorway, Craig stood, leaning on the door frame.

"Oh, well sure, okay, thank you." said Hannah, slightly flustered. Olivia shook her head.

"Nothing for me." she declined his offer, Craig then made his way to the kitchen, smiling as he did.

Tristan was just off the phone when Quentin came down the stairs.

"Well, that's me just had my leave extended on compassionate grounds." Tristan said with a shrug and sat of the bottom step rubbing his temples.

"What's wrong? Apart from the obvious of course?" Quentin said as he sat with the younger man, his knees creaking and protesting as he did.

"I don't know how to feel," Tristan said slowly "on one hand I have lost my father, on the other I am worried for Eva, even if she did do it." he shook his head and sighed.

"It's okay," Quentin said reassuringly "What yo

are going through was only natural, I remember when my brother Ronald committed suicide, I blamed myself for it and if I am honest, I still do to an extent, what if I helped him out a bit more, what if I had done things differently. The truth is there is not one right or wrong way to deal with all this but if you ever need to talk, I am there for you, okay?" Tristan sat in silence for a few moments and turned to Quentin, tears slowly forming in his eyes and gave the older man a rather awkward hug.

"Thank you." was all Tristan could manage to say.

CHAPTER 15

As he went to answer the doorbell, Jason adjusted the belt on his jeans and frantically smoothed his hair down with his hands. He stood just behind the door and took a deep breath and opened it, Linda stood in the doorway looking very serious.

"Oh, hi Linda," he said cheerfully "How are you?" Linda walked in without being asked.

"I'm okay Jason, Quentin asked me here just to make sure things are okay, but I came here because I need a favour." She said and went to make her way to the sitting room."

" Linda.. hold on... wait.." Jason started to say as he followed her, when she walked in Linda saw Astrid standing, she was wearing Jason's Rangers shirt, a large silk scarf worn like a sarong and her riding boots.

"Hello." she said shyly.

"Hi Astrid, okay Jason, what is the score in the Sexual Olympics?" Linda said in a knowing tone while pinching the bridge of his nose.

"I don't know what you mean," he protested weakly "Astrid was dirty from the stables and got soaked sorting out the horses drinking... okay okay, seven." Jason admitted after seeing Linda's cold hard stare and flopped down on the sofa.

"Sorry," Astrid said with a nervous smile as she sat next to Jason "We weren't expecting anyone to visit. Please don't tell anyone."

"I won't," Linda said as she sat on the chair and rubbed her temples "I should be used to Jason and his antics by now, I was just asked to make sure things were okay here and I wanted Jason's help."

"What is it?" Jason asked as Astrid cuddled into him. Linda took a deep breath before beginning.

"You know that guy that was found dead yesterday? The one who owned the big construction firm?" she started.

"Not personally but yeah I heard of him, why?" Jason said looking perplexed.

"Well, It is his place the Galloways are staying at..." Linda went to continue.

"...Oh bloody hell, what has Darren got himself into this time? They were going somewhere to take part in a foxhunt, that boy should be banned from them. That's the second he has been to that something bad happens." Jason leaned back and looked up at the ceiling in despair.

"Hey, neither Darren nor Tegan had anything to

do with it, okay Tegan found the body but they have another suspect"

"Oh thank God," Jason said with a sigh of relief "Well that's something, who is it?"

"His own daughter apparently but Quentin has asked me to look into the her husband." Linda said as she sat forward on the chair. Jason looked at her curiously.

"And how can I help?" he said cautiously. Linda got up and started to pace.

"Have you heard of Thistle computing?" she asked.

"Yeah," Jason said after some thought "It is on Union Street, why?"

"That is the husband's business, apparently it wasn't doing well financially until recently and Quentin is a bit suspicious of it all."

"Why?" Jason asked, not quite following Linda's train of thought, that is when Astrid spoke up.

"Maybe he wants to get some of the inheritance money from his wife?" she said but Jason shook his head.

"But his business is doing well, remember?" he countered but Astrid shook her head.

"Loans?" she suggested with a shrug.

"Could be," Linda said, agreeing with Astrid "there is one way to find out more."

"Oh?" said Jason cautiously "I'm not going to like this am I?" Linda shook her head.

"Probably not," she admitted "But I can't get much information online."

COLD BLOOD

"So what is your plan?" Jason asked.

"Well. We, well when I say we I mean you, go into the store, pretend to be interested in buying a computer, get the sales assistant talking, maybe they will give a clue or two."

"And why me? Why not you?" he asked sullenly.

"Jason, nobody in their right mind would suspect you of fishing for information," Linda said with a shrug "plus they did work for Galloway Haulage so thy may remember me."

"Oh," Jason said "Okay I'll help. What time tomorrow do you want to meet up and do this?"

"Tomorrow?" Linda said in a surprised tone and looking at her watch "I was going to go now, we should get there before closing time."

"All three of us?" Jason asked.

"Of course." Linda said, matter of factly.

"Just let me get, well, you know.." Astrid said awkwardly.

"Okay, Jason and I will wait for you at my car." Linda said as she stood up.

"We will get you outside my little Bremen beauty," Jason said.. to Linda but Linda grabbed his arm and nearly dragged him out the room "Hey, let go." he said, she eventually let go of his arm once they got outside.

"Jason, we do not have time for you to try and fit in another.. session." She said sternly, Jason looked shocked but then just sighed.

"Okay you win, did you say your car? Since when did you drive?" he said.

"I passed my test a few months ago and that is my car over there," she pointed over towards the silver Skoda Octavia.

"A Skoda? Really?" Jason said as he shook his head.

"Yes really." Linda replied as she got in the drivers seat, Astrid came out having put her jodhpurs and green quilted jacket on. Jason opened the back seat with an elaborate flourish to let her in and was just about to sit in the back himself when Linda ordered him to sit in the front.

"Okay, okay," he said as he got in the front passenger door "Why are you so determined to do this?" Jason asked as he buckled his seatbelt.

"Jason," Linda said as she started the car "Do you remember what happened that time at college someone accused Anita of copying Mark's work? The boat in the lake picture."

"Yeah, what that know it all prick tried to do was overkill," Jason said then said to Astrid "Mark was a guy who thought he was the best in the class and liked to let everyone know it."

"Do you remember how it was all resolved in the end?" Linda said knowingly, hoping Jason would get the hint.

"Yeah, Darren, after getting Anita's permission, went through her work and found out she had a unique way of editing sky behind the boat."

"Exactly." Linda said, there was a little frustration creeping in.

"Linda, Darren only noticed because he did

similar," he then explained to Astrid "Darren had a rather unique way of working, especially when it came to photo editing assignments, It got the same results but his work was too idiosyncratic for anyone else to copy."

"I see what I did, I started too small," Linda said to herself then to Jason said "Remember when we asked why he helped Tegan?"

"Yeah, he said he couldn't stand to see an innocent... oh." the penny dropped "You think he is going to try and prove this guy's daughter is innocent?"

"Yeah, pretty much" Linda replied, thankful that Jason finally understood "His total over riding sense of right and wrong is bound to kick in and who knows what will happen." Jason nodded.

"Oh, yeah, of course." he said and rubbed his temples.

"So this is something Darren always does?" Astrid asked looking a little confused.

"You could say that," Linda said, keeping her eyes on the road "Unfortunately it has the potential to cause problems because even if it is an issue everyone wants to move on from.. he can't, he needs to find out the answer, make things right in his head."

"He once told me it is like, mentally it is similar to having a constant pressure in his brain and he gets a feeling like a weight pushing on his chest when he gets that way." Jason added.

"I see." Astrid said but in reality she found it all a bit strange.

Don't get me wrong, he has calmed down a lot since he and Tegan became a couple," Linda said reassuringly

"But he still has his moments."
"And to think you tired to talk him out of going to that protest," Jason said, amusement evident in his voice "Imagine what would have happened if he hadn't."

"Okay, okay, a broken clock is right twice a day," Linda sighed, it was true that Jason did tell him to go, despite Linda's own objections "And I would rather not think about what might have happened instead but don't get too cocky, You aren't exactly known for giving good advice."

"Name one example." Jason said daringly.

"Just one?" Linda arched an eyebrow "How about the time you suggested that for Ellen's birthday I hire someone for a threesome? Or that time you tried to ask out Vanessa, who is profoundly deaf, by taking her to a concert of all things, or what about..." Linda continued listing his many poor attempts as dispensing advice and stupid ideas as Jason just put his head in his hands.

Quentin was on the phone making more arrangements for the funeral as Olivia walked into the sitting room.

"Quentin have you seen my.." she was about to say but then saw it, her riding crop. She had left there after talking to Hannah earlier "Never mind, found it." she then held it up so he could see, Quentin politely waved her off and continued talking on the phone. Olivia was still in her riding gear and was thinking of going out for another quick ride before it got too dark, Lolita did not like being locked up in stables too much, too much of a free spirit. Olivia walked past Craig who had just finished a call on his phone.

"Anything important?" she asked, pointing to the phone.

"Oh?" he said slightly surprised "Nothing major, just typical business stuff, I'm sure you hear a lot of that sort of thing from your husband."

"Quentin can be quite the workaholic at times but he has his moments," Olivia said "When Tegan was younger, well when I say younger, right up until.. she met Darren anyway, I would pity the person who would dare to try and get between Quentin spending time with his daughter, be it taking her to Celtic Park or watching Star Trek or some other show they both liked on the big screen TV."

"I didn't think Tegan was the type to be into football." Craig said, genuinely surprised.

"Into football?" Olivia laughed "Oh that girl is Celtic daft, I still remember her crying tears of joy when Celtic stopped Rangers winning ten in a row." Craig looked even more surprised, granted for any true Celtic fan that day did mean a lot as their greatest rivals Rangers had just equalled Celtic's record of nine league championships in a row and were on course to eclipse that achievement, things were not made any better that season by Celtic losing their first two league games.

"Really?" he shook his head.

"Yes, She was there at the stadium with her father, she was still wiping the tears away with her scarf when they came home." Olivia said knowingly.

"Wow," Craig said, still shocked "I'm sorry, I just

can't imagine that meek looking girl I saw yesterday, yelling and shouting at a football match that's all."

"Don't worry, happens all the time, most of the time she is that timid meek girl everyone sees but take her to the football or put her on a horse and you get a completely different person, it has always been the way with her." Olivia explained.

"She is a credit to you both," Craig said with a sigh "Eva however... let us just say things haven't been good, even before all this"

"Oh?" she said curiously "How so?" she then leaned against the wall.

"Where to start?" Craig started "When we met she was this amazing young woman, wild and rebellious sure but, let me ask you, you would do anything for you husband? Right?"

"Of course," Olivia said without needing to think twice.

"Eva wouldn't, even on our wedding day," Craig said vaguely, he wasn't about to tell Olivia he raped his own wife because he wanted sex on his wedding night but she was too tired "No matter what I do for her it is never good enough, it got worse once I bought her that damn horse."

"I take it you don't ride?" Olivia asked.

"No, never much cared for it to be honest." he admitted.

"Neither is Darren but he has made it a point to help Tegan as much as he could with her passion for riding, though he hasn't attempted to ride himself." Olivia said as Craig shook his head.

"Even if I really wanted to, it is a bit late now," he replied "Even if I ever found it within myself to forgive her actions, Eva could be in prison for a long time."

"It will be difficult but she will need you there for her." Olivia said with a surprising conviction to her voice.

"How can you be so.." he was about to say when Olivia cut him off.

"Craig, You need to remember Tegan, although she was fully justified in doing so did kill her own cousin. For years we loved Lucy like she was one of our own. She was family and even now I wished there had been another way things could have went, I wish she was still alive and if she was would we still try and help? Try and offer her an olive branch? Yes we would." Olivia explained

"I'm sorry, I didn't mean to.." Craig apologised.

"It's okay," she said, straightening up and idly playing with her crop "Look, I better go, Lolita will wonder where I am." she said.

"Oh, I won't Keep you." Craig said "Have you seen Hannah?"

"She is in the kitchen I think." Olivia said and she headed out the door, there was something about Craig that was increasingly unsettling her, but she couldn't work out what it was exactly.

CHAPTER 16

Despite the pain in his knees, Darren kept up a good pace. Eva looked over at him curiously.

"Darren, can I ask something?" she asked.

"Sure." he said, Eva looked over at Tegan before asking.

"If your knees are that bad, why don't you get surgery, maybe knee replacements?"

"I did ask once, at the doctors up in Dundee. Apparently they can't do that." Darren shrugged.

"Why not?" Eva asked, this time Tegan answered.

"They say it is his age, he is too young or at least that is what they told us."

"Yeah," Darren said "Pretty much that, I can cope, if that is your worry."

"I'm sorry, I guess I still feel bad for getting you two caught up in this." Eva said as they got to the

COLD BLOOD

treeline, suddenly Tegan crouched down amongst the tall grass, pulling Darren down too. Eva followed suit.

"What is it?" Eva asked in a whisper then looked over and saw Tegan almost shaking, Darren saw it too and pulled his fiancee closer.

"Over there." he pointed. On the other side of the large grassy clearing they could make out two very small figures moving amongst the trees, they looked like the were well ahead of the trio and moving away.

"Is that the two...?" Eva started to say in a whisper, Darren nodded

"What will we do?" Eva asked.

"Well, continue the way we are going, judging by the map we will have more woodland cover, the way they are going looks like fields, right?"

"Yeah," Eva nodded "Though we will have to cross some fields eventually too." Darren nodded in acknowledgment then shifted his body from a crouch to a sitting position and Tegan cuddled in, her head on his chest as she listened to his heartbeat.

"Tegan, it's okay, I doubt they saw us," he said soothingly "They haven't changed direction anyway." They waited a while, at least until Darren was sure he couldn't see any movement, Tegan still gripping him tight..

"Is everything okay?" Eva asked as she crawled over.

"Yeah," Tegan said, a slight tremor to her voice "I guess all this is bringing back some old memories." Eva sighed and hung her head in despair.

"I am sorry.." she started to say but Tegan turned

and looked at Eva intently.

"Don't apologise," She said "Please, we are all in this together now."

"Exactly," Darren agreed "It is Craig who should be sorry for all this, not you. So stop blaming yourself."

"Your right," Eva said as she slowly nodded "I guess I'm not used to this."

"Surely you've had friends." Darren asked.

"Not many, lost a lot of friends when I became a sab. The group I was with weren't too sure of me a lot of the time due to my background, no matter how hard I tried to prove I was just as against hunting as they were so none really shed a tear when I stopped it all." Eva sighed sadly "And you know the rest, apart from Jazz, you two are the only people outside of my family that really seem to have shown you give a damn." Tegan released her grip on Darren and went over to Eva, putting her hands on Eva's shoulders.

"Eva," Tegan said "I actually thought after that last time we spoke that you hated me because I still wanted to hunt, otherwise I would have gotten in touch."

"Really?" Eva asked with a hint of surprise.

"Of course I would have, you are my friend are you not?" Tegan asked with a smile. Eva threw her arms around Tegan.

"Of course you are, Both of you." Eva said in a tone that suggested there should never have been any doubt.

Union Street was busy with the crowds at the sales.

Linda was complaining about the amount they paid for parking.

"So what is the plan?" Jason asked as he looked at Linda for confirmation.

"It is simple, you go into the store and do your thing, find out what you can." Linda said wearily, how many times did she need to tell him?

"And where are you two going to be?" he asked pointedly.

"We will be down there at that bus stop." Linda indicated "Pretending to be waiting for.."

"A bus?" Jason said in a sarcastic tone.

"Yes." Linda said, deliberately deciding to ignore his comment.

"Okay, wish me luck." he said, Astrid gave him a quick kiss.

"Good luck." she said, he just smiled back in return.

Quentin sat down in the sitting room, thankful for the quiet after a long day of making and answering phone calls. He hadn't heard anything from Linda yet, he wondered if she had found out anything yet. Quentin looked down at his phone wondering if he should phone her.

"Are you waiting for a call?" said Hannah from the door.

"Something like that." He replied.

"Dinner will be ready soon." she told him, Quentin looked out and could see Olivia, on Lolita head towards the stables, Hannah looked out too "Good timing by the looks of it."

"It is yeah." he said distractedly then put his phone in his pocket, he will call Linda later.

Despite there being a sale advertised, Thistle Computing was quite empty as Jason walked in and pretended to browse. The shop assistant, a tall lady in her twenties called Karen came up to him.

"Can I help you at all?" She said in a tone that suggested she wasn't all that keen on helping and looked at her watch in a theatrical way as if hinting to him he doesn't have long left to select something "We are closing early today."

"Whys that?" Jason asked.

"Short staffed, was her cold reply "So.. Can I help you?"

"Erm, yes actually you can, I hope." Jason said and flashed a smile "I have been in every PC store in town and the staff have always been less than helpful.. and way less attractive." and he flashed a smile, Jason was in his element.

"Oh," she said, clearly surprised about how easily he mentioned the last part "What were you looking for?" he tone slightly more helpful and she smiled at him, Jason had to think quick.

"I need a good gaming PC," he blurted out "My old PC isn't up to it any more, if it is not Command and Conquer Tiberian Sun crashing when I go play online, it would glitch playing Counter-Strike." all this time listening to Darren talk about video games was paying off, Karen smiled.

"Tell me about it," she said, beaconing him to follow her as she took him over a row of display computers "So, GDI or NOD?" she asked.

"Huh?" Asked Jason, a little confused.

"For Command and Conquer, which side do you play as?"

"Oh, right," Jason said and picked one at random "NOD."

"Ah," Karen said, her voice sounding like she approved of his choice "Well, in that case you are best going for one of our custom built models, the Powerplay X, it has.." and she rattled off a bunch of facts and figures he had no interest in retaining but nodded and smiled "… And we always use AMD processors over Intel, any questions?" Jason eagerly stepped slightly closer with a smile.

"Oh, I think you answered most, You really know your stuff, the guy in the last shop was trying to get me to buy a computer that half the memory and a faction of the hard drive space." Karen brushed a few strands of hair away from her eyes.

"Well most of these guys work on commissions and don't care about anything really," She leaned forward and whispered in his ear "Most of them couldn't tell the difference between Half Life and Quake if their lives depended on it." and she laughed, Jason joined in, keeping up the pretence.

"Must be great working here," Jason said as he looked around "like a kid in a candy store." she gave him a warm smile.

"It an be good.. she paused as someone was walking in "Hey, we are closing!" she snapped at the prospective customer who turned about and walked out "I'm on my own today because the boss gave everyone else time off, Just a moment." she ran over and flipped the sign from open to closed then headed back to Jason.

"So, you were saying." Jason said, all smiles. He looked at her she wore a black tshirt with the company logo in blue and the smart black trousers, the look was finished off with her black and white converse trainers, she looked at him and shrugged.

"It's okay I guess, the boss can get a bit creepy at times but nothing crazy, just the odd compliment that sends shivers up my spine, was nearly out of a job a few months back and if I'm honest I might still look for a new job." she said and smiled sadly.

"Aww," Jason said and gave her a hug like it was second nature, she didn't protest, instead hugged him in return, after what seemed like forever they broke the hug "What happened?" Jason said, his voice sounding concerned.

"look, you can't tell anyone this but our boss was having huge money issues, I don't know why. Anyway he informed me if my attitude to him didn't change, I'd be the first to go if he was to make anyone redundant." she said looked down.

"Oh yeah?" Jason said, guessing what she was driving at.

"But suddenly he starts talking on his phone a lot to some guy called Michael, some investor or someone I assume, then one day out of the blue... all our worries are over, apparently. I get to keep my job, for now anyway, his words. I'm not the only female here he is creepy to. Poor Louise gets it as well. Want to know the worst bit about it?" Karen said, she looked like she was grateful to have someone to talk to.

"Go on." he said, realising it would be suspicious and impolite to leave just yet.

"The few times his wife has came in, she is a beautiful woman, long red dreadlocks, not braids but proper dreadlocks mind you, lovely to talk to when he isn't standing over her that is."

"What do you mean?" Jason asked, suddenly interested.

"Well," Karen started "she would go from this cheery bubbly lovely lady to this timid woman who looked scared of her own shadow when he would walk in the room, If you ask me, I wouldn't be surprised if he was beating her up. I'm sure I'd see her with bruising and the amount of concealer on her face.." she gave Jason a knowing look.

"Ooh," Jason said, now that was interesting "That doesn't sound good at all."

"It is horrible, especially when he flirts, or at least attempts to flirt, with staff and customers right in front of her." Karen said sadly "You can tell she really wants to say something but seems really terrified to do so, poor woman."

"I take it you haven't seen the papers?" Jason asked carefully.

"No, why?" she asked.

"No reason," Jason said and went to change the subject "So, where would you want to work? Apart from a computing store?"

"I don't know really and to be honest I'm not really all that bothered where I end up, what do you do?" she asked.

"Right now I work in a call centre but can't see myself doing that for too much longer," he replied and looked at his watch "I should probably go.." he started to say but Karen stepped forward and in a flirtatious tone said "The shop is empty and technically due to shut for another twenty minutes..."

Luke stopped a moment and shook his head.

"What is it?" Raymond asked.

"Oh nothing, It is just when we were walking past that clearing earlier, I thought I saw movement but couldn't be sure." The big Englishman looked uncertain.

"Think it was them?" Raymond looked at Luke curiously.

"More likely a wild animal, it was a blink and you miss it, probably a fox." Luke said after some thought.

"Well, it is foxhunting season I suppose, we should keep going, it's getting too dark to be moving about.

"Yeah, I suppose." Luke said, gazing up at the darkening sky.

"Where is he?" Linda muttered to herself, they

had been been pretending to wait on a bus for ages, so long that Astrid was away to the nearby McDonalds to use the toilet. She had half a mind to go in the store and find out what was keeping him when Jason walked out with his usual swagger and stupid grin on his face.

"Okay, what has got you in a good mood.." She started to say then suddenly realised "The sales assistant was a woman wasn't it?" Linda groaned, it seemed like having Astrid in his life hadn't fully tamed his lustful ways.

"What?" he said looking confused "Oh yeah it was, she told me quite a bit actually."

"Is that all she did?" Linda said with a hint of disapproval in her voice.

"What is that supposed to mean?" where is Astrid anyway.." he said but then seen her come cross the road towards them "Never mind I see her." he then waved at her and smiled.

"So what did you find out?" Linda asked.

"Will tell you back in the car." he said and started to make his way back to the car park.

With the sky getting darker it was getting harder to move about, plus Tegan was starting to get worried about Darren's knees again, she had noticed his walk had became stiffer a sure sign he was in severe pain.

"We should probably look for somewhere to rest for the night." she said.

"No, not yet," he said as he continued to walk awkwardly but Tegan put a hand on his shoulder.

"Darren, stop... please. For me?" she said to him pleadingly "We need to rest, you need to rest." Darren's shoulders sagged.

"I know, I just wanted to.." he started to say but Tegan was having none of it.

"No Darren," she said turning him round to face her "You are not putting yourself through this again, I know what you are like? Remember?" Eva just stood looking at the couple, Tegan had told her how Darren barely slept, pushed himself beyond his own limits, suffered a serious concussion and literally put his life on the line all for Tegan. Eva could see why Tegan was as concerned about Darren's well being, she had seen first hand just how selfless he was.

"Darren," Eva said "Tegan is right, we need to rest up for tomorrow, I mean I do have a lot to do.."

"..We have a lot to do." Tegan corrected.

"Okay," Eva smiled "We have a lot to do when we get back."

"Okay," Darren replied, realising it was futile to argue "Let's find a spot to rest up for the night."

"..So yeah, that is pretty much all I found out about him." Jason finished as they sat in the comfort of the Skoda.

"It doesn't tell us that much but at least we have a first name for whomever I assume fronted the money to keep him going, did she say if it was a loan or investment?" asked Linda, Jason shrugged.

"Didn't say, but it was the whole treatment of his

wife bit that really got me, I dunno why but that unsettled me and if it had that effect on me and I was only haring it.."Jason started to say.

"...Darren is bound to notice too and that will set off alarm bells with him, plus you know what he is like about that sort of thing," Linda finished for him "Yeah, I know what you mean, I'll call Quentin once we get you two back to Netherfield House." she said as she started the car.

CHAPTER 17

It didn't take Raymond and Luke to find a place to stop for the night, they found and area where the trees were quite close together which would protect from the rain and there was enough flat ground to lie somewhat comfortably.

"This place looks as good as any to settle down for the night and it is getting too dark to be roaming around." Raymond said as he pulled the sleeping bags out out of the rucksack followed by a four pack of Tennents lager "Here you go." he then handed one to Luke, who regarded it dubiously.

"Oh this stuff," he grimaced as he stared at the can "Not got anything decent? Or is it only this Scottish rubbish?"

"Oh and I suppose you English can make better can you? Have you tasted Carling?" Raymond said as he opened his can "If you want you can give it back, more for me."

"Oh no, I didn't say I would not drink it now did I? Needs must and all that." Luke said as he opened his can and took a long drink.

"Don't you think its a bit risky to build a fire? It's going to get a lot colder I think" Raymond wondered out loud.

"A small fire might be okay if you really want to run the risk of them seeing it," Luke shrugged "It is totally up to you."

"They don't know we are looking for them do they? May just assume it's other campers." Raymond insisted, Luke got up and tried to find some wood to make a fire with a groan as he had just gotten comfortable.

"I'm getting too old for this crap." he muttered to himself.

Soon Darren found somewhere they could camp for the night in safety but once he pointed it out, Eva did not look all that impressed.

"Are you sure it's safe? Can't we just use the tent?" Eva said in a sceptical tone as she looked at what Darren had found, A tree stump had been partially uprooted and the exposed roots gave the appearance of a shelter of sorts, they would have to crawl on all fours to get in between the gap.

"It should be, also we aren't using the tent as it would take way too long to set up and take down,"

Darren replied as he tested the stump to see if it would move, it wouldn't "Plus they would be looking for a tent." Eva shrugged, it did make some sense. Tegan was getting the sleeping bags out of the rucksack and unzipping them.

"I'm almost afraid to ask but what are you doing?" Eva asked curiously.

"I'm going to use one for us to lay on and the other to cover us, we may all need to huddle for body heat," Tegan said "you can help if you like." Eva decided to help and they had managed to create a somewhat comfortable area. Darren had taken Eva's blanket and was intertwining it between to roots to make a more complete roof for them.

"Eva, do you remember where did you got this?" he asked Eva.

"Some shop in Kilmarnock." she shrugged "It's ac Black Watch tartan I think, or at least that is what Craig said it was." but Darren just looked at her and shook his head.

"It's actually Douglas tartan, admittedly they do look similar but trust me, I know my own clan's tartan." he replied.

"Oh, I see," Eva said "I did wonder but of course Craig always knew best." she sighed.

"Was it really that bad living with him?" Tegan asked.

"Mostly yes, I mean there was a couple of times where it would feel like he has realised how horrible he had been and we would talk, thinks would seemingly goo back to how they were at the beginning then it would go back to normal. It would be a small thing, something as simple as his dinner being cold could set him off/"

"Sounds like a nightmare," Darren said as he finished the makeshift roof.

"It was, the worst part was he would gloat and mock me, even though I'd be in tears begging him to stop or worse, he couldn't resist the urge tell me why he was doing it that particular time... it was like he didn't care..." She started to tear up, Tegan walked over and instinctively hugged her.

"It's okay," Tegan said soothingly "It's going to be okay."

"I hope so," Eva replied. Wiping away tears with her sleeve. Tegan took Eva's hands in hers and looked her deep in her eyes.

"It will be okay, trust us.." Tegan said then looked at Eva with a worried expression on her face "Eva, your hands are frozen." Eva looked at Tegan and shook her head.

"Trust me I'm okay, really." She tried to say but Tegan was already unzipping her Umbro jacket and handed it to her.

"Put it on, you'll need it." she said with a hint of authority, the sort she would use on an awkward patient in hospital.

"Are you sure, won't you need it?" Eva asked, Tegan shook her head and gestured to her Celtic goalkeeper top.

"This is really comfortable and warm, trust me, I'll be fine." she said, Eva could see Darren smile in the background, he remembered Tegan had the same concerns when he wore it when they were being pursued in the lead hills and he more or less said the same thing to Tegan.

"I'll take your word for it." Eva said as she slipped the jacket on.

"So, what do you think ladies," Darren said as he stood back and looked at their handiwork "Not too shabby."

"Sure beats a length of tarpaulin and a couple of large boulders." Tegan shrugged. Eva looked at them curiously as if trying to work out if they were joking or not

"You didn't really spend a night in something like that.." Eva started to say but Darren shook his head with a smile.

"Two nights actually, with heavy rain." He told her.

"Oddly," Tegan added "In a way it was kind of fun, considering the situation we were in." she cuddled into Darren, smiling as she thought about those two nights they spent just talking for hours, getting to know each other while the rain lashed the makeshift tarpaulin cover.

"Yeah, it was." Darren said as he stroked Tegan's hair. After a few moments Tegan sighed and looked up to the sky. Darren had known Tegan long enough that he didn't need to ask what she was doing, he found himself looking for Orions Belt too.

"I think we should probably get in," she said "It's getting darker and the temperature is really starting to drop."

"Yeah, seems like a good idea to me. Eva said in agreement.

The station's coffee was horrible but it was keeping Detective Duff awake, she had been tasked with looking into the histories of everyone associated with the Ingliston murder case.

"I bloody hope you got some good news for me," she could hear Detective Sergeant McManus before she seen him come in "The papers are already having a field day with this one and every reporter seems to have a half baked theory." he said as he slammed a Daily Record on her desk in frustration.

"Well let us see, we found no prints on the murder weapon so it was either wiped or the suspect had gloves on. As for suspects, apart from his daughter with her past history, I can't think of anyone else with reason to do it so she is still our prime suspect. Although in saying that, there are some financial issues with her husband which may interest you." she said as she looked up from her computer screen.

"Oh, what like?" McManus said, his anger changing to curiosity.

"It does seem Craig Robertson was apparently in some financial difficulty until he got an influx of cash a few months ago." Duff said as she looked through her notes.

"So he had a difficult period, what company doesn't." McManus shrugged.

"It is the fact he got a rather large cash injection that came from a company called... lets see... Tradala Limited, ever heard of it?." Duff said as she struggled to find the correct sheet of paper that she wrote the name down.

"Never, doesn't ring a bell" McManus said after some thought.

"Neither have I, I have tried looking into the company but I'm struggling to find anything about it online too," Duff admitted with a sigh "But I am going to continue looking into it though. The money could be an investment or a loan..."

"And if it is a loan, having extra money.. say from a recent inheritance would allow him to pay it off? Is that your thinking?" McManus finished with a sceptical tone.

"I know it is a long shot but apart from the daughter nobody else has anything remotely looking like a motive.

"Okay, look into it if you must, "McManus said wearily " But our first priority is to find her, I take it there is still no luck there?"

"No," Duff replied "It's like she has vanished into thin air." McManus groaned.

"If she doesn't show up in the next few days we will need to go out there and start searching the surrounding area." He said with a sigh.

"You don't think..?" Duff started to say but stopped herself, the chance it could be a murder suicide was one of many possibilities she had not considered "Surely not."

"At this point in a case like this anything is possible." McManus said as Duff stood up to get another coffee.

"Coffee?" she asked.

"Sure, why not. Milk three sugars," McManus replied. He hated cases like this where the suspect is nowhere to be found "You know, I wouldn't be surprised if there is some more twists to this case, I can just feel it."

CHAPTER 18

Darren insisted on checking out the immediate area before settling, Eva was at the back of the makeshift shelter and was propped up on one elbow.

"So Tegan," she started to ask "Do you still compete?" Tegan, who was laying on her back turned her head to Eva and sighed.

"I do but not as much as I used to," she replied A combination of wanting out the limelight after all that happened, focusing on university and the pressure was getting too much."

"Oh," Eva said "Weren't you hailed as a potential prospect for the United Kingdom Olympic Team?" she then asked.

"Being in the Olympic team was never my dream, I just love riding and competing, the papers had heard that there had been some talk that if I continued doing as well as I had been that being in a future Olympics was inevitable Of course, naturally some papers blew it out of proportion as they do, now I just do some select competitions when time allows."

"I have been thinking of getting back into competition riding." Eva said "Craig always kept putting me off, telling me stuff like I'd be too rusty, my time has been and gone for that kind of thing and I should just grow up."

"Darren would never say anything like that to me, if anything I am surprised about how much he does support me in my riding," Tegan told her "You know what, you should compete again."

"Oh yeah? And go up against you and Princess?" Eva said shaking her head "do you remember how badly Lucy took it when you won your first competition against her on that horse."

"I do, but Eva please trust me if you are half the rider you used to be, you will do amazingly well, trust me on this." Tegan smiled, she was right, very few could compete with Eva when she was in the zone when they were younger "Who knows you may end up in the sights of the Olympic team."

"Which one? United Kingdom or Hungary? Because you know if given the choice I'd choose Hungary." Eva said knowingly.

"True, but trust me, you should start competing again." Tegan repeated earnestly "look, if you want you can go to them with me so you have someone you know there, okay?" Tegan looked at Eva, a young woman who has had every bit of spirit and confidence knocked out of her, in some ways literally, she remembered the old Eva and if she was honest there were subtle signs of that showing.

"Coast is clear," Darren said as he crawled in,

"Darren," Eva said "Do you think I should start competing again?"

"Did you enjoy it before?" Darren asked.

"I did yeah." Eva replied.

"Well there you go then, go for it." he said with a smile and tried to settle as best he could, Darren had decided he would the one nearest the opening, it was just another way he was being protective of them and Tegan knew better than to argue even though she knew he would be the one most exposed to the elements even with the sleeping bag over him, instead she just kissed him softly and pulled him closer.. for body heat of course.

Once they were back at Netherfield House, Linda got on the phone to Quentin.

"Hello Linda, Did you find anything?" Quentin asked the minute he answered his phone.

"Quite a few things actually," Linda said as she sat next to the phone "He was in financial difficulties but after some phone calls with someone called Michael, I assume he is an investor or something, things started looking up." she could hear Quentin sigh down the phone.

"Well, it is something, anything else?" He asked.

"I'm not sure how relevant it might be," Linda

said carefully "But, after I spent time online and came up with practically nothing on him or Thistle Computing, except the official website that is, we went to his store on Union Street and managed to speak with one of the sales assistants."

"Go on... wait, what do you mean by we, did you take Ellen?" Quentin asked.

"No," Linda said, holding the phone away from her ear "Jason."

"You involved him?!?!" Quentin shouted " him of all people? Why? What possessed you to include that halfwit?"

"I'm known to the staff, remember? And I will be the first to admit he is a halfwit but he is a useful halfwit." she said, trying to justify Jason's involvement in the investigation "And in all fairness that is how we got the name Michael, was through Jason's.. unique style of investigative technique."

"Do I really want to know? Or is it best I remain blissfully ignorant." Quentin groaned.

"Blissfully ignorant would be the wisest option in this case I think." Linda replied

"Okay, fair enough, At least he is being useful for once," Quentin said as he calmed down "Please, do go on."

"Well, it seems Craig is known for being a bit of a creep towards the female staff and customers, then there is the fact that some of the staff are convinced that he beats his wife." Linda then went on to explain everything Jason had told her.

"I see," he replied after a long pause "It actually

does explain some of the things I have seen here, thank you."

Quentin put down his phone and went downstairs into the study where he saw Craig sitting at Bruce's desk working on a laptop. Upon seeing Quentin he stopped typing.

"Just catching up on work." Craig said.

"Anything interesting?" Quentin asked.

"I don't know about interesting but I have just signed a contract to supply and maintain computers for a structural engineering firm." Craig said

"Oh?" said Quentin with interest.

"Some company called The Structural Partnership or something like that? Heard of them?" Quentin shook his head.

"Doesn't ring any bells," he said honestly "Are the a big firm?"

"Not really no," Craig said "But they are looking to expand the workforce. I spoke to one of the owners, a Mister John Leckie. That man drives a tough bargain but it is an ongoing contract and one of many in the pipeline."

"Always good to hear a small company do well." Quentin nodded "What other stuff is in the pipeline anyway? if it is okay to ask that is." Craig shifted awkwardly in his seat.

"Just a few small businesses showing an interest really," Craig said eventually "So what brings you in here anyway? He asked.

"Oh, just in for a book I remember Bruce telling me about," Quentin replied as he went over and scanned the bookshelves "Still no word from Eva?"

"No, nothing at all." Craig said sadly as he rubbed his temples "I really don't know what is going on with her."

"You know, she always did have a hint of a rebel in her," Quentin told him knowingly "It is a shame though."

"How so?" Craig asked a little confused, Quentin pointed to a picture of what happened to be a younger Eva at a youth competition and she was holding a few rosettes of various colours.

"She was always at the top or thereabouts, she had an instinctive way with horses, some said it was the Hungarian in her. Most of these events usually turned into a competition between her and Lucy over who would win."

"Lucy?" Craig said bemused "As in your niece? Not Tegan"

"Yes, out of the two of them, Lucy and Tegan that is, it was Lucy who took competitions more serious at first. Tegan did compete but it wasn't until she got Princess that.. something clicked and she started winning. When a strong bond between rider and horse like what she has with Princess happens it is amazing what can happen."

"Oh." Craig said as he sat back suddenly intrigued.

"Yeah, then of course Lucy dropped out of competitions due to.. personal reasons and then Eva stopped once she started her rebellious stage..." Quentin continued.

"...A stage she never really grew out of I fear," Craig sighed and stared at the ceiling "When I started to get to know her, Do you want to know where, or actually more importantly what she was living in when I first met her?"

"Go on," Quentin said as he made his way to the drinks globe and opened it, Craig was starting to open up, this could be interesting "Would you like some Scotch?" he asked as he selected the bottle of Glenfiddich for himself.

"Please," Craig said then continued "She stayed in a caravan that was in some farmers field just outside Kilmarnock. It was hooked up with electricity and stuff but still, she could be living in a place like this and earning big money competing but has instead preferred to live like a gypsy, selling silly little paintings to make ends meet." Craig shook his head, disgust evident in his voice.

"Her mother comes from a Hungarian gypsy background and was a very strong willed, passionate woman. You really need to remember that and also understand that at least for as long as I known Eva she always had an artistic mind." Quentin reminded Craig, he could hear the disdain in Craig's voice over Eva's life choices.

"Yeah, but..." Craig started to way but Quentin countered.

"Surely you must love her regardless." He said as he handed Craig a glass. Craig just gave him a look that said he wasn't so sure.

"I wish it was that simple, I really do but to be honest, the more I think on it, when she goes to jail.." Craig started.

"..If she goes to jail." Quentin quietly corrected him.

"Anyway," Craig continued with more than just a hint of annoyance evident in his voice "I really just can't see our marriage surviving this if I am honest, obviously I'm not going to do anything yet, at least not straight away but it has been playing on my mind for a while now, I think recent events have just all but confirmed my choice."

"Why?" Quentin said curiously as he took a sip of scotch.

"I thought it was pretty obvious, I genuinely believed marriage might mellow her rebellious streak and she would settle and get a proper job. But no, instead she spends most of her days painting in the garage that she uses as an art studio or if she isn't painting she is on her horse riding most of the day and now it looks like she came here with a pretext to settle old family scores." Craig then drained his glass in one fluid motion, stood and picked up his laptop. "Please, excuse me." he said before walking out. Quentin watched the younger man leave, one thing was now painstakingly obvious, Quentin was now doubting Craig's motives for marrying Eva in the first place.

As Jason walked Linda out to her car, she had something

she had to ask.

"Jason," he said "just how did you come by all that information?"

"Well, I had to use a bit of my charm, you know how it is." he stated

"Jason you didn't.." Linda started to say but Jason interrupted.

"No!, I mean I was tempted yeah.." he could sense she didn't believe him "Look, you can believe what you want but I even refused her phone number when she offered it. Regardless of what you think I really do love Astrid."

"Okay," Linda said in a dubious tone "Something else is on your mind isn't it?"

"Yeah," he admitted "I'm more concerned about how Darren will react to everything, you know what he is like."

"I know," Linda said in agreement "My worry is he won't be as lucky this time around."

CHAPTER 19

The temperature dropped quite dramatically and soon the three of them were huddled together in the makeshift shelter.

"I don't remember it being this cold last night." Tegan said, she was in the middle between Darren and Eva, Eva was cuddling into Tegan's back as Tegan snuggled into Darren as best they could, the open sleeping bag above them offered some comfort but not much.

"We were in a tent last night, that made a difference." Darren mused mournfully as the biting cold wild wind blew into the shelter.

"I don't know how you two managed to do this sort of thing for nearly a week." Eva said with a slight tone of complaint.

"Well, we did have no choice I suppose," Darren

informed her "To be honest it was risk of failure that was driving me."

"What do you mean risk of failure?" Eva said, confusion evident on her voice.

"He didn't want to fail me," Tegan explained "And you never have, ever." she said to Darren softly and kissed his cheek.

"So, I hope you don't mind me asking but is Darren your first.." y'know?" Eva asked with nervous curiosity.

"Pretty much, though I did go on a date with Stuart Ramsey." Tegan said, Eva's face was an expression of total disgust.

"That creep?" come on what happened?" Eva had to know.

"He took me to a restaurant, I walked out on him in the after the starter course and we never really spoke again." Tegan said with a sigh.

"I'm surprised you even agreed to go." Eva said stifling a laugh.

"I know, I know." Tegan sighed.

"What about you Darren?" Eva asked.

"Tegan is my first and hopefully only one." he said with a conviction in his voice that made Eva actually quite envious.

"Eva," Tegan started to say after thinking about an old memory "I have to ask after all these years, whatever happened between you and Maurice Reeves?"

"Why did you need to bring that up?" Eva groaned.

"Oh," Darren asked curiously "What's this all

about?"

"I admit Maurice was a nice enough guy," Eva said carefully "He competed in the same events as us, was always chatty and a good laugh, he got on with pretty much everyone. Anyway, he asks me out one time in that way you do when you are only fourteen."

"Wait for it." Tegan whispered to Darren, Eva heard but just smiled.

"We went out a few times, going to the cinema, hanging about, that sort of thing but he never even tried to kiss me or anything so one night I asked him what was wrong, long story short I just grabbed him and kissed him. After the kiss he just looked at me, shook his head and told me no, not for him."

"What was wrong with that, maybe you weren't his type?" Darren mused.

"He did it in front of everyone at a competition." Tegan explained.

"Oh, I'm sorry, I know what its like to be humiliated in public. It was standard practice for me at school." Darren said in an apologetic tone.

"It's okay Darren," Eva said "There things happen, whatever happened to Maurice anyway?"

"I think he is living down south with a guy called Barry Hampton, apparently they met when Barry was a ski instructor at Aviemore," Tegan said "Kind of divided the family."

"Oh yes, his mother was quite strict but his father was all for Maurice finding his own way."

"I think my mum said they divorced a few years ago," Tegan said "It was quite a messy divorce too from what she told me."

"What over that?" Eva said in shock "come on, looking back the signs were all there but, he was and I'm guessing still is a decent guy."

"Well I know he is happy and that is the main thing," Tegan said then remembered something. "Oh Gemma Carson and Nigel Ellis still a couple."

"Oh no." Eva rolled her eyes.

"Who?" Darren asked "Not heard about those two before."

"You don't want to." Tegan said with a sigh.

"You know how where ever you go there is always that one really annoying couple who think they are the only ones to have ever discovered love? That is them." Eva explained.

"Always holding hands, pet names for each other, that sort of thing and they even would try and kiss each other when they would both be on horseback, very cringe worthy." Tegan added

"They sound delightful." Darren said, sarcasm evident in his voice.

"Oh they were horrible," Eva said as she tried to get comfortable "Of course Nigel only asked out Gemma after Lucy rejected him something she would remind him of."

"Sounds like her." Darren nodded.

"To be honest I tried to stay away from the rest as much as possible, it got too much with all the gossip and mud slinging. Then there was the cruel nicknames."

"Oh?" Darren said, sounding intrigued.

"Yeah, just about everyone ended up with some

sort of nickname, usually a nasty one."

"Odd, I've attended a few competitions with Tegan and never heard..." Darren started but Tegan stopped him.

"That is because you have only seen me compete in a few local events up near Dundee, plus a lot of the people we competed with have either cut down the amount of events or stopped completely," Tegan sighed "I did have one but only knew about it after Lucy told me one time, everyone called me, at least behind my back anyway... " she took a deep breath "..Hummer, they called me Hummer and you can guess why." Darren responded by hugging Tegan close and kissing her forehead, he could feel her shaking.

"I know you told me the competition scene can get nasty but that is just horrible." he said as he stroked her hair to try and relax her.

"The only one who didn't have one was Lucy, only because she refused to let anyone refer to her by anything other than name," Eva mentioned "I'm very surprised that Lucy actually accepted a nickname at college."

"What was your nickname if it is okay to ask." Darren asked Eva.

"Nothing remarkable, just referred to me as the Gypsy once they found out about my mother."

"About that." Darren said, wondering out loud "If your dad ran a construction firm and your mum is a gypsy, how did they meet?"

"A site he was working on had a gypsy camp nearby, some of the young men from the camp asked if there was any work going. Despite complaint from the other workers my dad agreed, he never turned down hard workers, long story short, one had an accident and dad took him tot he hospital personally then took him back to the camp, and his sister, my mother, fell for dad at first sight and would find excuses to go to the site even though it was frowned upon by the rest of the community."

"I remember hearing my parents mention something like she had an ultimatum, your dad or her family." Tegan said.

"She chose my dad, within a week they had moved on from the camp and I don't think they went back to that site since." Eva said sadly.

"That can't be a good feeling, knowing there is an entire site of your family you may never see, I know it is tradition, I have gypsy blood in me too thanks to my great grandfather but still.." Darren said.

"Oh?" said Eva suddenly curious "Romani or Irish."

"Romani." Darren said after thinking about it.

"Me too." Eva said with a hint of delight. "Anyway, what about you Darren? Surely you have some old stories." Eva said curiously.

"Not much to tell, at school I was seen as a sci-fi nerd who plays video games, had hardly any friends and was ridiculed repeatedly for various things..." he started.

"like what?" Eva asked but Tegan replied.

"He was manipulated, people took advantage of his giving nature, mocked for being awkward," there was a genuine anger in Tegan's voice, Darren's treatment by his peers growing up was a real sore point for Tegan, she couldn't understand how people could be so cruel to a guy like him. It didn't help that when they were both kidnapped Lucy, whom all Darren wanted to do was get to know her better, personally and gleefully attempted to kill him as he was not really needed as part of the ransom plot and couldn't be let go "Sorry Darren." she said then hugged him a little tighter.

"Pretty much what Tegan said, my design skills made me useful to people, but not much more no matter what I did, I even made the school under eighteens football team, nobody cared."

"It was really that bad?" Eva asked, Darren nodded and continued.

"It took me until college to find lasting friends, There's Linda. Linda is a bit older, in her thirties, great company though can be a bit over protective of me and Jason.. more on him in a moment.. and her and her partner Ellen are a lovely couple."

"I have been teaching Linda to ride whenever she visits, which is usually once a month a least."

"Then there is Jason, a worry to us all. Lovely guy, but he's a scruffy looking, horny madman who acts before he thinks a lot of the time."

"I see," Eva said slowly "So you are a sci-fi fan? What do you like?"

"Star trek, Deep space nine is my preferred, Star Wars, Babylon Five, Predator, Alien, Stargate and recently found a show called Farscape.."

"..No way," Eva interrupted "Jazz loves that show and really got me into it too."

"Oh yeah, I forgot you were a huge Star Trek fan," Tegan said, remembering "Do you still love watching Voyager?" Tegan asked Eva.

"Of course, any excuse to look at Robert Duncan McNeill." Eva said with a silly grin

"Tom Paris?" Darren said shaking his head "Really?"

"Yeah," Eva said in a tone that suggested she was surprised he would question it "Of course for me nothing truly beats Commander Riker from Next Generation." Eva then looked at Tegan "You still have that magazine cutting of... "

"Corporal Hicks from Aliens, oddly enough yes I do." Tegan said, suddenly embarrassed. Darren observed just how relaxed Eva and Tegan were around each other, he knew she had few if any friends growing up and had seen how awkward in general Tegan was in company so this was, despite the situation, good to see and he was glad that Eva was coming out of her shell too.

"So, where did you go to school Eva? Saint Aloysius like Tegan?" Darren asked. Eva shook her head.

"Wellington School in Ayr, dad would pay for us to be driven there and back too," she sounded embarrassed by it all "When I got to high school I did ask my dad just to send me to a local school but he insisted, plus Tristan was already there too." Darren did wonder how close Eva and Tegan would have been if the two of them had went to the same school as he had noticed both were actually not very comfortable with high society. Though it did seem that whereas Tegan retreated into herself, Eva rebelled in a very public fashion.

"where did you go to School?" Eva asked.

"Nowhere fancy," Darren replied "Saint Ignatius Primary and Saint Aidans Secondary, both in Wishaw, Saint Ignatius did have a really good latin motto, Ad Majorem Dei Gloriam."

"What does that mean?" Eva asked curiously.

"For the greater glory of God." Darren explained "If I'm honest my school life is nothing to write home about." he shrugged

"Don't put yourself down," Tegan said pointedly "Darren played in the Saint Aidans football team at under eighteen level." she told Eva.

"Oh?" Eva said nodding "Interesting." Darren then looked out and saw how dark the sky was.

"It's getting late, we should probably rest up, it is going to be one hell of a day tomorrow." He declared. Tegan and Eva agreed so he set the alarm on his watch for an early wake up "We want to be on the move as early as we can." Darren said as he settled with Tegan in his arms, Eva cuddling into Tegan's back.

Quentin was getting ready for bed but his mind was on other things.

"Olivia," he said as he finished brushing his teeth in the ensuite "I'm convinced that Craig has to be up to something." Quentin entered to room wiping his mouth with his hand, Olivia sighed and put the book she was reading, Riders by Jilly Cooper, and looked at Quentin intently.

"I know you have lost a close friend, but you are doing it again." she said as tactfully as she could.

"What do you mean?" he said with look of bewilderment.

"Remember when your mother died? You spent months convinced there was some sort of medical malpractice, that they had botched the surgery. Look what happened with your Brother Ronald, you couldn't accept he had committed suicide.. want me to go on?" Olivia looked at him sternly.

"I know, I know," Quentin said as he climbed into bed "But this time there is something genuinely not right. I am sure of it. Everything about him from his business dealing to his treatment of Eva.. something is up."

Okay, I will admit his treatment of Eva was deplorable," Olivia said "He doesn't seem to care for her at all, if anything he seems more interested in comforting Hannah than anything else."

"Oh?" Quentin said in surprise "What do you mean?"

"Well apparently he is always there, offering to help, giving compliments.. that sort of thing." Olivia explained.

"I see." Quentin said, taking a mental note that this was something to keep an eye on

CHAPTER 20

Darren and Tegan were wakened by yelling, Eva was was screaming in her sleep.

"Eva," Tegan said as she turned to face the dreadlocked girl in the confined space and tried to shake her awake "Wake up, you are having a bad dream.. Eva."

"W..w..what?" Eva said as she slowly came to, shaking her head as if to shake off the sleepiness "Oh, Oh on, I'm so sorry, I must of had a really, really horrible nightmare."

"What is it?" Darren asked as he woke up and rubbed the tiredness out of his eyes.

"It's okay, I'm fine.. I'm fine," Eva said, as much to reassure herself than anyone else.

"What was it about?" Tegan asked.

"What was what about? The nightmare?" Eva countered.

"Yeah, I mean, whatever it was caused you to scream in your sleep. Tegan explained calmly, Darren could tell she was in nurse mode. Eva looked downcast and gave a sigh.

"In my dream," she started, her voice quivering "It was my dad's funeral, everyone was there but it was like I wasn't there, everyone was ignoring me. After the coffin was lowered, Craig pushes me in and starts to shovel dirt in, trying to bury me alive, he starts laughing, I want to stand up, try and get out but I can't..then everyone else joins in.. laughing..taunting.." she broke down in tears and Tegan hugged her.

"Everything will be okay." Tegan said, trying to sound reassuring.

"How?" Eva said pitifully "Both my parents are dead, I have a husband who hates me and probably killed my father..."

"Eva," Darren said "You have a bright future, what about Jazz?"

"I'm scared about that too as it would mean starting all over again.. what if he decides I'm not what he wants.." she started to reply.

"Listen, Eva, yes it will be difficult at first but if he loves you and I think he does, it will be worth it, trust me." Darren said confidently. It took a while to calm Eva down but eventually between them, Darren and Tegan managed it.

"I'm sorry," Eva said "I just.. I guess it is Craig, he has gotten into my head I guess. He has put me down so often, never ever supports me in anything I do and we rarely if ever do anything together yet you know the strangest thing?"

"What's that?" Tegan asked, still hugging her.

"The one thing he done for me and for some reason I still don't understand why he even did it, he made me a partner in his stupid bloody company, its technically half mine, not that I know anything much about computers and I have never really shown an interest in them or his company."

"Why did he do that? I does seem a bit odd if I'm honest." Darren asked curiously.

"Something about making it a family business..." Eva began to say but Tegan shook her head.

"Tax." she said abruptly.

"Excuse me?" Eva said in surprise.

"A tax dodge?" Darren asked, he was equally surprised.

"It's not a dodge, well not technically, see my uncles old shares in Galloway haulage? Even though my father bought them from him.. they are in my mum's name, mum told me why one time but can't remember all the details, only that its something to do with tax."

"Oh, I see, I did wonder why he was so insistent that we do that, to be honest I have only been in the place a few times and even then I try not to spend too long there, or anywhere public with him."

"Why?" Tegan asked softly.

"You saw what he was like last night, he was tame then. It is a lot worse when we do go out and he is with friends..it is always his friends of course.. I spent the whole night being belittled and berated and expected to laugh it off.. it's degrading.. humiliating.." Eva started to tear up again and Tegan just pulled her close and did her best to reassure her.

"Calm down, he can't hurt you here." Tegan tried to sooth they heard a noise like something moving about.

"Ssh," Darren said in a whisper "try and keep as still as you can, hopefully who or what it is will just keep walking." Everyone kept absolutely still. After a few moments, the sound got closer and closer until, of all things, a fox stuck it's head into the makeshifts shelter and looked at them curiously. Tegan breathed a huge sigh of relief and smiled.

"Reynard, not you again," she said, Darren was about ton say it is probably not the same fox from back then but the look Tegan gave him suggested he was better keeping his mouth shut "Did we wake you, you sly fox? Sorry if we did." Tegan realised she was sounding mad but she didn't care. The fox sniffed around then ran off into nearby bushes.

"Okay, that was strange," Eva said as she shook her head "A foxhunter chatting to a fox."

"I know, it's crazy," Tegan sighed "But would have been rude not to say something." Eva just laughed in response.

"Well, I admit that is one way to put it." she said eventually. They lay in silence a few moments before Eva spoke.

"You know what's really crazy?" she said slowly "This is the first time in a while I've felt... truly free I guess."

"I can imagine," Tegan said "living like that5, under Craig sounds like a nightmare."

"You know something," Eva said looking at Tegan "That is exactly what this feels like, waking up from a nightmare."

"You should try get some sleep." Darren said wisely "And don't worry, you won't have to go through that nightmare again, not if I have anything to do about it."

No matter how hard he tried, Jason couldn't sleep so he decided to get up and get a drink of something. They had been using one of the spare rooms in Netherfield house, Jason thought the place was quite haunting at night as he made his way to the kitchen. With only the fridge door light to see he tried to find a glass for his apple juice when the main light came on and Astrid stood at the doorway, she was still wearing his Rangers top with pyjama shorts.

"Something wrong liebchen? Can't sleep?" she asked.

"No, he replied "Been thinking about Darren and hoping he isn't in over his head.. again," Jason sighed as he poured the juice into a glass "You want some?" he asked, Astrid nodded.

"I need to know, how are you two friends?" She asked, Astrid had a very blunt way of putting things at time. Jason put it down to English being her second language, well most of the time anyway. For all he know she could be equally blunt in German too, unfortunately for him he was too busy admiring the girl sitting next to him in German class at school to pick up more than the odd phrase here and there.

"I can't believe I haven't told you this," he said as he poured her a drink and slid the glass over "It was my first day of college and we are all outside class and everyone is talking to each other.. except him, Darren is just standing there and not one person is even bothering to try to talk to him. Anyway I decide to see how he is and by the end of the day we are friends. Once you get past his shy exterior, he is a great guy to be around, he is easy going with a good, if a touch cynical sense if humour."

"I ask because you seem different from each other." Astrid admitted.

"What you mean I'm a confident easy going guy and he is an awkward bag of nerves? A lot of people tend to underestimate him because he does come across as shy and nervous but trust me that is a very big mistake one too many people make unfortunately." Jason countered.

"Some thing like that. It seems he and Tegan are.. perfect match." Astrid said, struggling with the right term to use.

"No argument there," Jason said knowingly "She seems a lot worse then him when it comes to shyness it seems."

"Tegan has always been that way as long as I been here," Astrid added "It took her long while to talk to me."

"Though I will say something." Jason said as he poured himself another glass "They do make a lovely couple." and he then drained the glass in one and quickly refilled the glass again, putting the carton of apple juice back in the fridge.

"They do, don't they?" She echoed, Jason looked over at her and smiled then once again drank the juice in one go, walked up to Astrid and put his arms around her waist."

"But not as good a couple as us, my little Bremen beauty?" He said and he gave her a devilish smile and kissed her "Let's get back to bed shall we?"

"Do you think she will be okay?" Darren whispered, Eva had fell asleep quite quickly but he and Tegan had stayed up just to make sure she was going to be okay.

"She should be," Tegan said "I'd see this a lot on my placements, patients getting night terrors and I mean really bad ones, they are screaming blue murder but when you wake them up, it is almost like someone has thrown cold water over them."

"She seems to have been put through a lot, physically and mentally," Darren looked at Tegan and sighed "Tegan, you know I'd never do anything to hurt you." he sounded and looked worried.

"Darren, what's wrong." Tegan asked, suddenly concerned.

"It's just.." he stammered "Hearing about how bad things were for Eva.. I don't want you getting second thoughts..I wouldn't blame you... y'know..." he trailed off, Tegan just looked at Darren sadly, shook her head and pulled him in close.

"Darren, you have always been the kindest, most caring person I ever met and you have always, always put my safety and needs before yours no matter what. Even when I have told you not to. I want to be your wife more than anything in the world. Nothing on earth is ever going to change my mind. Okay? I promise you." she said reassuringly, she could hear him softly crying "Darren, I love you."

"I love you too." was all Darren could manage to say.

Luke found it hard to settle, his large frame made it hard to get comfortable in the sleeping bag so he elected to open it out and instead just cover himself with it like a blanket.

"Can't sleep?" Raymond asked.

"No," Luke replied "Why the hell are we even doing this anyway? Isn't all this a bit much?"

"I know what you mean but you know what Michael is like once he has his mind set on something," Raymond sighed "I met this Craig guy once, not impressed by him."

"Why is that?" Luke asked curiously.

"Well," Raymond started "I was sent over one day to get some of the paperwork for the transfer, Michael wanted the exchange to look like a legit business transaction."

"Sounds like Michael wants to go legit.. period." Luke noted.

"I get that feeling too, the whole business with

Andy hadn't helped either. Anyway I get there and there he is, on the phone to his wife and... well I would never dream of talking to my Sinead like that, ever." Raymond continued

"In what way? Luke seemed genuinely interested.

"He was shouting at her, like proper hatred shouting but he hung up before I could hear specifics but he tried to casually brush it off as nothing major. Then later on as I was leaving, this young woman came into the store and, the look he gave her.. sent shivers down my spine, it was... creepy." Raymond said, a shiver going down his spine.

"Sadly I know what his type are like," Luke said sagely "Treat the wife like crap but flirt with everything in a skirt"

"Yeah, something like that." Raymond agreed "anyway we better get some rest." Luke stared at him dubiously.

"I'll try, no promises though." Luke said in a sour tone.

"I thought you were some big hunter, used to stalking animals though the wilderness and all that." Raymond said, teasing the big man a little. Luke just shook his head

"I am, but usually I come prepared. Tent, decent sized sleeping bag. It is the little things that count." Luke replied.

"Well Peter has the tent." Raymond offered with a shrug.

"Fat lot of good it is doing us here is it? I mean.." Luke started. Raymond looked up at the night sky as he

COLD BLOOD

let Luke rant, the big Englishman did have a point but he wanted to travel light. Plus cooped up in a two man tent with a guy the size of Luke was not Raymond's idea of a fun He had to admit there was a certain beauty to sleeping under the stars, Raymond quickly found the north star and then he looked for and found the plough or Starry plough as he knew it as. It was a constellation very familiar to the Donnelly family as they were of Irish ancestry and he had seen the constellation depicted a lot in it's use on some flags used by the Irish republican movement. Raymond then turned his attention back to Luke who was finishing his rant "..but yeah, if you had told me what you had planned I would have been better prepared for it."

"Luke?" Raymond said calmly.

"Yes?" Luke replied.

"Get some sleep." Raymond said pointedly as he settled down for the night himself.

Detective Constable Duff had just got home to her home in the Anniesland area of Glasgow, it was a small two bedroom flat she lived in by herself. It had been a long hard day and even then there was something bothering her as she headed over into the kitchen and put on the kettle and lazily spooned some instant hot chocolate into a mug.

"Why does the name Tradala Limited sound so damn familiar?" she said to herself in a frustrated tone. It had to be a case she had worked on before, or at least something he had heard during one. Duff poured the hot water into the mug and stirred the contents as she walked into her sitting room and flopped on the sofa unceremoniously. There was a lot about the Bruce Ingliston that didn't sit right with her, she was so tired she fell asleep on the sofa within a few minutes of sitting down.

Darren had fallen back asleep quite quickly but Tegan couldn't, she was worried about Eva, it seemed all house yeas since she left home, first with the sabs then with her husband had not been the kindest, not truly fitting in with one and being abused by the other. She looked over at Eva who looked by all accounts to be sleeping peacefully, Tegan stayed awake a little while longer just to make sure.

CHAPTER 21

It was still quite dark when they packed away the things used in the makeshift shelter.

"I'm sorry for waking everyone up last night." Eva said sheepishly.

"No need to apologise," said Darren as he packed the sleeping bags away "It's understandable." Eva noted both he and Tegan looked a little tired and exhausted but weren't complaining.

"So, what's the plan?" Eva asked curiously as she helped Tegan fold the blanket.

"Well," Darren said, thinking "We need to get Craig to confess somehow but I don't think the three of us turning up to the house is the best idea as I said before so we need a way to get you there without anyone seeing you," he turned to Tegan "Not even your parents can know."

"Why not?" Tegan asked "Surely they would be able to help us out." but Darren sighted and shook his head.

"Your dad has been told Eva killed one of his best friends, how would you feel if you were him and saw her turn up?" Darren countered. Tegan looked at him for a moment and nodded.

"I suppose" she said "To say I wouldn't be happy would be a huge understatement." Darren nodded in agreement.

"Exactly," he said thoughtfully "Once we get Eva to relative safety we can then start thinking of the next step."

"Which is?" Eva asked.

"We need to find a way to get Craig to confess of course," Darren smiled "Trust me, I will find a way, I don't know exactly how I will yet but I'll find a way somehow."

"I really do hope so," Eva said with a deep sigh "I really do."

With a groan Luke woke up to see Raymond already up and eating a nutrigrain bar.

"Hey where did you get that?" Luke asked, Raymond looked at him bemused for a moment then realised.

"Oh," he said, throwing an unopened bar at the Englishman "There you go, I packed them as I figured we might need them." Luke took it and tore the wrapper off greedily.

"Got any more?" he asked as he crammed as much as he could in his mouth, he hadn't eaten in some time but Raymond shook his head. They soon packed up and were on their way.

"So," said Raymond "Had any thoughts on how to finish the job?"

"Yeah," Luke replied, thinking as he walked "can't be anything that leaves obvious marks, probably snap her neck and dump her body somewhere she could have fell." Raymond always marvelled at the casual way Luke talked about killing he had always been that way. It was almost like he took more of a professional pride in knowing what method to use as opposed to some of the others the Donnelly brothers knew who took personal pleasure in it and if Raymond was honest, he never liked killing women or even the suggestion of it which is why he chose Luke as he knew the big guy wouldn't make it more gruesome than it already had to be. For that he was grateful.

"Well just do me a favour," Raymond said grimly "Make it quick."

With a renewed sense of purpose Detective Constable Duff set to work, Her main goal this morning looking for any trace or mention of a company called Tradala Limited.

"Come on, there must be something." she muttered to herself as she sipped on coffee she got from the vending machine, it wasn't the best tasting stuff but it did the job. Then suddenly as she sat the plastic cup down, the answer came to her. Duff leapt up and marched purposefully over to one of the filing cabinets and started looking through some old cases. Soon she found exactly what she was looking for.

"Of course," she said out loud "I bloody knew it." and she went back to her computer, now she had the vital information it was a lot easier to find out more. Duff realised that McManus needed to know. About this new development.

Despite the current situation it was turning out to be a pleasant walk through the trees., Darren was forging ahead with purpose while Eva and Tegan followed on behind.

"He is really determined isn't he?" Eva half asked, half commented.

"He is that," Tegan said It doesn't help that he has this really strong irrational fear."

"Oh?" Eva said, her voice had a hint of surprise "what is it?"

"He has an irrational fear of somehow failing me, failing to match up to what I want and need. It is hard to explain but he has been like that since the moment we met. I've done my best to reassure him time and again that he doesn't need to do it but I have only been partially successful." Tegan explained, Eva listened and nodded.

"I remember you telling me, he was really willing to literally put his life on the line for you," Eva stopped and turned to her "Tegan, take it from me, you are a very lucky lady, you found someone who loves and cherishes you and will refuse to let you down. If only I had found someone like him." Tegan smiled at Eva and continued on behind Darren.

"I'm sure Jazz could be that man for you.. if you let him." she said. They had notice Darren had stopped in his tracks.

"What is it?" Eva asked curiously, Darren pointed ahead.

"We have to cross that open field." he said, field was a loose term as it was a grassy area with slopes, gulleys and various other things.

"We can't risk being seen." Eva said, worry evident I her voice.

"Well, we will just have to be really quick then," Darren uttered and stepped out "Come on!" he shouted back towards Eva and Tegan, who just looked at each other.

"After you." Tegan said, trying to sound cheerful but a hint of nervousness was creeping in.

"I'm sure we will be fine." Eva said and gave Tegan a reassuring smile, Tegan shook her head and ran up to Darren and grabbed his arm tight.

"You okay?" Darren asked as he pulled her close, Tegan had her head on his chest listening to Darren's heartbeat

"Sorry, just was reminded of.." she trailed off as Darren stroked her cheek.

"It's okay, you know I won't let any harm come to you." he said reassuringly "come on, the sooner we cross this place the better."

He was on his second cup of coffee when Duff entered Detective Sergeant McManus's office. He looked up and saw that Detective Constable Duff was practically bursting with excitement

"You might wanna see this." she said setting a file down on his desk triumphantly.

"Can't you summarize?" McManus half asked, half ordered.

"Oh, Sorry," she said, all flustered "You remember that a case a couple of years ago when we found there was a company importing drugs into the country via Ireland?"

"Oh yes," McManus said slowly with interest " I remember that one, it was a particularly tricky case, Go on."

"Well, you will also remember it wasn't a real company at all but a front for a local gang." she said smiling.

"Oh yeah," McManus nodded as he remembered "Wasn't the companies name a literal translation of the word 'trading' in Irish Gaelic or something along those lines?"

"Yes, Tradala Limited." She said in a rather smug tone.

"And pray tell what gang was it who owned the company?" he asked though he had a pretty good idea himself.

"The Donnellys, the company is owned by Michael Donnelly" Duff announced. McManus looked pensive, in his mind this revelation changed a lot about the case.

"So, let me get this straight," He said leaning back on his chair "What you are saying is, essentially that Craig Robertson, son in law to Bruce Ingliston, is in financial trouble and ends up going to the Donnellys for money. Now he owes them at least.. how much?" Duff picked up the file and flicked through the various documents.

"Around one hundred and seventy five thousand." she read out loud "Plus whatever interest they have decided to attach onto it.".

"I can see why he went to them, no legitimate bank or loan company is simply going to fork out that amount just like that without him making a major commitment. Anyway so they will undoubtedly want their money back..."

"And when you look at all the figures," Duff said, interrupting "He isn't making nearly enough to pay it back."

"So he needs money fast." McManus nodded as he spoke.

"I know it is only speculation but I think he deserves a second look." Duff agreed.

"There is another angle here." McManus sat forward deep in thought "Don't you think it is a bit suspicious?"

"It does a bit." she replied.

"More than just a bit," McManus said and he gave Duff a knowing look "Think on it, the Galloway girl and her fiance had managed to not just elude on of the

Donnelly boys but he is also humiliated in a very public trial."

"And then they just so happen to be guests at the same house where a man who apparently owes money to the Donnellys, possible chance of revenge?" Duff said nodding.

"Exactly," McManus said "And if I am honest, if it wasn't for the brutality of the murder I would say some how the Galloway girl was the intended target and Ingliston just got in the road."

"I think it might still be worth bringing him in for some further questioning, even if only to find out how involved he is with the Donnelly clan." Duff mused.

"I agree, it is a question that needs answering, I doubt it is a complete co-incidence. There is something about him in general that doesn't sit right with me," McManus agreed "Bring him in, let's see what he has to say."

They managed to get across the clearing quite quickly, Tegan was a nervous wreck the whole time, griped Darren's hand so tight it hurt and her eyes darting everywhere. The minute she got to the treeline she sank to her knees and started to cry, Darren got down and comforted her as she started to softly hum Loch Lomond.

"Tegan, what's wrong?" Eva asked, Tegan looked up as she held onto Darren tightly.

"I thought I was over this sort of thing." Tegan said once she had managed to compose herself enough to talk.

"Hey Tegan, it's okay, you didn't get much sleep so that won't be helping," Darren said softly "we will take a quick rest here for now, we don't have long to go anyway." he winced in pain and his knees cracked as he tried to get comfortable on the ground by he stretching his legs

"Okay." Tegan said as she composed herself "Just a short rest".

"This isn't right," Eva said sadly "You two shouldn't be putting yourselves through all this for someone like me."

"Eva, don't start with all that okay?" Darren said as he leaned his back against a tree and Tegan lay her head on his chest."We aren't about to abandon you now." Eva sighed, looked around and sat on the ground next to them, she suddenly had a rather bemused look on her face.

"Do you hear that?" she said softly, Darren listened, yes he could hear something, then he looked down, Tegan had fell asleep on him.

"Mystery solved," he said quietly with a smile "We kinda stayed up a while after you went back to sleep, Tegan was really concerned for you, she must have stayed up after I went to sleep too." Eva smiled at Tegan as she slept, using Darren's chest as a makeshift pillow Eva crept up closer and leaned on the tree trunk too. Darren stroked Tegan's hair.

"Will she be okay?" Eva asked softly.

"Yeah, I'll let her sleep a while," he replied "It is just like she would come home from being on a placement at a hospital and I'd put on a DVD for us to watch and she would be sleeping within five minutes and still in uniform." he smiled fondly, she looked on and smiled too. It was obvious they loved each other. Deeply. Eva took off the jacket Tegan had gave her the day before and covered her with it.

"She was always the caring type," Eva noted "Even when we were younger she was the kind hearted one, a rare thing on the competition circles." she then started to fidget with her dreadlocks.

"Something on your mind?"Darren asked, noting that she seemed to play with her dreadlocks when she was nervous or deep in thought.

"Sorry," Eva said and rubbed her temples "But my head is still spinning with everything that is been going on." Darren smiled in a sympathetic manner.

"It must feel like your life has been turned upside down." he commented.

"Something like that. I know my life hasn't been much to shout about but .. this... " she said with a tone of helplessness and hung her head, letting her dreadlocks hide her face.

"I know the feeling. You think your life is stable, not great but stable and suddenly.. Boom!" Darren said "I was like that too until two thugs grabbed me in a field and before I know it I'm in the back of a van and when I look up.." he looked down at Tegan and his voice softened "... I see her, from that moment on my life changes, initially for the worse but eventually for the better." Eva just threw her arms around Darren. And hugged him awkwardly and after a few moments released the hug.

"So.. she said trying to find something to talk about that had nothing to do with the current situation "You are a designer?"

"Yeah, mainly logos and custom stuff" he said proudly with a smile "I also specialise in photoshop too. I see computer design as like digital artwork." now that definitely interested her.

"Oh, what do you mean?" she asked.

"When you create your artwork, it feels like an achievement. Right?" he asked,

"Yes," she nodded "Jazz thinks I have a unique style, he described it as looking like a photo from a distance but becomes more abstract painting as you get closer. When someone buys it I feel like I actually achieved something special, that someone has a unique work or art created by me and me alone."

"Good, that is how you should feel, it is the same with me, creating digital art, it is calming actually and it is so satisfying when you finally get something just right. I can be a bit of a perfectionist." I stayed up one night until three in the morning fine tuning and perfecting a design for a library book sale poster, was worth it though." Darren shrugged.

"Sounds like me, Craig hates the amount of time I paint but it is one of the few things I openly defy him on. That and the horses are my passion, I refuse to let him strip me of that.

"Well," Darren said as he clumsily pulled the map out of his pocket and studied it one handedly "If I am reading this correctly we should be at Glen Tachur soon, then we can think about the next part of the plan." Eva looked on in admiration, there was something about the confidence and conviction in his voice that made her trust him implicitly.

Raymond and Luke were making good time but Luke was getting frustrated, there was no trace of them to be found and if he was honest it was feeling like a wild goose chase.
"Surely we must have caught up with them by now." Luke said as he batted a branch with his hand.
"I know, I don't get it myself," Raymond agreed "We are getting close to the house too by the looks of things..." there was a rustle of leaves in the bushes and Raymond stopped and wordlessly signalled to Luke where the noise was coming from.
"Over there," he whispered "I'm going in on three... two.. one..." Raymond said, then took a deep breath before before rushing into the bushes, followed by Luke...

CHAPTER 22

Raymond came dashing out the other side of the bushes only to be greeted with a rifle barrel pointed right at his head.

"Hey," he shouted "Peter what the bloody hell are you playing at? You could have shot me." Peter lowered the rifle and sighed.

"Sorry but no sign of them yet and I.." peter tried to explain

"Thought we were them?" Raymond shook his head.

"Something like that," Peter shook his head "I take it you had no luck either."

"Yeah," Luke said as he come through he bushes himself.

"So, what now?" Peter asked curiously.

"Wait for a few hours then phone Michael,"

Raymond shrugged "it is the only thing we can do I suppose."

Eva had mixed feelings about being as close to Glen Tachur again, Tegan kept apologising for falling asleep no matter what Eva said.

"Tegan it's okay," Eva said "Look you were tired, I understand."

"I know but we could have gotten you home sooner, what if we had been caught?" Tegan replied in an apologetic tone.

"But we weren't caught were we?" Eva tried to reassure her "You looked like you really needed a rest." Tegan eventually gave a reluctant nod and gave Eva a shy smile.

"I did," she admitted "Sorry, I'm so used to telling Darren to take a break and not burn himself out. I guess I forgot to take my own advice, I was worried you'd have more night terrors." Eva stopped and and turned to face Tegan.

"I appreciate everything you are doing, I really do," she said, putting her hand on Tegan's shoulder "I don't think I could ever thank you enough." and she hugged Tegan tight. Darren, who had been walking on ahead came back.

"I have been thinking," he said slowly "trying to get Eva into the main house might be tricky especially with everyone hanging about the place, so I was thinking about one of the outbuildings..."

"Well, here is the coach house I guess," Eva

interrupted but then shook her head "But won't they notice someone is in there." but Darren already had that worked out.

"We,and by that I mean Tegan and I could ask to sleep there tonight." Tegan and Eva looked at him dubiously so he continued "Well, think on it, our room is right next to your parents.." he gave Tegan a knowing look.

"Oh, I see." Tegan said as she slowly realised what Darren was getting at. Tegan was always awkward about getting up to anything too sexual under the same roof as her parents. Indeed the first time they even had sex was when they moved to Dundee.

"So, next question..." Eva started to say but was stopped by Darren, they could hear voices, Darren crept forward and saw the front bumper of Raymond's Vectra not too far off., he beaconed Eva over.

"Is there any way we can get around without them seeing us?" He whispered.

"If we head down there," She said after thinking a moment and pointing towards a line of trees that was well away from the Vectra's position "That will take us to the main driveway. And they shouldn't be able to see us.. good eye spotting that by the way."

"Okay we will do that." he said nodding.

"What if they see us.." Tegan said, her anxiety starting to get to her but Darren just walked over and held her close.

"You are sure they won't see us." Darren asked as Tegan rested her head on his chest, listening to his heart.

"I'm sure, I rode horses all over this area." Eva

said confidently.

"Okay, sounds like a plan." he said/

"Then what?" she asked but when she saw the look Darren gave her Eva shook her head "I'm not going to like it am I?"

It wasn't the most comfortable thing but it was better than the hard ground Luke thought as he lay on the back seat of the Vectra. Peter and Raymond had packed away the tent an were sitting on the grass, leaning on the rear bumper. He could swear he heard something but could have been leaves rustling and besides he was too tired

"You alright in there?" Raymond shouted.

"Yeah, just trying to get some sleep." he shouted back and closed his eyes.

Craig had just got off the phone to the police when Tristan came down the stairs.

"What's wrong?" He asked Craig who just looked at him and shook his head.

"Police want me to come to the station," he sighed "Just for some further questions." he wasn't about to reveal too much to Tristan.

"It is to be expected, I'm sure they will probably call me in next. Get as much information about where Eva might be and stuff like that."

"Yeah.. Stuff like that," Craig echoed "Only one problem, Eve did take my car didn't she?" Tristan nodded and looked deep in thought.

"You could use dad's car, for now anyway." he offered.

"Really? Are you sure? The Jag?" Craig looked genuinely shocked as Tristan took the keys from the rack next to the front door and gestured for Craig to follow him. The silver Jaguar XJ, Bruce Ingliston's pride and joy was sitting amongst the parked cars.

"There you go." Tristan said as he dropped the keys into Craig's hand, then looked over Craig's shoulder "Hey look who's back.", Craig turned around and was shocked to see Darren and Tegan walk up the Driveway alone and unharmed.

"Hi!" Tristan shouted over to them "Where is the car?"

"Ran out of petrol." Tegan said with a nervous smile, Tristan chuckled then replied.

"I'm not going to as how" then he asked "Anyway, how was the camping trip?"

"It was good, thanks for recommending the spot to us." Darren said smiling casually.

"We had a good view of the stars." Tegan added shyly. Craig looked at them dubiously.

"Did you see anyone else there?" he asked.

"No, but there had been signs someone had been there just before us but didn't see or hear anyone, we actually found another spot the second night that was more secluded," Darren said, thinking quickly "Which reminds me, Tristan, is the coach house free to use?" Darren asked.

"Well, no-one lives in it right now if that's what

you mean, why?" Tristan asked, Darren sighed and shook his head.

"Our room is next to Tegan's parents and we don't want them hearing us.. you know..." he started, Craig and Tristan looked at each other and nodded knowingly "... But we were too self conscious to do it in the tent, so I was thinking..."

"Oh, of course, I'll get you the key for it." Tristan said and he headed back to the house. Craig looked at Darren intently.

"Are you sure you didn't see anyone else when you were out there?" he asked.

"Well we did see the odd person walking about in the distance, why?" Darren said curiously. Craig looked a little confused.

"It;s nothing." he shrugged.

"No, it's okay you can tell us." Darren replied innocently.

"Well, I thought as Tristan told me that park was a particular favourite destination of hers, I thought that..." Craig started but to her surprise Tegan jumped in and answered.

"I did worry about that, I guess that's why I couldn't really relax." she said, Darren smiled inwardly at the comment, if he had said it Craig may have been more suspicious.

"Yeah," Darren agreed "To be honest I think going camping just brought back too many memories we'd like to forget if you get my meaning.". Craig could clearly see Tegan did look stressed, though for a different reason than he thought.

"Sorry to hear that," he said, slightly crestfallen "I still haven't heard from her and right now I just want to talk to her, ask her why." Darren, resisting the urge to tell Craig what he really thought about him, put his hand on older man's shoulder.

"She will turn up somehow, unless she has fled the country." Darren offered

"I suppose," Craig sighed "And you are right it's not like she can flee before we left I was looking for some work documents and saw her passport still was in the drawer we keep them in."

"Which one?" Tegan asked "Did she ever get a Hungarian passport?".

"What do you mean..." Craig said in a surprised tone then quickly composed himself "Yes, yes she did. It was her UK Passport I saw. Anyway, I better get going, The police want to talk to me about Eva." he said, telling half the truth.

As he got into the car, Craig pulled out his phone and called Michael, after too many rings for Craig's liking Michael answered.

"Okay Craig what is it?" Michael didn't sound impressed.

"Apparently that Galloway girl and her man hadn't came across my wife." Craig said,as he put the seatbelt on.

"Are you sure? My brother found their car at the roadside." Michael didn't sound convinced.

"Well they are here now ans it is just the two of

them. They said they didn't see her at all, apparently." Craig sighed.

"Do you believe them?" Michael asked pointedly, Craig thought about it as he watched the two of them enter the house.

"Although I hate to admit it but I think they might actually be telling the truth, I can't see her helping my wife after what she had been through herself, if anything she seemed afraid to bump into Eva." Craig shook his head, if they had met Eva and if they believed her that she didn't do it, the last place they would bring her would be back here. Regardless of if they thought he was the real murderer or not.

"Hmm, I'll tell my brother to stand down, if and when I can get a hold of him that I guess. So I take it your wife hasn't gotten in contact with you either?" Michael asked carefully.

""No, she hasn't." Craig said with a hint of frustration.

"If she does, let me know." Michael said with hint of menace to his tone.

"Why?" Craig asked.

"Why? I offered to.. take care of her haven't I?" was the reply.

"Oh? of course I will." Craig responded "I have reason to believe that she might try to flee the country actually if she hasn't already."

"Oh?" Michael said, sounding a little confused.

"I had honestly thought I had locked away her passport but it turns out she has another one." Craig explained.

"How?" Michael asked.

"She is half Hungarian you see." Craig said as he shook his head, he should have figured she would try something like that.

"I see," Michael said "Cairnryan is near you isn't it?"

"It is yes, why?" Craig asked.

"Might ask my brother to hang around there for a bit, just in case." Michael said, it was doubtful that with the police being on high alert that she simply got onto a ferry quite yet but she could be lurking about, waiting for an opportunity to get on.

"Oh, okay," Craig shrugged "But I promise to let you know the minute I hear from her

"Good." and Michael hung up, Craig shook his head and put his phone on the passenger seat before driving of to talk to the police, he thought it was probably for the best he didn't tell Michael about that part, at least for now.

Raymond just got off the phone to Michael and explained the situation to the others.

"How long are we expected to mess about near Cairnryan?! Asked Luke dubiously but Raymond just shrugged

"A day or two at least, but I will be buggered if I am spending Hogmanay there and I told Michael that." Hogmanay is the Scottish name for New Years Eve and Raymond had a huge party planned and nothing was going to get in the way.

"hey, I'm not sleeping rough again, you can forget that." Luke moaned.

"Don"t worry, I'll find a hotel or something, okay?" Raymond said as h got in the drivers seat and sighed "I'll pay." he added, peter and Luke exchanged glances and smiled,a couple of nights in a hotel paid for by the Donnelly family and they were not about to complain.

As they walked over to the house Darren whispered to Tegan.

"So just how did you know about the two passports?" Tegan just gave him a look.

"It was a lucky guess, she always talked about getting a Hungarian one when we were younger." she shrugged.

"If that's the case where is it?" he asked but Tegan shrugged again.

"No idea, will have to ask her." Tegan replied as they stepped inside.

"Quentin was just coming out of the sitting room when he saw Tegan walk in.

"Hello there Stranger, I have missed you" he said giving her a hug "Didn't hear the car."

"Well, you see... about that.." Tegan said looking sheepish.

"Oh no tell me that you didn't crash it?" Quentin asked with a shake of his head.

"No, no," She said quickly "I just ran out of petrol." Quentin just sighed and looked at her in mock disappointment then went over to get his Range Rover keys.

"Come on," I have a small can of petrol in the car boot, I'll take you there but you have to drive it straight to a petrol station yourself. And fill the tank up. I have to go and sort out some things for the funeral"

"Okay," Tegan said and went over to Darren "I'll be back soon ." and kissed him on the cheek before following her dad outside. Tristan came back with the coach house key.

"Here you go." he said with a smile.

"Thanks." Darren said then rushed up the stairs to get a much needed shower and grab some stuff to take over to the coach house.

COLD BLOOD

CHAPTER 23

Before she pulled into the driveway, Tegan stopped next to bushes at the side of the road and Eva stood, her tartan blanket draped over her, it was covered with leaves and grass and she was looking unsurprisingly very nervous indeed.

"Thank goodness, I thought you were never going to come she said as she hurried to the car." Tegan opened the car boot as quick as she could and helped Eva climb inside.

"Sorry, took forever getting petrol," Tegan said in an apologetic tone "Not used to the hassle of refilling the car yet." she then smiled weakly, Eva lay down and let Tegan cover her with a blanket from the car and got into the drivers seat.

"I saw that car drive past, the Vauxhall." Eva said as Tegan started the engine.

"Oh?" Tegan said, did you see what way it went? I didn't see it pass me."

"No idea, I just ducked my head back down in case they saw me." Tegan nodded and was almost about to engage first gear when she suddenly remembered something.

"Oh," she said eventually "Do you have your Hungarian passport?" Eva looked confused for a few moments then opened her backpack and pulled out a passport out.

"Got it here." she said before putting it back in the bag carefully.

"Wait, you actually carry it with you?" Tegan sounded surprised.

"Craig keeps the passports locked up after one time I threatened to leave him," Eva said sadly "But luckily I hadn't told him about this one so I always keep it on me, It made me feel a little less trapped. I must sound like such a weirdo."

"No," Tegan said sadly "It doesn't, anyway we better get back, Craig is away for now so it should be easier. To sneak you in." and she engaged first gear and headed up the drive as Eva ducked back under the blanket.

As Darren was about to head out the door with his backpack filled with essentials they would need for overnight when Olivia and Hannah were just returning from the stables after an afternoon riding.

"Hello Darren," Olivia said with a smile ""How

long have you two been back?"

"Not long, just waiting on Tegan bringing the car back," he saw their faces then added "long story but everything is fine." Olivia just smiled and shook her head.

"So, where are you off to?" Hannah asked with a smile.

"The Coach house.." then he explained as politely as he could "... So I'm going up to make it all cosy, Don't worry Tristan gave me the key." he glanced over to see the Lupo come up the driveway.

"What will do you do for dinner tonight?" Hannah asked.

"Is there any takeaways that deliver up here?" Darren asked. Hannah nodded.

"Yes, a nice fish and chip shop, hold on I will find the menu, we have one in the house." Hannah said as she jogged in as best she could in her riding boots and emerged soon after with a local chip shop menu with a phone number "It was Bruce's favourite place to go." Hannah looked like she was trying not to be too emotional.

"Well, have.. fun," Olivia said and give Darren a wink, out of Tegan's parents, it had been Olivia who was the first to really warm to Darren as Quentin needed more convincing that he was right for his precious daughter. Olivia also guessed Tegan had issues about having sex under the same roof as her parents.. "Don't do anything I wouldn't do."

It was tricky to get Eva inside without noticing, what they eventually did was Tegan went in herself when they were sure for definite nobody was looking then Darren came in with Eva who was still wearing Tegan's jacket and just put the hood up to hide the dreadlocks. Once they were inside. Darren was careful to lock the coach house door behind him and joined Tegan and Eva in one of the bedrooms. It has been decided it was best for them all to stay in the same room in case anyone saw multiple lights on, Eva for her part was okay with sleeping open fold down bed that was in the room and was doubling as a chair. As Darren joined Tegan sitting on the bed Eva looked around.

"They have done some work to the place since I left." she said absently to herself, Darren noted both Tegan and Eva kept their boots on, in fact he noticed that Eva's boots were field ones and had the laces at the ankle.

"Eva, I have to ask, It is about your boots do the ankle laces make that much of a difference?" Darren felt he had to ask, Eva looked puzzled then looked down at her boots.

"oh, I see, apparently they are supposed to allow more flexibility in the ankle..." Eva started.

"Apparently." Tegan snorted.

"… But personally I haven't really noticed too much of a difference, you never liked field boots did you Tegan?" Eva asked "Always dress ones for you if I remember." Tegan nodded.

"Couldn't be bothered with the laces, too fiddly, besides you remember that time Lorna Dempsey snapped the laces on hers just before she had to go out and compete."

"Oh yeah," Eva said, the memory flooding back "Then she had that horrendous jump that ended with her falling off awkwardly."

"She was lucky to get away with a just bruises." Tegan nodded. Darren shrugged.

"I only asked because I got a pair for Tegan for Christmas and she insisted I look for some dress boots." Darren shrugged.

"Oh I see," Eva said "What brand did did you manage get her?" Darren shrugged and Tegan answered instead.

"Rhinegold Olympics I think," Tegan replied "They are the ones that have a zip up the back."she said knowingly.

"Ooh, fancy." Eva said with a smile. Now that they were in relative safety Darren could see Eva noticeably relax but then she suddenly looked dejected.

"I really wish I could call Jazz.".she said sadly.

"You can," Tegan held out her mobile phone "Use my phone."

"It's not that, I can't remember his number off by heart, it was saved on my phone," Eva explained "I also kept a note of it and my other numbers in a small notepad but I left it in the main house when I ran out."

"I could go in and try and get it for you." Darren suggested.

"No!" Eva said "You have done too much for me already. It's fine, honestly." she attempted a smile and only half succeeded "Anyway, what is Dundee like?" she said to try and change the subject.

"Well..." started Tegan, who proceeded to tell her all about their experiences in Dundee.

Jason had been preoccupied all day.

"What's wrong liebchen? Still thinking of your friend?" Astrid asked as she sat next to him "Why not call him?"

"How?" he asked "It's not like I can phone up that big house.."

"Why not?" she asked.

"I don't know, I just don't like talking to people on the phone I don't know." he said with a sigh.

"But you do that for a job is it not?" she said pointedly.

"Well, yeah.. but still, doesn't mean I like doing it." he complained.

"Call Tegan," she replied, not giving up and held up her own mobile phone "I have her number." and tossed the phone to him. "There, I will be out with the horses." she then got up and headed out. Jason looked at her as she left and shook his head, she already had Tegan's number brought up.

It was getting dark and Craig was thinking he should be heading back, he had been sitting in the car for twenty minutes just trying to calm down after what happened. That stupid female officer more or less accusing him of being a part of the Donnelly gang at one point, That older detective was no better. He checked his phone, no missed calls or messages. Should he tell Michael that they know it was him who gave Craig the loan. No, what if Michael thought Craig had told them to somehow implicate the Donnellys in the murder? He shook his head.

"Craig, you are getting paranoid," he said to himself "Just remain calm, they can't prove a damn thing." he then put on his seatbelt and carefully drove off.

"There is something more to this," Duff said in frustration "there has to be." she sat down and rubbed her temples.

"I know," McManus said as he reviewed the notes he took "He claims Michael Donnelly gave him the loan based on Craig having some big deals coming up and he was the only person who could have gotten Craig the money quick."

"I believe the quickness part but the rest of it, from what I saw those deals aren't enough to pay off the debt unless he has others he isn't declaring on the books." Duff mused.

"Or he has ones that haven't been finalised yet," McManus said in a neutral tone "Regardless, I'm not sure it is enough to make him a suspect." Duff looked like she was going to argue her point but eventually backed down.

"Sorry," she said eventually with a heavy sigh "It's just here is something about the way he acts that is unsettling, the way he looked at me. I don't know if he was disgusted or leering." an involuntary shiver went down her back.

"I did notice he directed any reply to your questions to me," McManus said as he headed to the coffee machine "Unfortunately for us misogyny is not illegal, just bloody rude. Want a cup?" he asked, she nodded.

"Yeah." she said distractedly.

"However," McManus said carefully "I don't want you to give up on him, it is obvious he is hiding something. I'm not sure Craig Robertson is the murderer but he is up to something." Duff nodded.

"Don't worry, I will." she said with a hint of pride in her voice.

She looked everywhere but couldn't find it, Tegan was sure she told Darren to bring her phone over as they were going to order food and she swore she had put it on the bedside cabinet but no sign.

"Darren, did you see where I put my phone?" she asked reluctantly, Tegan hated asking for help looking for stuff, it could get frustrating at times especially if he may now were whatever she is looking for is located but by his own admission Darren could get that way too.

"Well, was it not on the cabinet?" he replied after some thought.

"Well it is not.." she started to say when they heard a noise "..My phone!" she said in realisation. Eva, who was returning from the bathroom had the phone in her hand.

` "Looking for this?" she asked and handed Tegan the phone. Tegan looked at the incoming number in confusion.

"Its Netherfield." she said as she answered "Hello?"

"Hi," It was Jason "Is Darren there?"

"yeah, hold on," Tegan replied then handed the phone to Darren with a confused look on her face "It is Jason." Darren took the phone off her.

"Hello?" he said.

"Hey mate," Jason said joyfully "How are you? I heard about the news from up your way."

"I'm okay, Tegan is too." Darren replied "How are things with you?"

"Ah you know how things are and don't worry I have stuck to our agreement. I hope you aren't getting into too much trouble."

"No, we went camping for a couple of nights.. no we didn't get up to anything before you ask." Darren anticipated Jason's thoughts.

"Okay, okay." Jason relented "Take it you guys are staying there for the funeral stuff?"

"Yeah," Darren confirmed "Tegan's dad is helping with that and then there is the hunt."

"They still going through with that?" Jason asked

"Pretty much yeah, show must go on and all that I suppose." Darren shrugged.

"Fair enough," Jason said "You alone?" he asked.

"No," Darren said and got up to move to another room, signalling to Tegan he would be back soon "now I am."

"Right, listen I don't know your thoughts on the situation.. but Linda was asked by Tegan's dad to look into the daughter's husband, you know the one who apparently killed.."Jason started to say.

"Jason I know who you mean, why would he want to do that?" Darren was intrigued.

"Something suspect about the guy..." Jason then proceeded to tell Darren everything he knew "… so Yeah just be extra careful around the guy okay?"

"Okay I promise." Darren said

Darren came back in and put the the phone down next to Tegan.

"I'll phone the chip shop," Tegan said "I will get drinks too. You still want the Haggis supper?" Tegan asked (In Scottish chip shops anything with chips is referred to as a 'supper')

"Yeah, what are you having?" Darren said.

"Sausage supper." Tegan smiled and then turned to Eva, who, despite the possible danger was discreetly looking out the window, the room roughly looked on to the main house, she looked deep in thought but suddenly smiled and replied.

"Steak Pie supper please..." she said then stopped, her facial expression one of horror.. Darren walked over.

"Eva what is it?" Darren said then he then followed her gaze and saw a silver Jaguar had pulled up next to the other cars in the main driveway and out came none other than Craig Robertson.

CHAPTER 24

Darren guided Eva away from the window and sat her on the bed, the poor woman looked like all the colour had drained from her face.

"No," she muttered then pulled Darren close in a desperate tight hug, Darren just looked at Tegan in surprise and she gave him a look that suggested he went with the flow "What if he comes here, what if he finds me..." Eva continued.

"It's okay he is going inside the house." Tegan interrupted as she looked out the window. Eva broke the hold she had on Darren, closed her eyes and took a couple of deep breaths.

"I'll be fine," she said shakily as she slopped onto the bed "I think...." Eva suddenly sad back up and looked around "Do you hear that?"

"Hear what?" Tegan asked.

"It's like a voice shouting..." she looked over and saw Tegan's phone, still flipped open, still connected to Jason.

"Darren , what have I told you about hanging up on this thing?" she asked shaking her head and picking it up.

"Hello!" Shouted Jason as loud as he could down the phone "He forgot to hang up."

"Sorry about that," Tegan said then realised "You could have hung up you know."

"I know and was going to but then I heard... Eva." Tegan looked over at Darren, looking worried then handed it to him whispering that Jason must have heard Eva.

"Okay Jason what is it?" Darren said wearily.

"Oh nothing, just my best mate seems to be helping a potential murderer." Jason replied "What's the story?" Darren, realising there was no point in lying detailed everything.

"… So there you have it." Darren finished

"Typical Darren," Jason said "I know you'd do something daft like this. So what's your plan?"

"need to find a way for him to confess.." Darren started.

"Just your word against his mate, unless you manage to record it or something."Jason countered "He isn't exactly going to confess to the police because the great Darren Douglas says so, is he?" but Darren was zoning out, maybe there is a way to get Craig to tell the police, Jason had been able to hear them when the phone was sitting on the cabinet.. he thought back to what Eva said about Craig and what he was like.. maybe there was a way...of course.

"Jason, call you back." was all he said and hung up abruptly.

"What is it?" Tegan said, looking confused.

"Eva. I have an idea to prove your innocence to the police but you will need to trust me."

"I do." she said looking up at him sadly.

"Well first things first, do you know anywhere safe near Cairnryan we can go?" Eva shook her head but Tegan nodded.

"Fairhaven farm," she said "It belongs to the McCafferty family. They would sometimes come to hunt with my dad."

"As in Liam McCafferty and his wife Mary?" Eva said as she sat up "He takes part in a lot of hunts around here too, but why would his place be safe?"

"He and his wife always go to Ireland after Christmas for a big hunt in County Limerick so it will be empty." Tegan replied "But wait, the house will be locked, Darren we are not breaking in." Tegan said sternly.

"No," Darren said, but I have to assume they have a barn or stables." he said apologeticly.

"I think they have a stables on the farm." Tegan said, thinking "why?"

"Because that is where Craig is going to come and meet Eva," Darren said, the girls facial expressions were ones of shock but he continued "Well that is what he thinks once you phone him and tell him where you are. Ask him to come and help you as you are planning to skip the country on a ferry or something and need his assistance."

"What if he just phones the police.. or worse.." Eva tried to say but Darren shook his head.

"he will come, I get the feeling he will want to set you up rather than just inform on you. I think he will definitely want to gloat first. Eva, trust me. It is worth a try." Darren said almost pleadingly.

"What do you think?" Eva asked Tegan as if looking for a second opinion.

"I think you would have to really convince him to come and see you." Tegan shrugged "But if Darren thinks it could work it is worth trying."

"What if Craig sees me here?" Eva said "I mean when we go to the car at least."

"We bring the car as close to the door as possible for one," Darren explained "As for making sure he won't see you, I have an idea." he picked up Tegan's phone again and called the last number.

"..and the best way I can help is with a distraction?" Jason said, just as he did, Astrid walked in and he grinned "Oh I have an idea, when you get a text from this number, go.. trust me." Astrid looked at him curiously.

"What is it liebchen?" she asked.

"We are going computer shopping, well you are anyway." he said, his grin widening

COLD BLOOD

As Craig walked into the sitting room he could see that Hannah, Tristan, Quentin and Olivia were looking through photos.

"I don't remember seeing this one before." Hannah said holding up one of the photos, it was of Bruce and Quentin and it looked by the outfits to be either late nineteen seventies or early nineteen eighties. Quentin reach out for it and took a look.

"Oh yeah," he said, his eyes took on a faraway look "Bremen, it was West Germany at the time. It was a European business conference, he went there to try and get more overseas contacts and I was there with Ronald.. he was the one who took the picture.. "

"...Was that the one I couldn't go to because I was pregnant with Tegan?" Olivia asked curiously.

"Yeah," he turned the photo over and saw a note written 'best night ever' and another memory came flooding in. Something in Quentin's face changed, a flicker of emotion before he set it down.

"What's wrong?" Hannah asked.

"Oh, nothing, just .. realising we will never have moments like that again I guess." he said shakily but spotted another photo.

"Craig, this should interest you." Quentin said, he seemed composed and relaxed again.

"Oh and why is that?" he said as he sat down in vacant chair. Quentin showed him a photo of three young girls, they looked no more than thirteen and they looked like they were at a competition.

"That is Eva there," Quentin pointed to the quietly pouting, disappointed looking girl to the left with her helmet still on in the photo "And there to Tegan on the right." he pointed to a the girl who had her black hair in a tight bun but some strands of wavy hair had worked loose, Craig noticed she wasn't even looking direct at the camera.. or anything for that matter, it was like she was avoiding eye contact with everyone.

"Who it the one in the middle with all the awards?" Craig asked, Quentin sighed.

"That's Lucy, she had just beat Eva by a mere point that day." the girl in the middle, Lucy had her hair out and had the blonde curly locks were cascading over her shoulders and she had a rather smug smile on her face.

"Ah." Craig said and took the photo, looking at it blankly

"Here are two more of the girls." Hannah said as she looked through the album in front of her. Quentin took a look, one was similar to the first but this time Eva had the first place awards and Lucy's smile was anything but sincere and Tegan was still looking as awkward as ever. The other picture was different, there was only two of them this time, Tegan and Eva and they were a few years older. This must have been after Lucy stopped going as this time Tegan was the one with the first place awards and was at least looking in the camera's general direction with a shy smile and there was Eva, arm around Tegan and smiling warmly at the camera. It was a stark contrast to the awkwardness of the first two photos.

"Bruce was usually unable to attend so he trusted me to take as many photos as I could." Quentin said with a sigh "Look there's one of you Tristan." and he held up a photo for the younger man to see. Once again it was at a competition, Young Tristan had already took off his helmet and boots and had put on some old well worn Adidas trainers and he was happily holding up a third place award and there was Eva, brash and happy grinning, she looked about eleven and had several first place awards.

"Think I could take that one?" Tristan asked Hannah, he didn't need to but wanted to be polite "A reminder of.. happier times." his voice sounded a little overly emotional, Craig shook his head.

"And if it does turn out she is the.." he started to say.

"..She is still my sister," Tristan snapped "Just like you are still like a brother to me. I know you have given up on her innocence but I haven't." Tristan took the photo and went up the stairs.

"They were very close when they were younger, the photo probably brought back old memories." Olivia explained. But Craig wasn't listening, he found himself looking over at Hannah, who had found a photo that must have been when she and Bruce were dating, Craig had to admit she looked even more radiant back then. He found himself once again just staring at Hannah admiringly, a look at was unsettling Quentin. Olivia stood and stretched.

"Well I will get some dinner on.." she said Hannah went to protest but Olivia insisted "No I will cook tonight." and she went to the kitchen. Craig looked in deep thought, as if hatching a plan.

Later on after dinner, Hannah was putting away the box of photos when Craig came up to her.

"Can we talk?" he asked, looking around to see if anyone else was in the room, they were alone.

"Sure," she said "You can talk to me about anything."

"I had been thinking, this has not been a great week, for either of us," he started, Hannah nodded in agreement "I think once things calm down a bit I know someone with a holiday home in Spain."

"Maybe a break from everything will be exactly what you are needing," she replied with a slight smile "Go for it I say."

"Well, about that," It is a big enough place, three bedrooms.. if you wanted.." he said trailing off he didn't want to sound too opportunistic, as Bruce wasn't even buried yet.

"Oh," Hannah said, a little flustered "But won't that be.. weird? Going with your mother in law?" but Craig shook his head.

"No, we'd have separate rooms and it would be just as if we were two friends, nothing more." though his smile suggested that wouldn't be the case, luckily for him she didn't notice.

"I see," she said slowly "I will need to think on it, that you for the kind offer." she then made her way out the room as Craig looked out the window. He shook his head, going as friends, not likely, not if he had anything to do about it.

Quentin and Olivia had went out for a stroll noting one of the bedroom windows of the coach house was on.

"I feel a little better knowing Tegan is back here, even if she isn't in the same building as us." Olivia said as she linked her arm in Quentin's "You know, you never did tell me what went on in the Bremen trip."

"Oh? okay" Quentin said, slightly tensing then in a voice he hoped sounded calm went on to explain "You know, Just the usual, you know how Bruce like to have a drink."

"Come on, I know there has to be more to it than that. I know you all too well Quentin Galloway." Olivia said sternly.

"Okay, I didn't want to say in front of the others but Bruce had invited a couple of the staff from the hotel we had been staying at," Quentin sighed "both were women and if he hadn't thrown up over one of them he probably would have done something he would regret, she had sapped him and stormed off. I made sure the other girl got home while Ronald took him back to the hotel, when I got back Ronald and I had to get Bruce cleaned up."

"Well," Olivia said relaxing a little, Bruce was notorious for his hard partying lifestyle when he was younger "At least he didn't end up in a police cell like he did at the Denmark trip I suppose, why didn't you tell me?"

"If Katalin found out he was even looking at other women, surely you remember what she was like once that Hungarian temper is released." Quentin reminded her

"I see." Olivia said nodding, she had to admit it was true, Katalin was the sort to wear her emotions on her sleeve and could be very passionate when she wanted to be.

"I think Eva's birth was the thing that finally settled Bruce in a way Tristan didn't." Quentin said with a sigh.

"I'm not surprised. He wasn't actually there for Tristan's birth if you remember, he was stuck up in Aberdeen due to bad weather." Olivia added, remembering.

"But he was the first to hold Eva in his arms and he said that was the moment everything for him changed." Quentin said

"It is a real shame how it all turned out." Olivia noted.

"I know, tell me about it." Quentin agreed as they headed back inside.

It was late and the Coach house was quiet. Tegan had woke up needing the toilet and was just returning when she saw Eva standing in the empty sitting room with the lights off.

"Eva, what's wrong." Tegan said softly Tegan had changed into her shorts for bed but still wore the Warner Thirty Four jersey.

"Just worried," Eva said as she stood still in her jodhpurs, bare feet and a tshirt Darren had loaned her for the night "I guess I am just worried about this plan of

Darren's, it is very risky."

"It is," Tegan admitted "But the thing is, Darren has a way with making things just.. work even if it makes no sense to anyone else. I can't explain it, now come on, you need your sleep." Tegan said and went to go back to the bedroom. Eva went to follow, took two steps and burst into tears.

"Why? Why did he have to do this.. my dad..." she got out through floods of tears, Tegan just held her close.

"It's going to be okay." Tegan said as she just let Eva cry a while, it was twenty minutes before they got back to bed.

CHAPTER 25

When he woke up, Darren saw a note left by Tegan saying she was off to see Princess. It made sense as she hadn't see n the horse in a few days and it would be suspicious if Tegan didn't do something with her.

"Morning," came a sleepy voice from the fold down bed and Eva sat up and stretched "where is Tegan?"

"Off to see Princess," he said as he read the note, he saw Eva suddenly look worried "It"s okay, if anything it is better if she does, everyone knows how much she loves that horse." he said hastily.

"I guess," Eva said with a sigh "I just constantly worry you two will get in trouble because of me." Darren sat up in the bed, resting his back on the headboard.

"Don't worry about us," he said with a smile "You will be fine. Besides we need to do this, can't let him away with literal murder."

"I know," Eva said, looking deep in thought "It is actually angering me. He is in my family house, eating, drinking, socialising with my family and friends and I am hiding out in an outbuilding like some fugitive. It's not right."

"And that is why he won't get away with it." Darren said with determination.

The smell of freshly made coffee greeted Hannah as she came into the kitchen, Olivia was sitting at the table with a mug and was finishing of some toast.

"Morning." Olivia said cheerfully.

"Morning to you too," Hannah said as she sat down "Something strange happened last night when you went out for a walk."

"Go on." Olivia said, leaning forward with interest.

"Well, I was putting the photos away when Craig approached me. He told me after everything settles down he was doing to a friends house in Spain for a while."

"Nothing really wrong with that." Olivia said, wondering what was so noteworthy about it.

"He invited me.. as a friend." Hannah replied.

"As a friend," Olivia echoed, giving Hannah a dubious look "As a friend? Oh come on Hannah, there is something going on with him.."

"Like what?" Hannah said defensively.

"I don't know but are you saying it is normal for a man whose wife has, as far as we know, killed her father ask his mother in law to go on holiday with him, just the two of you?"

"No, but it has been a crazy few days, maybe he isn't thinking straight." Hannah tried to rationalise it but was finding it tough to do so.

"Just be careful around him, please." Olivia said, full of concern.

"I will, I promise." Hannah said.

"I'm back." Shouted Tegan as she locked the door behind her.

"How was Princess?" Darren asked as Tegan sat on the bed and sighed.

"She was great, took her out for a short ride."

"How was Marco?" Eva asked.

"Marco was okay, I did check on him too." Tegan replied with a smile then turned to Darren "So, now what?"

"We wait until we hear from Jason." Darren responded as he got up to get dressed.

"Dammit." Eva said as she struggled with getting her boots on, without bootpulls she was having a lot of difficulty. She looked at Tegan and at Tegan's rubber boots.

"You are lucky, I bet those slip on easy." she said, Tegan looked down at her boots and wiped some wet straw off the toe of the boot with her sleeve. Then looked at Eva as she tried to get her pair on.

"Yeah, they do./. usually. I've had this pair for years and they are so comfortable. You want help?"

Tegan offered.

"Please." Eva said as Tegan stood and gestured for Eva to sit.

"Now you see why I didn't take mine off." Tegan said to Darren as she knelt down in front of Eva to help pull her boots on.

"Ready?" Eva said looking down at Tegan.

"Yeah, you pull, I push," Tegan said knowingly "Pull in three... two... one.."

Despite the fact it was still quite early, Glasgow city centre was already busy and the Thistle Computing store was no exception, Karen was run off her feet when a young brunette lady entered the store wearing rubber riding boots, black jodhpurs and a green Nike hoodie.

"Hello," Karen said "How may I help you?" the young woman looked at Karen sharply.

"I doubt it," the woman said coldly with a German accent "I ordered a computer from here two weeks ago and it has not arrived."

"I see.." Karen started to say.

"No you don't, I demand to speak to the manager."

"He is away.." Karen tried to tell her.

"I demand to speak to the manager." the woman shouted again.

"Look I can check your order on our system, what is your name?" Karen asked.

"Astrid Berthold," the young woman said confidently, there was no orders under that name that Karen had heard of.

"It appears your order is not on our system." Karen informed her.

"How can this be?" Astrid said, her anger rising "Your manager, he served me himself. I demand to speak to him now! Dummkopf!"1 Karen relented.

"Okay, I will try and get him on the phone, but he won't like it." and she went over to the phone and rang his mobile phone. Astrid took hers out and started typing a text.

"You do that," Astrid sounded impatient "Well? Hurry up! Schnell!"

"Hold on," Karen said in a stressed tone when suddenly she heard the phone being answered "Hello Mister Robertson.. yes I know I haven't to disturb you but this is a little urgent..." she didn't see Astrid hit the send button to on her text.

"Astrid Berthold? And she definitely ordered a computer from us?" Craig said in a confused tone, "Hold on I will check my laptop." he sighed, he had just sat down in the empty sitting room and now he had to go back up and get his laptop.

Tegan's phone buzzed with a Text message.

"it's Astrid," Darren said looking at the text "We should go." Luckily they had managed to get Eva's boots back on her, albeit with a lot of effort but they got there in the end. Darren grabbed his backpack he had put a few items they may need in it and everyone made for the

door.
    "I'll bring the car around." Tegan said, somewhat nervous.

Craig got to his room and got out the laptop bag and fired the machine up.
    "Bear with me." He said over the phone, he couldn't remember an order by that name, but to be honest his mind was on other things

The Lupo stopped outside the coach house door and Tegan opened the boot door, Eva hurried out and climbed in, hastily throwing a blanket over herself as she did, without missing a beat. Tegan slammed the boot door down and got back in the drivers seat as Darren locked the coach house door and got into the passenger side as Tegan drove off down the driveway.

Eventually the laptop had fully loaded and Craig had his personal list of orders," nope, no Astrid Berthold on the system." he shook his head "Just have to tell her and if she doesn't leave just phone the police on her. I can't be bothered talking to some crazy bitch about a computer she didn't buy." he then hung up and sighed It wasn't the best way to start his morning, dealing with a bizarre complaint. Hopefully things will get better.

Karen shrugged and put the phone down, she went to turn around and tell this Berthold girl that the manager had no Idea who she was and would not be available to talk when she saw that Astrid had already left

Astrid walked down Union Street and got out her phone again texting Tegan to tell her hat her time was up and sent it but kept her phone in hand as Jason walked up to her, as he was standing at the nearby bus stop.
"Well?" he asked, just then Astrid's phone buzzed, it was a text that simply read 'got out, thank you', Jason looked at the phone and smiled.
"See?" she said proudly.
"Tegan must be driving, That's Darren, he is one of the few people I know who rarely if ever uses any text speak on MSN Messenger." Jason said with a smile "Come on let's get back to the house."

"Okay, Texted Astrid back so she knows we are safe." Darren said as he put the phone down in one of the cup holder spaces near the gearstick "So where is this place anyway." he asked.
"Fairhaven Farm?" replied Tegan "It is about ten minutes drive north on Cairnryan if you follow the road from Girvan to there. That is the way dad always took when we would visit."
"How long will it take?" Eva asked as she poked her head out from under the blanket.
"Roughly a couple of hours," Tegan said "so get

comfortable." Darren looked back at Eva.

"You're okay, you get to lie down." he quipped, Eva shrugged and turned on her back, using the backpack Darren had brought as a pillow., she strained her ears and could hear the CD Tegan had playing in her CD player.

"Is that Runrig? I knew you liked them when we were younger." Eva asked.

"Yeah, you liked them too if I remember." Tegan replied.

"I do, unfortunately Craig doesn't and apparently 'lost' my Runrig CD's when I moved in with him," Eva sighed. "The sooner this whole mess is over with the better. Is life always this exciting for the two of you?" she asked.

"No, despite how we met, Our idea of fun is usually a good night for us is a takeaway and some good sci-fi on the TV." Darren said with a smile.

"You know what I could go tonight?" Tegan said as she kept her eyes on the road.

"Probably the same as me, chicken Curry with no onions and egg fried rice from a Chinese takeaway, right?"

"Yeah," Tegan nodded.

"Sounds good to me." Eva added.

When they got back to Netherfield, Jason and Astrid found Linda standing waiting at the door.

"Just thought I'd pop in and see how things were going." she said "Where were you?"

"We ere in.." Jason started but saw that Linda was in no mood for lies "It is a long story, we better get inside." he said sheepishly as Astrid opened the door to let everyone in.

Craig came down the stairs with a confused look, he genuinely could not remember an order under that name.
"Penny for them." A voice came behind him, it was Tristan.
"What?" Craig asked.
"Your thoughts, a penny for them."
"Oh!" Craig said "Sorry, not with it this morning, just had work on the phone, some woman came in demanding to know why her order hadn't been sent out yet."
"Seems a standard complaint in your line of work I'd assume." Tristan said with a shrug.
"Ah," Craig said knowingly "But this woman had not even ordered one from us."
"That is strange." Tristan admitted.
"Yeah, tell me about it." Craig agreed.

"… So that is the full story, you can't tell Quentin, I promised Darren I wouldn't tell anyone."Jason said after explaining the full story, Linda just put her head in her hands.
"I expected this from him, but why didn't you try and talk sense into them?" Linda eventually said to Astrid who shrugged.

"Jason trusts Darren, I do too." Astrid said in a direct manner.

"Oh I trust Darren believes he is doing the right thing but Jason should have told me earlier." Linda said shaking her head.

"I only found out last night." Jason said meekly.

"And you didn't think to tell me, Where is Darren and Tegan now?" Linda asked.

"I don't know, he didn't tell me that part of the plan." Jason admitted "Only that he needed to distract that Craig bloke."

"Jason!" didn't you even try to ask? What if he is wrong and he is helping a killer escape, what if he and Tegan are her next victims? Think Jason, think." Linda said in frustration.

"You do not believe she is the killer do you?" Astrid asked.

"No," Linda admitted "After what you two have told me it doesn't sound likely."

"So what exactly is the problem?" Astrid looked confused.

"I'm just worried that once again, Darren has gotten in way over his head, he was lucky before.." her voice trailed off and she closed her eyes "Sorry, but Darren is like the little brother I wish I had when I was growing up."

"What about me?" Jason said, looking hurt.

"your like a brother too, just more annoying." Linda said "You are a worry to us all."

"Charming." Said Jason as he flopped back on the sofa and crossed his arms in a mood as Astrid laughed.

CHAPTER 26

As she sat the coffee cup down on her desk, Detective Inspector Duff sighed, this case was driving her crazy. No sign of the prime suspect and she was getting more and more convinced that the suspect's husband had something to do with it but no evidence was presenting itself to her.

"Come on," She said to herself as she stared once again at the screen and hoping for some divine inspiration "What are you up to Craig Robertson?"

"I do have one question," Eva said lazily from the back "Do you have the number for the officers working on my dad's case? Or how you planning to get them to hear Craig's confession?" Darren rummaged in his pockets and after a while pulled out a rather sorry looking business card.

"He gave us all these, it's a Detective Sergeant McManus." Darren said showing Eva the card.

"Oh I've heard of him,"Eva said ans she handed the card back "A few of my Sab friends have had run ins with him."

"What was he like?" Tegan asked "He seemed a bit gruff to be honest."

"That is an understatement, he is one of those old school detectives," Eva told her "Proper hardline with suspects."

"I can only hope he hears me out." Darren sighed "Otherwise I don't know what we will do."

After the unfortunate incident before where she ran out of petrol, Tegan had became paranoid about running out again. As she filled up the car Darren and Eva put the first part of the plan into action. Wearing Tegan's green jacket with the hood up, she headed to a nearby phone box.

"Are you sure about this?" she said to Darren.

"I'm sure, All you need to do is to get him to come to you. Tell him that you are fleeing the country and need his help. Just say anything to get him to to come." Darren said, Eva just looked at him sadly.

"Sorry, I guess I'm just nervous." she admitted, as she was about to step into the phone box, Darren had a sudden realisation.

"Eva," he asked suddenly "You do know your husbands mobile number, don"t you?" Eva just looked at him and smiled sadly.

"Oh I do, It is one of the few I know off by heart, I pretty much had to." and she gave him a look that suggested he didn't want to know the penalty for daring to forget it. Eva then turned around and stepped into the phone box. She took a breath and keyed in Craig's mobile phone number...

He was catching up on some work on his laptop when Craig heard his phone ring.

"Hello?" he said lazily as he answered.

"Craig? It's me Eva." Came a voice.

"Eva," he said in shock and stood up "Where are you, what the hell happened."

"Craig, they think I killed my dad, I have to get away." she said, sounding as if she was on the verge of tears.

"Just come home, hand yourself in. surely.." he started to say.

"No," she interrupted "Not with my history, my criminal record. I'm telling you I need to get away."

"where are you going to go?" he asked curiously.

"Ireland at first, then I don't know where after that. I have my passport I just need some money and clothes, please can you help. Please. I know things haven't been the best between us but I really need your help please." she sounded desperate.

"Okay, okay, where are you?" he said, a smile creeping on his lips.

"Fairhaven farm, just follow the road to Cairnryan

from Girvan. Please hurry." she said.

"How did you get there? Police found my car at Galloway Park." he lied.

"I went there at first but managed to make it to an old hunt saboteur pal's place," Eva said, thinking on her feet "She stays near the park and took me as far as here... look it doesn't matter right now, will you help me, please?"

"Okay, okay I'll help. I will be down there as soon as possible," he said soothingly. Craig was too excited about the prospect of finally getting rid of her to ask too many more questions.

"Thank you." she said then hung up. Craig smiled.

"Oh, I'll be there alright," he said to himself "And I'll help.. just not in the way you think." and he picked up his phone and dialled Michael Donnelly's number.

Eva stepped out of the phone box wiping some tears away with her jacket sleeve.

"Are you okay?" Darren said with concern.

"I will be," she said shakily "I guess he mistaken my nervousness for fear." Darren gave her a reassuring hug.

"Let's get back to the car," he said "I think Tegan is ready to go."

"How did it go?" Tegan asked as she rolled down her car window.

"He will be there." Eva said as Darren opened the car boot for her, Eva climbed in quickly after looking around to see if anyone had seen her.

"Okay what now?" Tegan asked as Darren then got in.

"Well," he said as he took Tegan's phone out of the cup holder "Now we contact the police." and he entered the number that was on Detective Sergeant McManus's card...

She was getting nowhere and she knew but Duff was sure that Craig Robertson was hiding something, he had to be. She was about to go and get another coffee when the phone in Detective Sergeant McManus's office rang out. He was away so Duff went in and answered.

"Hello, is that Detective Sergeant McManus?" came a voice.

"No, it is Detective Inspector Duff, McManus is away right now, who is calling." she replied.

"Okay, It is Darren Douglas, I think I know who killed Bruce Ingliston and it isn't Eva Robertson." said the voice.

"I see.." she started to say.

"Expect a phone call from this number around seven o'clock, you have the ability to record calls?" Darren asked.

"Yes, why?" Duff was intrigued.

"You will need to record this next conversation, trust me, will you do that?" Darren said, sounding slightly flustered.

"Okay, we will do that, where are.." she started to say but the phone line went dead.

"So?" Tegan said as she started the car and started to drive off from the petrol station.

"It is all set." Darren replied "I hope, I didn't talk to McManus, it was the other officer, the woman."

"Oh her?" Tegan said "That is a good thing surely? She seemed reasonable to me. Darren I really do hope this plan of yours works for all our sakes."

"So do I," Eva said softly as she lay back down and got comfortable for the remainder of the trip "So do I."

Craig had just hung up on Michael and rushed to get ready. As he grabbed the keys for the Jaguar. Hannah was coming back from the stables.

"Going somewhere?" she asked.

"Yeah, something came up at work, I won't be too long." He said with a sad smile.

"Well, have fun, or at least try." she smiled.

"Thank you," he said and kissed her cheek "see you later." and he headed out to the car. Hannah let out an involuntary shiver, there was something about the kiss tat unsettled her.

The Royal Hotel in Stranraer wasn't the most glamorous place in the world but Luke didn't mind as it wasn't him paying for it. He was laying on the bed relaxing when there was a knock at the door. Luke Answered to find Raymond standing there.

"We gotta go." he said with a sigh.
"Oh?" Luke replied "why is that?"
"Got a call from Michael," Raymond explained. "They know were she is."
"And?" Luke said wearily, they had been going to the Cairnryan every time a Ferry was due to take on passengers and so far nothing. "Can you be sure this time."
"Michael didn't say, just get your jacket and come on," Raymond said with a sigh "Peter is already at the car."

As she lay in the back of the Lupo covered in the blanket, Eva's mind wandered. She thought about the tie she met Jazz. She was so nervous at the train station she busied herself with her phone, relentlessly checking messages and keeping her head down until he showed up. Eva remembered gripping him tight and just standing there in each others arms for a few good minutes before either of them even spoke, from that moment on every little thing they did just felt right, proper. Eva even remembers sitting in the pub, having a meal and just thinking how right it all seemed and how this is what her life could be like. Jazz truly loved her and treated her with a kindness and care no man had ever shown her before. She wished that he had only told her his feelings sooner. He must be worried sick about her if she has been all over the news. If only she had her phone. If she was totally honest Eva wasn't the best at remembering details like phone numbers or addresses and the likes, she had to write them in a notebook, which she forgot to take with her when she ran out of Glen Tachur. The only one she could remember by heart was Craig's but that was only because she wasn't allowed to forget it. Eva knew one thing for absolute certain. She loved Jazz and when all this was over, contacting him was one of the first things she was going to do.

"So let me get this straight," Detective Sergeant McManus said as he sat at his desk rubbing his temples "The Douglas kid phoned here and told you to expect another phone call soon?"

"Yes, That is what he said." Duff replied "And he actually asked if we could also record the conversation? Is that correct?"

"Right," McManus said as he gestured to the equipment on the desk "I assume that is what all this is in aid of?" Duff nodded.

"He seemed really insistent." she replied.

"Did he say where he was?" h asked wearily, not liking this at all.

"No." she admitted.

"Did he say exactly what it was about?." He asked, getting increasingly irate.

"He said he has found out who killed Bruce Ingliston." she answered.

"Oh," McManus said, suddenly curious "And did he mention any names." He could see that Duff was trying to choose her words carefully.

"No," she eventually replied "But he did say it

isn't Eva Robertson."

"It isn't?" he echoed "So, to recap, we are now waiting on a phone call that will somehow, amazingly reveal who the murderer is. Something we have yet to prove ourselves..."

"I think its worth trying.."She tried to interrupt but McManus wasn't stopping.

"Oh but I save the best until last, not only does young Mister Douglas apparently know who the killer is, he knows it is not the only person with solid motivation to do so."

"What about Craig.." Duff tried to ask.

"Have you found any real proof that he is definitely involved in the murder?" McManus asked with a raised eyebrow.

"No," Duff said sheepishly "Nothing beyond that I have already told you. But we have to give this Darren Douglas a chance, what if he is right?"

"If he is, why not just tell us outright?" McManus countered.

"I looked at all the information on the Galloway abduction case, judging on what I read up about him Darren does not seem the type to do things in a conventional manner. It could be his various mental conditions but I do think it is worth a try, I know it seems a long shot but we have nothing to lose by trying."Duff said pleadingly.

"Okay, okay," McManus said begrudgingly "We will do this your way for now, I hope for your sake it works."

CHAPTER 27

As Tegan had expected, Fairhaven cottage was very much empty.

"Told you they would be away." Tegan said as they pulled up outside the house.

"They really go to Ireland every year to foxhunt?" asked Darren "Seems a bit of a hassle."

"I think they are either originally from there or at least have some family ties." Eva said after a bit of thinking.

"He is from Ireland I think." Tegan said as she got out the car, Darren got out his side and they helped Eva get out the car boot.

"Oh yeah," Eva said as she climbed out "Now I remember, isn't she from Northern Ireland though?"

"I think so. I do know he is Catholic and she isn't." Tegan said.

"Nice place." Darren said as he admired the house, it was a large bungalow and had a healthy mix of traditional and modern appearance.

"It is yeah," Tegan nodded "I always loved visiting here."

"Where is the stables?" Darren asked.

"Round the back." Tegan replied and they headed round to the stables,

"That looks impressive." Darren said as he saw the stables, both Tegan and Eva shrugged.

"I dunno, I've seen bigger." Eva replied in an offhand manner.

"Much bigger," Tegan agreed "This is pretty average. It was an 'L' shaped building with six stable stalls. After some looking around it was noted that none of the stalls had been properly locked and it was relatively easy to open them.

"Doesn't look like they have locked any of them right." Eva said opening the nearest one carefully. The interior was cleaned out with a patio table inside and a few assorted farmyard items and tools laying around, on some shelves set up at the back of the stall or suspended from brackets attached to the walls.

"Must be using this one for storage." Tegan mused.

"It's perfect." Darren said looking around We can wait in the next stall for Craig arriving and when he has said enough we can intervene." he said with rising confidence. Eva took the green jacket Tegan had given her off and laid it over the table.

"So this is where it is all going to happen."she

said with a sigh "How long have we got?" Darren looked at his watch.

"Well I'd say an hour at most." he said after working things out in his head.

"What now?" asked Tegan.

"Not much to do but wait." Eva said with a deep sigh and leaned on the stall wall, looking up at the ceiling.

"Hey, doesn't that car look familiar?" Luke asked as they came up to Fairhaven Farm.

"Well I'll be damned.." Raymond said shaking his head "How?"

"It's him," Luke said thoughtfully "Pulled the wool over everybody's eyes.. again."

"I'm beginning to think we should ask him if he wants to work for us," Raymond remarked sarcastically "I swear this guy is the bane of the Donnelly family's existence."

"So, what now?" Peter asked "Wait for that Craig bloke to show up?"

"like hell we will," Raymond said as he parked the Vectra and unbuckled his seatbelt "Come on, let's find them and get this over with, God knows what might happen if we wait any longer."

"Hey, did you hear that?" Tegan said, suddenly agitated.

"Hear what? I don't hear a thing." Eva said as she

tried to listen.

"It sounded like a car door losing," Tegan replied "He couldn't be here already surely."

"No," Darren said shaking his head "Craig shouldn't be here yet."

"He's right," came a jovial voice from the door "But we are here, Raymond Donnelly.. at your service." they turned to see Raymond standing in the doorway, flanked by Luke and Peter.

Raymond and his men slowly advanced menacingly on to the trio.

"It's nothing personal, but your husband is paying us a lot to do this."

"What?" Eva said in a panic "I thought he owed you money."

"He does, but you see, he also offered to pay us extra if we... dealt with you too." Raymond smiled humourlessly.

"Wait!" Darren said suddenly "This is crazy, there has to be another way." Raymond stopped and gave Luke and Peter a dubious look.

"Oh and I suppose you have a solution?" Peter said in a sceptical tone.

"Well.. yes," Darren retorted "At least I think I do."

"We could always hear him out." Luke said with a shrug.

"Okay," Raymond said as he looked at his watch "You have a minute."

"Well, Craig owes your brother money, right?" Darren started, As he spoke he could feel Tegan grip onto him tighter, she was too paralysed with fear to say a thing.

"Yeah." Raymond nodded.

"What if Eva agrees to pay the debt?" Darren suggested. Eva, realising what Darren was doing, nodded in agreement.

"Yes I should be more than able to pay that amount." she said.

"How so?" Raymond asked dubiously but Darren had the answer.

"I'm assuming he was planning to use her inheritance money to pay you guys off?" Darren said as he looked at Eva.

"That would be telling." said Raymond in a tone he hoped sounded neutral and then he turned to Eva "But if that was the case how does this new deal benefit us more than whatever your husband may have offered us?"

"I don't know," Darren admitted with a shrug "But from what I have heard it is technically her business too."

"Oh," Raymond replied, surprise creeping in "What do you mean?"

"The thing is, She owns half of it apparently." Darren informed him. Luke gave Raymond a curious glance.

"That's right," Eva confirmed "I technically own half of the company."

"See?" Darren said, desperate hope creeping into his voice "She says you back in return you let us live and don't help Craig with whatever he has planned." After a few moments Raymond let out a sigh

"Hold on," He said as he pulled out his mobile phone and walked off to the side "Make sure they don't go anywhere." she said to Peter and Luke. Eva moved closer to Darren and whispered.

"If this works..." she started to say. But Darren shook his head.

"Lets see if it does." he said as Raymond returned.

"Okay," Raymond said, his phone still in hand and looked at Eva "I spoke to my brother and he agreed to you paying off the debt if and only if you agree to sign over your half of the company to him."

"What? Why?" Darren said, he was taken totally by surprise.

"You heard," Raymond replied "All you need to know is that a stake in that company means more to my brother than what her husband could ever offer us." If the truth be told, Raymond knew Michael believed the real worth was the stake in the company. It would be far better and easier just getting her to simply sign it over than having to get involved in Craig's murderous scheme any further.

"Okay, sounds fair, as for my half of that seggfej's company, your brother is welcome to it." Eva said with surprising calmness.

"Good, glad to hear it" Raymond said with a smile.

"What if Craig tries to block it? Can he?" Darren said, looking confused.

"If it is half the company he can't do much."

Tegan said suddenly, it was the first she spoke since Raymond and his men turned up "That is one of the reasons my dad bought out my uncle, it was either he do it or my uncle would have sold it to someone else and dad wanted to keep it in the family." she explained to Darren.

"She's right," Raymond nodded "Besides if he did try to oppose it, we would just have to... persuade him, even if he is in prison, Hold on," and then Raymond went back on his phone and after a few moments said to Eva "It's a deal, we will be in touch to.. finalise things at a later date, don't worry I know how to contact you." Raymond said in a tone that suggested that they better not back out of the deal "Oh and one last thing, you guys never saw us, we have nothing to do with anything your husband done. got that?"

"Hey, all we know is Craig got into financial trouble and asked your family for money, he couldn't pay it back to resorted to trying to get his wife's inheritance. He did that on his own, you didn't tell him to do any of it." Darren said, Raymond looked over at him as if wondering if he was being sincere or just playing the game, either way Raymond was impressed and just smirked and said.

"You're smart kid, I like that," then turned to Luke and Peter "Come on, I'll buy you guys a drink."

There was little to no traffic on the back roads as Craig drove down to meet Eva, all he had to do was keep her there until Michael's brother showed up. Part of him wondered what they had in store for her. The truth was he was surprised how little he actually cared what happened her, after all he was going to come into a lot of money, Craig smiled at the thought of that.

As Raymond started his car, Luke turned to him.
 "So, we really just leaving them to it?" he said, Raymond nodded.
 "Michael's orders, we get what we want without taking as many risks and after that whole affair with Andy we have to be a bit more careful for a while." Raymond explained.
 "Let's hope for their sake they are able to keep up their end of the bargain." Peter said looking back at the trio.
 "They will," Raymond said confidently "Thy know what the alternative will be." and gave Peter a knowing look.
 "Raymond. so, where exactly are we off to now?" Luke asked.
 "Well if you remember we did pay for a couple of hotel rooms didn't we? We might as well just use them for at least one night." Raymond said with a smile before driving off.

Nobody was able to fully relax until the Vectra drove into the distance. Tegan looked on the verge of tears and just cuddled herself tighter into Darren.
 "That was some really quick thinking there." Eva

said to Darren, looking at him with admiration "Thank you."

"I just figured they wouldn't care about who gave them back the money just as long as they got it back, I'm just glad I was right." he shrugged then looked at Tegan "Are you okay?" he asked softly.

"Yeah," she nodded though her voice was shaky "Please can we not do that again."

So," Eva asked "What now? Craig should be here soon"

"Well, you go inside and we wait until he shows up. If he tells you everything, which I think he will if he thinks the Donnellys are going to come in and finish the job, just shout for help and we will be there for you, okay?"

"Okay." she said dubiously as she tried to take in what just happened.

"Oh almost forgot," Darren said and asked Tegan for her phone again and tossed it to Eva who caught it with both hands "You'll need this, ring the last number dialled the minute you hear his car pull up." Eva nodded gravely

"That reminds me." Tegan said suddenly "I'll park the Lupo at the other end so he can't see it." And she went out to move the car.

"I'm nervous Darren," Eva said shakily "I'm not really sure I can do this." Darren just stepped forward and put his hands on her shoulders.

"Eva, you got this, okay? Tegan and I have every faith in you." he said softly.

"Thank you, that means a lot." Eva said softly and

he gave her a hug, after a few minutes Tegan returned.

"Car is hidden. Parked it the other side of the house so nobody should be able to see it" she said "You okay Eva?"

"Yeah," Eva said, releasing the hug "I guess I have last minute nerves." Darren looked around and sighed.

"Okay, we better get ready," Darren said then turned to Eva "Good Luck."

As they sat in the adjacent stall, Tegan cuddled into Darren.

"I suppose this is familiar territory for you," he said sniffing the air "Smell of horse dung and wet straw..."

"Yeah, something like that," Tegan said, resting her head on his shoulder "That coach house was nice wasn't it?" she said suddenly.

"It was yeah, reminds me of that place at Netherfield House," he agreed "Nice and cosy."

"The Coachman's cottage?" Tegan said "Yeah it does."

"Isn't that the place your parents have said we could move into if we like? Once you graduate that is." Darren asked curiously.

"It is yeah," Tegan confirmed with a smile.

"Well, I think..." he was about to say when they heard a car pull up.

"Is that him?" Tegan whispered, suddenly nervous and gripping Darren's arm tight. Darren got up into a half crouch and looked. Yes, there was Craig getting out of the car.

"He's here." Darren said.

"I hope this works." Tegan said, her voice trembling.

"So do I." he whispered back.

It was time, Eva dialled the number and put the phone on the table, her mind was racing with so many thoughts, would this plan of Darren's work. What if it didn't work, did he have a backup idea, what if everything went wrong, what if Raymond double crossed them? she was so lost in her thoughts that she didn't hear Craig come in.

"Oh Eva, I have missed you." came an all too familiar voice behind her.

CHAPTER 28

Eva turned around and saw Craig, smiling warmly with his arms wide.

"Eva my darling, I have been so worried about you." Craig said as he stepped forward and forcefully pulled Eva in for a hug.

"I'm sorry, I would have came back but then I heard about my dad, everyone thinks I did it, don't they?" Eva said shakily "I really need to get out of here don't I?"

"Yes," Craig said "But I know you didn't, how could you? Though I admit you could have if you had put your mind to it. I mean after the first blow knocked him to the ground it was easy from there." Eva suddenly looked up and stepped away horrified, it wasn't just the fact he did it just as Darren had more or less convinced her Craig had done it but it was the way he said it... like he enjoyed it.

"You killed him, didn't you? She said eventually. Craig sneered as he knocked Eva to the ground with a vicious backhanded punch.

"Too bloody right I killed him," Craig looked unhinged "Look at you poor pathetic little Eva, you had to rebel, had to be different. What's wrong? Daddy love your brother more than you?" he put his foot on her chest, pinning her down "Imagine my luck to find out that stupid bitch selling off the paintings in the local shop was none other than the daughter of the man who ran BICon, one of the richest men in Scotland. Did you think I married you for love? Sorry darling I just wanted the money and I'll get it too. Your inheritance and life insurance." He gave a mocking laugh "two thousand and two is going to be my lucky year."

"But.. but.."Eva stammered.

"But what? Oh yeah about the life insurance part, obviously, my darling Eva, you cant be alive for me to claim it," he head footsteps behind him "And the men here to help me with that crucial detail have just arrived, you took your time." he said with a hint of impatience "Time to take care of business I think."

"I'm sorry Craig but I can not do that," said a voice behind him that sounded familiar, but not who he thought it would be he turned to see Darren smiling at him.

"What are you doing here?" Craig asked, looking confused.

"I thought that would be obvious," Darren said, his smile broadening "Helping a friend."

"A friend? Her?" Craig said shaking his head "Don't be stupid, why would anyone want to befriend this waste of space?" Craig saw Tegan was standing a little bit behind Darren and pointed to her "As for her over there, how long do you think she will stick with you. She is out of your league and you know it." Darren looked deep in thought a moments then looked Craig square in the eye.

"I love Tegan and she loves me, you won't understand that because you married a beautiful kind hearted woman and instead of giving her the love and respect she deserves..." Darren started.

"...Don't give me that bollocks, Love someone like her?" Craig said dismissively "She could be somebody yet she is happy being a nobody, who would want someone like that? Look, you are like me, we don't fit in with these formal dinners, foxhunting, big mansions in the country. People like them look down on people like us and you bloody know it." and he spat on Eva for emphasis.

"So? That makes it okay to kill her does it?" Darren said in disgust.

"Yes actually it does," Craig said "I was hoping for help but looks like I'll have to do it myself..." Darren didn't wait for him to finish and aimed a well placed left hook to Craig's head, He was momentarily stunned but shook it off.

"Shouldn't have done that." And tackled Darren to the ground.

Tegan rushed to Eva's side as the two men fought.

"Are you okay?" Tegan said to Eva in a frantic tone.

"I'll live," Eva said weakly as she looked on as Craig and Darren struggled, er hand landed on something metallic, a horseshoe and she found herself standing and advancing on her husband, who was too preoccupied to notice her.

"Eva, what are you doing?" Tegan shouted.

"What is it with you?" Craig shouted into Darren face as they fought on the floor "Must you interfere?" Darren was too focused on protecting himself as Craig aimed blow after blow to Darren's head but instead was connecting with Darren's arms as the younger man covered up "Screw this, Craig said and reached into his pocket, suddenly Darren felt Craig's body just fall full weight onto him, when he looked he saw Craig was out cold and Eva was standing over him. Horseshoe in hand.

"Couldn't let him harm another person..." she said in an unsettling neutral tone "Is he dead?"

Tegan walked over, knelt next to the body and checked for a pulse.

"No, just unconscious he will probably have a concussion though." Tegan informed her, Eva simply burst into tears. Tegan stood up and pulled her in for a hug.

"It's over, we got him." she said.

"Do we?" "Eva asked through tears "Do we actually have him?

"Only one way to find out," Darren said as he moved Craig' off him and got up, walking to the table, in amongst the junk on it was Tegan's phone and it was still in the middle of a call so he picked it up "Did you get all that?" Darren said with a smile.

"It was a bit faint but yes we got it and it is all recorded too," said the voice at the other end of the line, it was McManus "Where exactly are you, we will send some local officers to your location."

"We are at Fairhaven Farm, at the stables, Probably be a good idea for an ambulance too." Darren added as he looked down at Craig.

Soon the police and ambulance crew had arrived and they were taking Craig away. One of the officers, a tall thin redheaded man by the name of McCready informed them they would probably have to come to the station at some point to give full statements but was otherwise happy to let them go for now. As they walked to the car Eva suddenly stopped and looked at Darren and Tegan.

"I do not know how I will ever be able to thank either of you, without either of you, who knows what may have happened to me, arrested.. or worse." she looked down then shook her head "It feels like. I'm waking up from a nightmare." she then hugged Tegan. "Thank you, both of you."

"Eva, as I have said before, you are our friend, of course we were going to help, now let's get you home."

"Sounds like a plan," Eva said as Tegan walked over to the Lupo and opened the car boot, Eva looked at her "You are kidding, right? I don't need to sneak around any more."

"I know," Tegan said "But it would mean having to get the seat's back up.."

"It's okay," Eva said, climbing into the back "It was just a thought," She smiled at Tegan "It is a nice car by the way."

It was late by the time they pulled up outside Glen Tachur.

"Home has never looked so good." Eva said as she got out the car boot with Darren's help.

"What are you two doing back? Everything okay? It was Quentin, who had come out when he head a car come up the driveway "Have you heard the news, Craig has been.." he stopped when he saw Eva "Tegan? Darren? what is going on?"

"It is a long story." Darren said with a shrug.

"I'm sure it will be, lets get you three inside first, it's getting cold out here." Quentin said as he ushered them in.

"… And then we waited for the police to turn up and arrest Craig for murder." Darren finished, he noted the others were staring at him.

"So," Quentin started "Let me get this straight, you managed to work out Craig killed Bruce and not only that help Eva, who you were told was the rime suspect in the case, to get him to confess to it without telling anyone... all because you saw him use a purple phone?"

"Well that was the first clue.." Darren started but Quentin smiled.

"Darren my boy you are some man, I had my own doubts about him but you managed to work it all out. Anyone tell you that you have a real talent for this?"

"No." Darren shrugged.

"Well I'm telling you now," Quentin said and turned to Tegan "I'm proud of both of you." Hannah looked in shock.

"I don't want to think what plans he may have had for me." she shuddered.

"You have done my family a great service," Tristan said with a smile "You outed my father's killer and helped my sister in her hour of need."

"I just done what any normal decent human being would have done in my place." Darren shrugged but Eva turned and shook her head.

"No," she said "what you did, both of you was extraordinary, you did way more than anyone could reasonably ask and now, as Tristan says not only did you catch a killer but you freed me too, simply saying thank you just doesn't seem to do it justice I feel but it will have to do for now, thank you.." and she gave them both a heartfelt hug.

"I know someone else would love to hear from you." Darren said.

"Who?" Eva said looking confused but then she remembered "Jazz? But how? I don't know his number."

"Who is Jazz?" Tristan asked curiously.

"Long Story," Eva said then turned back to Darren "I really want to but how?"

"Oh, okay, didn't think about that." Darren said with a shrug.

"Wait, my notebook," Eva said, the realisation finally hitting home "Back in a moment and she rushed up the stairs, a few minutes later she came down, flicking through a rather well worn notebook "Got it, the notebook was right where I had left it." she said smiling, Tegan pulled out her phone and handed it to Eva.

"Go on, call him." she said as Eva shyly took the phone and started to dial, after a few rings someone answered.

"Hello, who is this?" the voice was that of a young male, a voice Eva knew by the look of the smile on her face.

"Jazz, it's me, iit's Eva..."

The next day was relatively peaceful at Glen Tachur, the funeral for Bruce was arranged for the third of January. Eva asked to move back home, at least until she could sort something out, Hannah happily accepted. After that initial phone call with Jazz, he and Eva decided that after the Funeral they would make a go of having a proper relationship, Tegan noted how happier Eva had seemed. Before they knew it New Years Day was upon them, luckily everyone decided a nice quiet Hogmanay the night before so nobody was nursing a hangover.

"Okay, let's see if I can do this one first time too." Tegan said as she gripped the bootpulls tight and pulled with all her might to get her riding boot on, Cavallo branded ones looked good but were hard to get on, luckily it slid on, Darren gave her a round of applause.

"Well done, both of them first time as well." he said with a smile. Tegan stood and stamped a couple of times with each foot just to doubly make sure her feet were in properly. She had just finished putting the spurs on when Darren turned her around and pulled her close.

"So," Tegan said playfully "how do I look?"

"you look more than beautiful to me." he said, kissing her with wild passion. She responded in kind but after a few moments stopped and smiled playfully

"Easy there," She said "Not until after the hunt, remember, then all.. well most anyway... of this comes off." and she winked at him. Darren looked at her and smiled, apart from the boots being different, she looked almost exactly as she did when they first met, the hair in a tight low bun, although you could still see evidence of the wavy nature of it. The white blouse in stark contrast to the jacket. The beige jodhpurs and her riding boots completing the look.

"I love you." he said simply.

"And I love you." she replied and kissed him on the cheek as she grabbed her helmet, riding crop and gloves. Suddenly there was a knock on the door.

"Come in." Darren said and in walked Eva, her Dreadlocks in a rather heavy looking bun Darren didn't want to think about how she managed to entice her hair into it and she was dressed almost the same as Tegan, but there was something about her look that Darren couldn't quite place.

"Hi," Tegan said then pointed towards Eva's feet "Hey, where did you get those?" Darren looked down to see that Eva was actually, for the first tie since he met her was wearing black riding boots.

"Oh? These?" Eva said as she showed them off "These are an old pair Hannah had, we share the same shoe size so she let me have them. It is the least I could do for my dad."

"he will be proud of you, you know that don't you." Darren said.

"I know," Eva replied and looked at her watch ""We better get down there, wouldn't do to be late now would it? I'll wait for you guys outside." she smiled and left, closing the door behind her. Tegan just looked at Darren and put her arms around him.

"You know, I was thinking," Tegan said "Maybe it will do us good to move back to Netherfield after I graduate." and smiled at him.

"I think so too, "he agreed. Tegan just looked deep into his eyes, They both knew moving back to the area permanently was a huge step, but one they needed to take. Tegan pulled Darren closer and kissed him.

"I Love you." she said after a few moments of silence.

"I love you too." he replied, Tegan took his hand "Now we better get out there, can't keep everyone waiting now can we?"

"No," Darren said with a smile "No, we can't."

EPILOGUE

Craig Robertson was found guilty of murder by a jury who barely took an hour to come to a verdict over the matter. Unsurprisingly Eva divorced Craig and ended up living with Jazz in a small farmhouse near Lanark with attached stables she had bought with some of her inheritance money, the location was chosen as Eva wanted to make a clean break of things and move out of Ayrshire plus it would be closer to her friends. Jazz had turned out to be every bit the man Eva made him out to be. Kind, caring and totally in love with Eva.

Thistle Computing actually flourished under the Donnellys especially once Craig was 'convinced' in prison to sign away his half of the company too. Not wishing to be hands on, they appointed one of the current sales assistants to be Manager for every day running. Karen ended up getting the job and her idea of diversifying by selling games consoles and games turned the stores fortunes around

After Tegan graduated from University that summer they decided it was time to return home, though Quentin kept the flat up in Dundee on as a rental property. The Coachman's cottage at Netherfield house was essentially a two bedroom apartment above a garage with attached office, thought Darren had the idea of turning it into a games room. Tegan had applied for nursing positions at various hospitals in the area, eventually landing a position at Wishaw General Hospital in Darren's home town of Wishaw, there were offers from Glasgow hospitals but Tegan ultimately wanted to be close to home. As for Darren, he managed to get another library job but on Quentin's advice started to look into doing private investigation work on the side as Darren seemed to have a genuine talent for deduction and analytics. They also made the decision after Tegan's Graduation that they would start seriously planning their wedding.

"That is Princess settled in." Tegan said as she joined Darren upstairs in the Coachman's cottage. They had moved everything down the same day, Princess and their household possessions. Tegan was wearing ther Celtic home jersey with Larsson Seven on the back, beige jodhpurs and her knee high rubber riding boots. She smiled as she saw Darren, who was wearing some old jeans and a tshirt with Boba Fett, his favourite Satar Wars character on the front. He was already unpacking some of their stuff from boxes, there was already some furniture in the apartment like a corner sofa and a large screen TV, a fully outfitted kitchen and double beds in the bedrooms. He had already put up some of the wall decorations. The signed and framed Andreas Thom Celtic jersey along with The framed Runrig and Aliens movie posters.

"How does it feel to be back home?" he asked as he looked through the boxes. Tegan walked over and sat down on the sofa then started looking through the nearest box herself.

"It feels good," she said looking up "I know it sounds crazy but although we had some great times up in Dundee it did feel a little bit isolating." Darren stopped unpacking and went over to Tegan, sat with her and put his arm around her.

"I know what you mean, we knew we had to do it but I guess we both knew in our hearts we would have to return at some point." he said as she rested her head on his shoulder and smiled.

"Yeah, I know what you mean," she said softly, looking around the room "You know, for years this place has been empty. I was surprised when dad started getting work done to it."

"Did you ever imagine you'd be the one living here?" Darren asked.

"No, if anything I thought he would rent it out or something but I can't think of anywhere else I'd rather be," she said then stood up "well the sooner we unpack..."

Together they managed to get through quite a few boxes and the sitting room was starting to look more homely, Tegan's showjumping awards were on display as was Darren's old school football league trophy. Their three CD changer sound system was set up and Darren was just finished setting up the PC when he looked into one of the smaller boxes and something caught his eye

"Look what I found," he said, taking it out the box "Remember this photo?" and he showed Tegan the first photo they ever had as a couple, which was taken by a newspaper photographer. They both looked dirty and dishevelled as they had only recently been rescued from the ordeal that had brought them together a few hours before but you could already see clearly the real love they had for each other.

"How could I forget," she said easing the framed photo down and wrapping her arms around his neck "From the moment you entered into my life you have given me everything you have and asked for nothing except love in return." Darren looked deep into her eyes and smiled.

"I have you in my life, what else could I possibly need?" he said.

"These for a start," came a voice from the living room doorway, Olivia stood there holding two sets of doorkeys "I can take the master set back now you have these. One set had a large metal 'T' keyring and the other a 'D', she set them down on the TV cabinet "Need a hand?"

"Please," said Tegan with a shy smile as she gave

Darren a quick kiss and whispered "later." and winked at him.

With Olivia's help they managed to get most of the boxes unpacked. It was getting late by the time Olivia had decided to leave.

"So, what are you doing for dinner tonight? Olivia asked.

"Oh, we will probably order in I think." Tegan said as she walked her mother to the door.

"I can understand that, not in the mood to cook are you?" Olivia smiled knowingly.

"Something like that." Tegan answered.

"Well I shall leave the two of you to enjoy the rest of the evening, good night and I will probably see you at the stables in the morning." the older woman said with a knowing smile.

"See you then. Thanks for helping out mum." Tegan said and waited until it was polite enough to do so and closed the door, locking it with her new key, she ran up the stairs and took Darren's hand, guiding him the the main bedroom.

"What are you up to?" Darren said in an amused tone.

"Well, It is our first night in our new home," Tegan said and took the big cuddly fox Darren had bought her in Dundee that they had christened Reynard off the bed "Wait there." Tegan said playfully and left the room, closing the door behind her.

COLD BLOOD

Darren sat on the bed patiently as he heard some noises coming from the other bedroom were most of Tegan's riding stuff had been stored for now. After a few minutes the door opened and Tegan walked in wearing her Warner Thirty Four jersey as an impromptu minidress and her Petrie riding boots her mum bought her for Christmas on bare legs, he knew from experience she was wearing literally nothing under the jersey. It was a look he always described as cute, gorgeous and very sexy all at once.

"I know how much you love this look," she said as she gestured to her riding boots and goalkeeper jersey "You really find this a sexy look don't you?" Darren nodded.

"You know I do," He said with a smile as he looked at her lovingly " Tegan, You are so beautiful."

"You always say that." Tegan said as she smiled seductively and eased his tshirt off him., Tegan then pushed him down on the bed and straddled him, boots clamped tight on his sides and she looked into his eyes lovingly..

"I say it because it is always true." Darren said in an honest tone, looking back at her lovingly..

"Oh Darren..." Tegan said softly "I love you."

"And I love you too." he replied and they kissed a long loving kiss…

The end... For now.